# PHOENIX

## Before the Day of Fire

J.H. MILLS

ENSŌ
STUDIOS

# Table of Contents

# PHOENIX

## The Shadow Government You Were Never Meant to Know

In the invisible heart of the Republic, beyond the reach of Congress, oversight, or sunlight, there exists an organization so vast, so interwoven with the machinery of government, that even its name is spoken in whispers among the few who dare acknowledge it.

PHOENIX.

Officially, it does not exist.

Unofficially, it is America's final failsafe—a sprawling network built to preserve the continuity of government in the event of national collapse. Its mission began as a noble contingency. Its legacy may yet define the end of democracy itself.

### Origins in the Ashes

Phoenix's story begins—officially—on July 26, 1947, when President Harry S. Truman signed the National Security Act. While history remembers it for birthing the CIA, the Air Force, and the Department of Defense, buried deep in its classified appendices was a single clause authorizing "continuity structures of indefinite jurisdiction."

That clause was the seed. Phoenix was the tree.

But the roots reach further back—to the American Civil War, and a covert fund known only as the Acadia Project. Wealthy Union sympathizers, fearing the collapse of the Republic, created a hidden network of off-book financing marked by a single word stamped on each ledger page: Acadia.

These men—Rockefellers, Morgans, Vanderbilts—forged the model of an invisible state: privately financed, publicly untouchable, and loyal only to its own survival.

That model would later be perfected under a new name: Phoenix.

## Site C and the Birth of the Underworld

After World War II, Operation Paperclip brought hundreds of German engineers to American soil. Among them was Dr. Xaver Dorsch, the architect of the Reich's underground fortifications. Under his supervision, construction began on an unmarked facility in Arizona known only as Site C.

Site C was not a bunker—it was a prototype for a civilization reborn underground. Within a decade, it expanded into HADES, an interlinked network of subterranean cities stretching across the continent. Connecting them was STYX, a maglev transit line capable of moving personnel and cargo from coast to coast in less than an hour.

To the public, they were myths—Cold War paranoia. To Phoenix, they were foundations.

## Funding the Empire Below

Originally fed by Pentagon black budgets, Phoenix's appetite soon outgrew government coffers. In the 1970s, it turned to private capital. Through a conglomerate known as Ouroboros—comprised of BlackRaven, Supercolossus, and Nation Street Capital—billions began flowing into off-book construction and research projects under the guise of energy infrastructure and data resilience.

Declassified memos suggest Ouroboros now wields veto power over Phoenix operations. In other words: the shadow government has shareholders.

## The Council and Project Citadel

The first governing body of Phoenix, known as The Council, operated under the early codename Project Citadel. Headquartered in a converted safe house outside Pinion Pines, Arizona, its members included military officers, engineers, and survivalists—along with a handful of former Nazi scientists who had quietly integrated into American defense projects.

Among them were figures history knows—Wernher von Braun, Dorsch—and others who vanished from public record. Together, they established the guiding doctrine of Phoenix:

"In the event the Republic falls, it must be reborn.

Fire is not an ending. It is continuity through purification."

That creed was later carved into the foundation stone of Site C, the first operational complex.

## The Modern Hydra

Over the decades, Phoenix expanded its reach through a series of internal divisions—each named after mythic figures of death and rebirth. JANUS managed information. OCEANUS built the deepwater vaults. BOREAS controlled arctic data repositories. And NYX, the most secretive of all, studied the intersection of artificial intelligence and human consciousness.

To the outside world, these programs appear as unrelated research contracts. But viewed together, they reveal a single architecture: a global system preparing not just to survive catastrophe, but to inherit the Earth afterward.

## The Exposé Begins

Whistleblowers speak of black sites, simulated environments, and "seed archives" designed to repopulate the world after the Day of Fire—whatever that means. One name recurs across all leaks: Neo Columbia, a planned reconstruction of the United States under a new constitution written by Phoenix itself.

If true, it means the organization no longer answers to the government it was built to protect.

## Conclusion: The Paradox of Survival

Phoenix embodies the oldest American dream— survival through ingenuity—and the oldest American sin: empire through secrecy.

In chasing the myth, I've interviewed former engineers, widows of missing technicians, and men who swear they've seen trains without operators gliding beneath the Nevada desert. The evidence is circumstantial. The pattern is undeniable.

This is only the beginning of The Dutchess Sentinel's investigation.

Because somewhere below our feet, a sprawling titan sleeps—waiting for its reincarnation.

## About the Author

Samuel "Sam" Griffin is an investigative journalist with The Dutchess Sentinel in New York. Known for his relentless pursuit of hidden truths, Griffin specializes in the intersection of government secrecy and corporate power. His ongoing series, Archangel, explores the ethical and existential consequences of privatized continuity programs and the moral vacuum at the heart of American resilience.

# Operation Nightfall Part 1

## The Ritchie Boys

"This is a war of the Unknown Warriors; but let all strive without failing in faith or in duty..." — Winston Churchill

### Camp Ritchie, Maryland

April 1945

The mountains still held the last of winter in their seams. Mist clung low over the training grounds, curling through the pines and around the obstacle course like smoke that refused to lift. Captain Jack Harper drove straight through it in a mud-spattered Willys, tires spitting gravel, the cold air cutting at the loose canvas.

He didn't bother parking in the designated row. He brought the Jeep to a stop in front of Headquarters Company, killed the engine, and sat for half a heartbeat with both hands on the wheel, jaw working. He hated being called back. End-of-war summons were never simple. They were either medals, cover-ups, or impossible errands.

This one smelled like the third.

Harper tugged his service cap on, stepped down, and took in Camp Ritchie the way a man measures a tool before using it. Men in field-gray training uniforms moved between barracks. A formation of recruits—boys, mostly, with the stiff-backed look of recent citizens—was being drilled on vehicle identification. A corporal held up silhouettes of German half-tracks and Panzer IVs, barking questions in English; every one of those kids answered in German without an accent. Downrange, rifle fire popped in tidy, economical spurts.

The war in Europe was, everyone said, in its last act. But this camp was still running at full burn.

Inside, the HQ smelled of old coffee and wet wool. A clerk glanced up, clocked Harper's captain bars, and pointed him toward the end office.

Colonel William T. Bennett waited behind his desk, sleeves rolled, tie loose, rimless spectacles sitting on a weathered nose. He had the build of a man who still ran with his officers instead of sending them. On the desk lay a manila folder thick enough to be trouble.

"Jack." Bennett didn't offer a smile—just a hand. "You made good time."

"Your message said 'urgent,'" Harper said, shaking. "The last time I got an 'urgent' I ended up in Poland arguing with a colonel who wanted to burn a laboratory."

"Did you win?"

"No. But I stole the files before he lit the match." Harper's gaze flicked to the folder. "What are we stealing this time?"

Bennett's mouth twitched. "We're not calling it stealing. We're calling it denial of enemy assets."

"That's what we called it in Poland, too."

Bennett gestured to the chair. "Sit down. This one has teeth."

Harper sat. The chair creaked. Bennett opened the folder and turned it so Harper could see. Inside were aerial reconnaissance photos—black-and-white swaths of alpine terrain, dotted with structures. One of them, at the base of a mountain, sat in hard shadow.

"Alpenhof Hotel," Bennett said. "Bavarian Alps. It's a health resort right now—spa, wine, ski-lodge for officers whose conscience doesn't bother them. But our people in Switzerland say it's been 'hosting' late-arriving Party traffic."

"Evacuation?"

"Evacuation," Bennett agreed, "and consolidation. According to London intercepts—and this is where it gets complicated—there's been signal traffic about three crates shipped south from Saxony and Silesia.

The words used repeatedly are Staatsgeheimnisse and Sonderakten."

"State secrets and special files." Harper's eyes narrowed. "Not art?"

"Not art." Bennett tapped the photo. "The Monuments boys can squabble over altarpieces. This came from our side of the house. G-2, OSS, even Navy Intel—they all threw flags."

Harper leaned back. "So you called the poor bastards at Camp Ritchie."

"I called the only bastard I know who can go in small, finish fast, and not start an international incident." Bennett's glasses came off; he massaged the bridge of his nose. "I also called the MIS. They approved you using two linguists."

"Two?" Harper said. "That'll slow us down."

"It'll keep you alive." Bennett set the papers aside. "I read your report out of Aachen, Jack."

Harper's jaw tightened. "I told them I needed another interpreter. They told me we couldn't spare the shipping space."

"And you lost him."

"And I lost him." Harper said quietly.

Bennett let the silence sit long enough. "We're not doing that again. Two is one, one is none. You said that in your after-action. We listened."

Harper's eyes flicked up. "You actually read those?"

"I actually read the useful ones." Bennett crossed to the window and looked out toward the drill field. "You're not the only one hunting these crates. Ultra says NKVD mountain units out of Czechoslovakia have turned west. SOE has an SAS detachment in the vicinity, too. Everyone smells the end. Everyone's grabbing table silver."

"Wonderful," Harper muttered. "Three dogs, one bone."

"This won't stay quiet for long. If the Soviets get it, we'll never see it. If the British get it, we'll see it with pages missing. If we get it—"

"We file it away in a vault under the Chesapeake and pretend it never happened."

Bennett gave him a flat look. "We safeguard it. And someone, decades from now, gets to decide what to do with it."

Harper didn't argue. He'd been in the business long enough to know that was the best answer he'd get.

"So," Bennett said, businesslike again, "you're taking your team—Ross, Duffy, Cruz—and two Ritchie boys I'm going to introduce you to. You brief, you're on a C-47 by sundown, you jump into the Alps before dawn. I can give you approvals. I can't give you time."

"Then let's meet them," Harper said.

Bennett nodded and opened the door. "Gentlemen!"

Two young men in field uniforms stepped in from the hallway, caps under their arms. The first was dark-haired, clean-shaven, with a narrow, intense face—the kind of intensity born of seeing something and deciding not to forget it. The second was taller, fair-haired, with steel-rim glasses and the posture of someone used to a library more than a battlefield.

"Captain Jack Harper," Bennett said. "This is Corporal Benjamin Levy. Born in Berlin. Father was a judge. Survived Kristallnacht by hiding in a coal chute. Got out in '39 on a Kindertransport. Speaks German like a native; English like someone who's going to lecture at Columbia. He can interrogate a brick."

Levy's eyes flicked over Harper—measuring— before he offered a sharp, precise handshake. "Sir."

"And this," Bennett continued, "is Private Karl Vogel. Vienna. His family left after the Anschluss. He knows the Alps from the south side. Knows the dialects from Innsbruck to Berchtesgaden, and he can tell you which Austrian officer went to which academy based on how he ties his boots."

Vogel looked embarrassed at the praise. "I just listen, sir."

"That's why you're useful," Harper said, shaking his hand. "Sit."

They sat. Harper stayed standing, hands behind his back—the habit of a man who liked to loom when he talked.

"Here's the short version," Harper said. "We're not chasing paintings. We're not liberating wine cellars. We're after three crates of paper the Germans don't want us to read. That makes it more dangerous than art. Art you can drop. Documents you burn."

Levy nodded once, jaw hard. "Do we know what's in the files, sir?"

"No." Harper's tone made it clear he didn't like that either. "We know Berlin burned documents by the truckload before you two ever set foot on this continent. We know some of the Party leadership has been trying to ship rather than burn. We know Alpenhof was supposed to be a layover—we have reason to believe the crates have already moved again."

"So why us?" Vogel asked. There was no insolence—just honest curiosity. "This sounds like something for OSS Switzerland."

"Because OSS Switzerland didn't spend three years teaching teenagers from Europe how to talk to Nazis," Harper said. "You two did. You know the music of it. You know when someone is lying because the cadence goes Austrian instead of Prussian. And because —" he looked from one to the other "—when it comes to critical resources, two is one, and one is none."

Levy's eyes flickered. "You've lost an interpreter before."

"Yes," Harper said simply.

Bennett cut in. "You two will report to Captain Harper for the duration of this operation. This takes precedence over your current assignments. Dismissed to the supply hut in fifteen minutes. Full kit, mountain load."

They stood. "Yes, sir."

Levy paused at the door. "Sir? One question?"

Harper raised an eyebrow. "Go ahead."

"Will we be... meeting Germans?" Levy said the word with careful neutrality. "Not as prisoners. As... allies."

Harper understood. "Probably. There's a local asset. Codename 'Edelweiss.' We don't get to pick our friends this week."

Levy's mouth was a straight line. "Understood, sir."

When they were gone, Harper exhaled. "Kids," he said, not unkindly.

"They're not kids," Bennett said. "They're Germans who remember being kids in 1938. That's different."

Harper nodded once. "All right. Get me to your toy store. I assume Rolly Farraday's in on this?"

Bennett actually smiled. "Oh, he insisted."

* * *

The OSS R&D shed sat at the edge of the parade ground like a structure that had rolled in from a circus and been forgotten—tarpaper roof, wide doors, radio aerials poking up like whiskers. Inside, it was organized chaos: workbenches, lamp arms, locks with their covers off, coils of wire, and a wall of rifles with tags.

Xander Roland Farraday—"X" to everyone who didn't want a lecture—was halfway up a stepladder tinkering with a field radio when Harper walked in. Farraday wore his uniform with the insubordination of a man who knew too much to be yelled at: sleeves rolled, tie crooked, captain bars a little tarnished. He had a cigarette parked in the corner of his mouth and a pencil behind his ear.

"Jack!" he called without looking. "Tell me something good."

"We're ending the war," Harper said. "You can go home."

"Lies," Farraday said, climbing down. "This country will find a reason to keep me in a shed until the sun burns out." He clapped Harper on the shoulder, clocked Levy and Vogel behind him, and grinned. "Ah! Fresh Ritchie brains. I love Ritchie brains. They speak better German than the Germans."

Levy and Vogel exchanged a look that said this is the man they warned us about.

"We're flying over the Alps," Harper said. "I need suppressed toys, mountain kit, and anything that will make Soviets rethink their life choices."

"Always Soviets with you," Farraday muttered, moving to a workbench. He laid out items like a magician. "All right. For your reading pleasure..."

He set down a long, ugly bit of stamped metal. "M3 'Grease Gun,' suppressed. .45 ACP. Slow, fat, and quiet. Treat her nice."

Next, a slender pistol. "Hi-Standard HD MS. Suppressed. Ten rounds .22. If you miss, Jack, I will hear about it and never let you live it down."

He held up a sphere the size of a baseball. "Beano grenade. Throw it like a ball. It goes pop on impact. Try not to bounce it off a helmet."

He dumped a small tin of what looked like aspirin tablets on the table. "And, God forbid you get caught..." he wiggled his eyebrows "...'K' and 'L' tablets. One's instant, one's theatrical. You can choose the ending you want."

Vogel swallowed. Levy didn't blink.

"And because I love you," Farraday said, reaching under the table, "button compasses, playing cards with maps of Austria baked in, and—" he pulled out a little matchbox "—camera. Sixteen millimeter. German officer thinks he's being clever taking your notebook, you still have film in your pocket."

Levy reached for the camera, almost reverent. "Kestrel is getting all this?"

"Ohhh," Farraday said, pleased, "they told you the name?"

"They didn't," Harper said. "Loose lips."

Farraday waved a hand and chuckled. "Everyone seems to be naming their pet commando units after birds these days."

Vogel, curious despite himself, said, "Why 'Kestrel'?"

"Because," Harper said, pocketing the camera, "we snatch small, fast, and mean. And we leave before anyone looks up."

Farraday lit his cigarette again, eyes on Harper. "You're going far for this, Jack."

"It's important," Harper shot back. "Something important we have to get from the Germans."

"Oh, I'm not worried about that," Farraday said. "I'm worried about you snatching this pretty present while the Brits and Reds show up for the same birthday party."

Harper's silence said he was worried about that, too.

Farraday sobered. "Be careful with the boys. Ritchie's full of ghosts. Half of them want to make it right. Half want to go back and put a bullet in the whole damned continent."

"I know," Harper said.

# Operation Nightfall
# Part 2

### "Edelweiss"

The C-47 rode the air like an old workhorse—steady but loud—its engines droning against the night. Outside the open side door, the world was a jagged silhouette: the Bavarian Alps rising like black teeth, snow still clinging to the high slopes even in April 1945. Below, no lights. Just forest, stone, and the occasional white seam of meltwater catching moonlight.

Inside the bird, Task Force Kestrel sat on the web seats, bundled into jump gear, faces gray-green in the red cabin light.

Harper did what he always did before a drop: he walked the line.

Lt. Ethan Ross, radio—calm, sharp, wiry, headset crooked around his neck, hands resting on his set like a man petting a nervous dog. Sgt. Mike Duffy, demolitions—bulldog face, Irish eyes, chewing gum slowly, arms folded over a canvas bag that contained more ways to ruin a Nazi's day than the Geneva

Conventions liked to acknowledge. Cpl. Hector Cruz—scout and sniper—dark eyes, dark skin, rifle broken down beside him, expression unreadable.

Then the two newest men. Levy sat tense but not panicked, helmet strap snug, eyes a little too bright—not fear, but readiness. Vogel, beside him, kept craning to look out at the mountains like he was trying to verify they were his mountains.

Harper crouched in front of them so they didn't have to crane up to see him over the engine noise.

"Last chance to ask why you didn't stay in Maryland," he said.

Duffy grinned. "The mess hall here's better."

Cruz's mouth quirked. Ross just shook his head.

Levy said, "We're fine, sir."

Vogel added, "Better than fine. That's the Lech valley out there. I think I know where you're putting us."

"Good," Harper said. "Then if I break my leg on the way down you can still get us to the hotel."

The jumpmaster—a tired-looking T/Sgt with a cigarette burned down to the nub—moved up beside Harper, shouted over the engines, "Ten minutes!"

The red light glowed steady over the door.

Harper clapped Levy on the shoulder, then Vogel. "Remember," he said, voice low, "we're coming in quiet. No heroics. We hit the DZ, stow chutes, go straight to rendezvous. We don't shoot Germans tonight unless they absolutely insist."

Duffy muttered, "They always insist."

Harper pretended not to hear.

He moved back toward the open door and looked down. The wind was sharp, cold, carrying the scent of snow and pine even at this height. Somewhere down there, in a forested fold below the mountains, was the Alpenhof—a peacetime playground built for people who had forgotten there was a war—and in its laundry room or wine cellar or private suite, a woman who called herself Edelweiss.

He checked his watch. Local time, 0307.

The jumpmaster held up five fingers.

Then four.

Then three.

The C-47 banked slightly. Mountains slid past like dark waves.

Green.

"GO GO GO!"

Harper went first, as always—out into the freezing air, the slipstream snatching him, black and blue and white tumbling, the plane vanishing overhead. The chute yanked him hard—a familiar punch—and then he was hanging, swaying, the silence immense.

Below him, the treetops rose dark and pointed. He pulled his risers, leaned, guided himself toward the small break in the trees—the one Ross's recon photos had promised would be there.

He hit snow that was only pretending not to be ice, rolled, came up on a knee, yanked the chute in fast and hard, bundling it like a man afraid of ghosts. The forest around him was deep and white-breathed and absolutely quiet.

A rustle—to his right. Cruz, landing clean, already low. Another shape—Levy, a little sloppy but unhurt. Duffy, cursing under his breath as his canopy snagged on a low fir.

Vogel came down last and landed like a man who had done this before—knees bent, roll, gather, done.

They formed a circle automatically, weapons out, listening.

Nothing.

Harper whispered, "Sound off."

"Ross."

"Duffy."

"Cruz."

"Levy."

"Vogel."

"All present," Harper said. "Bury the chutes. We move in five."

They worked fast, dragging parachutes to a rocky cut, stuffing them under branches and snow. Harper oriented himself with a compass, then with the stars, and then—for good measure—handed it to Vogel.

The Austrian glanced once, pointed downslope. "Hotel's that way. Two kilometers. Pretty easy going until the road."

"Lead us," Harper said.

Vogel set off. He was careful but not slow, picking lines between trees, avoiding crunchy patches, finding the old hunter's paths that never made it onto maps. The men followed in single file, weapons slung but ready.

As they descended, the forest thinned. Through the trees they could see a faint yellow halo— incandescent bulbs from a building that should have been dark at this hour.

The Alpenhof sat in a small winter meadow like a fairy tale that had accidentally survived a total war. Three stories, steep roof, carved balconies, its façade whitewashed and decorated in that kitschy Alpine style travelers loved. A few trucks in the side lot, a staff car. One sentry at the back door, bored, smoking.

"Not bad for a nation with no gasoline," Duffy murmured.

"Germans always save some for themselves," Ross said.

Harper held up a fist. They stopped in the treeline.

"All right," he said, low. "We do it like we briefed. Cruz, overwatch from the barn roof. Ross, back porch—listen for anyone calling Berlin. Duffy, you're contingency on the door. Levy, Vogel—with me. She knows you're coming, but she doesn't know you. Don't spook her."

Levy nodded. Vogel swallowed, eyes on the hotel like he was seeing two things at once: the target now, and the Austria he left.

They moved.

Cruz ghosted away toward the outbuildings. Harper, Levy, and Vogel kept low along the hedge, then cut across the snow straight to the rear staff entrance.

Harper rapped three times—short, short, long.

A beat.

Then the door opened a crack, spilling warm, butter-yellow light into the dark. A woman's eye appeared, sharp, assessing. Blonde hair pinned under a kerchief. White apron over a sweater.

"Wer ist das?" she whispered.

Levy's German was soft and immediate. "Freunde. Aus Ritchie. Wir kommen für die Kisten."

Her eyes widened just a fraction at Ritchie. Then she pulled the door wider.

"Schnell," she said. "Before someone sees."

They slipped inside.

The warmth hit them—radiator heat, kitchen heat, the smell of soup stock and coffee—and for a second all three men realized how cold they'd been. The woman—Edelweiss—shut the door behind them and drew the blackout curtain.

She was late twenties, maybe thirty. Strong cheekbones. Tired eyes. Hands like someone who actually worked in a hotel instead of just owning it. On her lapel, pinned small and almost invisible, was the tiniest edelweiss flower—pressed and lacquered.

Harper took off his cap. "Fräulein Schiller?"

"Ja. But call me Lena," she said, her English nearly perfect. "Only Army men call me Edelweiss." She looked past him. "No Americans with moustaches?"

"No moustaches today," Harper said. "You expected OSS Bern?"

"I expected someone to be slower," Lena said. "The crates are no longer here."

Levy's head snapped up. "Wie bitte?"

Harper's stomach sank. "When?"

"Yesterday," Lena said, already moving, ushering them down a short service corridor toward the laundry. "We heard over the Feldfernsprecher—field phone—that the Soviets were already in Bohemia. That British commandos were asking questions in Innsbruck. Berlin issued an immediate relocation order. The crates were loaded onto a truck with three guards and taken to the mine at Oberstück. They said it was only temporary. 'Until the Americans go away.'"

"Do they ever listen to themselves," Duffy muttered from the doorway, having slipped in behind them.

"Oberstück," Vogel said, frowning, pulling his mental map forward. "That's—"

"Old salt mine?" Harper said.

"Converted," Lena said. "They used it in '42 to store art from Munich. In '44 the SS took control of part of it for—" she made a face "—'special material.'"

Ross, appearing from the porch, said, "Captain, I picked up chatter on the local loop. There's another Allied team in the valley."

Harper turned. "British?"

"SAS by the callsigns," Ross said. "Four men, maybe five, operating 'with approval of London.' They're late to the party."

"And the Soviets?" Harper asked Lena.

"NKVD special detachment out of Prague," Lena said. "Smuggled in through Salzburg as a 'repatriation liaison team.' We have eyes at the Bürgermeister's office. They were asking for directions to the mine an hour ago."

"So we're not early," Duffy said. "We're in it."

Harper looked at Lena. "Can you get us to Oberstück without putting your people at risk?"

"My people are already at risk," she said, simply. "I have been listening to German officers drunk in the dining room for five years. I survived that. I can survive one more night."

She led them into the laundry—big, tiled, steamed up, machines clanking—and to a side door that opened onto the hotel's lower terrace. The mountains stood close here, like walls.

"I can give you a guide halfway," she said. "But I must come back. I have a brother in Gestapo custody in Berchtesgaden. If they know I have disappeared, they will... finish him."

"We can't pull him?" Levy asked, the anger in his voice not entirely professional.

Lena shook her head, smiling sadly. "No. You cannot. That is not your war."

Harper nodded. "You're still coming with us to the handoff. And if the mine's noisy, you stay out."

"I am not helpless," Lena said, offended. "I can shoot."

"I bet," Duffy muttered.

Harper checked his watch again, then looked at his team. "All right. We move now. We try to beat the British to the front door and the Russians to the back."

# Operation Nightfall Part 3

## The Mine at Oberstück

Oberstück sat like a scar in the mountain—a blasted mouth at the base of a cliff, iron rails disappearing inside, concrete poured in the last three years to shore up the old salt seams. Two guard shacks, a searchlight on a pole, a winch house, and a single Opel Blitz truck idling with its headlights off.

Snow whispered down in a lazy curtain. The air smelled of stone, diesel, and explosives.

Kestrel arrived high on the slope, belly-crawled to the lip, and looked down.

"Two sentries," Cruz whispered. "One smoking, one watching the road. Both Wehrmacht, not SS."

"Truck's still there," Ross said. "Means they haven't moved the crates far."

"Or they just got here," Duffy said.

"Or," Levy added, "they're waiting for someone."

"Us, the Brits, or the NKVD," Harper said. "We're cutting in ahead of schedule."

He turned to Lena, who lay beside them, breath fogging. "This is as far as you go."

She looked like she wanted to argue, but she also looked at the men below—the rifles, the floodlight, the open mouth of the mine—and nodded once. "I will wait one hour. If you are not back, I was never here."

"Fair," Harper said. "If we come out hot, run."

"Viel Glück," she said.

They slid back into the trees, circled down behind the winch house. Cruz moved first, silent, cross-covering. Duffy ghosted to the generator. Ross found the junction box and looked like Christmas had come early.

Harper picked up a fist-sized rock and lobbed it down the service road.

It clattered and rolled.

"Was war das?" the smoking guard said, straightening.

"Ein Fuchs," the other said, bored.

Harper shot the smoker in the throat with the Hi-Standard—a small, wet pfft. The man toppled without a sound.

Cruz dropped the second with a short suppressed Grease Gun burst before he could shout.

Duffy yanked the main at the generator. The searchlight died. The mine mouth fell into shadow.

"Move!" Harper hissed.

They ran.

Ross covered the road. Duffy dragged the first body out of sight. Levy and Vogel went straight to the back of the Opel. The bed was empty, but full of sawdust, with three clean depressions where heavy containers had sat.

"Shit," Levy breathed. "We just missed them."

Vogel squinted at the tracks leading inside. "Then we're on the right trail."

"Then we head in," Harper said. "Quick and quiet."

From inside the tunnel came the flat, rapid cough of British-suppressed 9mm—the unmistakable sound of a Sten Mk II(S).

"Shit," Duffy muttered. "Looks like our cousins are already inside."

And over it, echoing faintly: men shouting in Russian.

Harper's eyes went cold. "All right," he said. "We go help them before the Russians have their way. Ross—stay with the truck and be ready to move. Levy, Vogel—with me. Duffy and Cruz, rear."

They plunged into the mine.

\*  \*  \*

The tunnel swallowed them. Harper moved in a crouch, Grease Gun tight to his shoulder, boots scuffing over salt-crusted floorboards. Flickering bulbs along the ceiling cast jaundiced light, each one humming faintly before surrendering to the dark. Somewhere ahead, a Sten whispered again—short, muffled bursts—and then the harsh echo of men barking orders in Russian.

The mine stank of cordite, oil, and nervous sweat.

They reached a junction where the passage forked. Harper flattened against the wall, listening. On the left: English with clipped consonants—SAS. On the right: Russian and the heavy tramp of boots. And somewhere past both, the cargo they'd come for.

He signed for Levy and Vogel to stay tight and pushed left.

They emerged into a cavern carved out of the salt seam—stacked pallets, fuel barrels stenciled Kraftstoff – Gefährlich. A dozen Wehrmacht lay where they'd fought, some half-buried under collapsed scaffolding. The fight had been fast and ugly.

A flashlight beam cut across Harper's chest.

"Hold your bloody fire!" a voice barked. "Americans?"

Harper raised a hand. "Captain Jack Harper, U.S. Army Intelligence."

Out of the shadows stepped a tall, square-jawed man in camo smock and a British beret dusted with salt. Welrod in hand, muzzle still hot.

"Captain Alistair Blake, Special Air Service."

The two men sized each other up in the kind of silence only soldiers understood.

"You're late," Harper said.

"You're early," Blake countered, accent dry as gin. "And you've brought an audience."

He glanced at Levy and Vogel.

Blake's sergeant, a burly Scot with a scar down his jaw, muttered, "Bloody Yanks bring the whole bleedin' U.N."

"Save it," Harper said. "You're taking fire from Soviets up the right tunnel."

"Not Soviets," Blake said grimly. "Chekists. NKVD. They've been shooting anything that moves since they came in the back door."

"Then we clean it up together," Harper said.

Blake hesitated—then nodded once. "Agreed. Temporary marriage. No lawyers."

Harper almost smiled. "Duffy, set a charge on that side shaft. If we have to leave fast, I want it closed behind us."

"Gladly," Duffy said over the radio, already unrolling wire near the entrance they'd come through.

Cruz climbed a stack of crates for overwatch, sights on the Russian approach.

The first NKVD probe came five minutes later—three men in quilted jackets and fur caps, PPShs up, faces grim. They didn't challenge. They just fired.

The joint team answered as one.

The confined space turned deafening: soft thup-thup of suppressed .45s, the dry cough of the Sten, the harsher crack of Soviet 7.62 coming back. One Russian went down hard. Another tossed a grenade that bounced once, twice—Duffy booted it into a side drift, and the blast tore a white gout of salt from the wall.

Levy ducked behind a support beam, reloading, breath ragged.

Vogel knelt beside a dead German NCO, stripping his map case. Inside: rough sketches of the mine—a main shaft, side galleries, and a deep vault marked Schacht IV.

He showed it to Harper. "That's where they're taking the crates."

Harper glanced at Blake. The Brit was reloading with calm precision, face streaked pale with salt dust.

"Then that's where we go," Harper said.

\* \* \*

They advanced through Schacht IV in short bounds, leapfrogging cover. The fighting shrank down to flashes of muzzle light, shouted commands, boots on timber.

Levy broke left to clear a corner and came face-to-face with an NKVD officer in a greatcoat. Both men fired.

Only one fell.

Harper reached him seconds later.

Levy was down, blood soaking through his parka, eyes wide with disbelief. In his fist he still clutched the faded photograph of his family, the edges soft from handling.

Vogel dropped to his knees. "Ben—"

Harper grabbed his collar, dragging him back as rounds chewed the wall. "He's gone, Karl! Move!"

Vogel stared at him, grief and fury colliding. Harper lifted two fingers. Then one.

Two is one. One is none.

They pushed on.

\* \* \*

At the heart of the mine, they found the vault.

Three metal crates sat on wooden pallets under an arc lamp. Fresh markings: Reichssache V. Two Russians lay dead beside them, papers scattered like confetti.

Harper crossed to the nearest crate and snapped the latches.

Inside—stacks of leather-bound journals, each embossed with a crooked swastika and the initials A.H.

Blake looked over his shoulder. "Bloody hell. Diaries?"

"Seems so," Harper said.

Blake exhaled, half laugh, half disgust. "We've been killing each other over a madman's bedtime scribbles."

Before Harper could answer, a new voice boomed from the tunnel mouth.

"Killing... like clumsy schoolboys," said a deep, accented baritone. "And now you will die together."

Commander Vasili Dragunov stepped into the light, flanked by his NKVD men. Scarred. Broad-shouldered. Eyes like polished coal. He carried a captured MG-42.

Harper didn't hesitate. "Down!"

The world dissolved into gunfire.

* * *

What followed was noise and smoke and falling rock.

Duffy hit his plunger. Charges he'd seeded in the side galleries boomed, forcing the NKVD to scatter. Cruz picked off men in the confusion. Blake laid down precise, murderous fire with the Welrod and a captured MP-40. Dragunov raked the room with the MG-42, bullets chewing stone, the weapon screaming in that way that made men duck whether it hit them or not.

Then the ceiling gave.

A section of the old salt seam, already weakened by wartime mining, came down in a rolling crash. Dust turned the air to milk. The tunnel behind Dragunov folded, cutting him and most of his men off in a choking whiteout.

Harper and Blake didn't wait to see who lived.

They grabbed the crates—two men per crate—and staggered back the way they'd come. Cruz limped. Vogel was white-faced and silent. Duffy fell in behind them, covering, dust-gray and coughing.

They reached the outer tunnel just as the last of Duffy's charges went, a rolling concussion that seemed to flatten the snow outside.

Blake turned to Harper. "You've got your bloody crates. Now get them out." He jerked his chin at Vogel—he'd meant your men, not the cargo.

"What about you?"

Blake gave a tired smile. "I heard voices back there. Someone's got to keep the Reds from following."

Before Harper could stop him, the Brit snatched a satchel charge and vanished into the smoke.

"See you in another life, mate," he called over his shoulder.

Harper took a step after him—orders, instinct, fury all colliding—and stopped. There was nothing to chase but dust.

A moment later, the mountain roared again.

Then went still.

* * *

Dawn found them staggering through a mountain pass into Austria, uniforms torn, faces gray with exhaustion. Behind them, the Oberstück mine smoldered quietly under a dusting of new snow.

The truck had gotten the crates most of the way, but the last stretch had to be done by hand, ropes over shoulders, boots slipping on ice. It took most of a day to reach their destination.

Task Force Kestrel arrived spent, just as the sun was rising.

The ruined medieval castle had been commandeered by U.S. intelligence. A major in clean khaki waited beside a jeep. He saluted Harper, eyes flicking with something like respect.

"You've done well, Captain. Washington will want to debrief you personally."

They cracked one of the crates. The major leafed through a diary, lips moving as he skimmed the opening pages—paranoid rants, self-mythology, to-do lists of a collapsing regime.

"Propaganda gold," he said. "Even madness has its value."

Vogel turned away, staring at the peaks burning pink in the sunrise. "We paid so much for this madness," he said softly. "Levy, Blake... all those lives... for what?"

Harper looked down at his gloves, crusted with salt and blood. "War is madness," he said. "And all who fight them are madmen."

He shut the crate.

High above, the wind moved through the broken towers, carrying the dull echo of a mountain settling its dead.

\* \* \*

## Afterword

The men of Task Force Kestrel returned home under sealed orders.

Their mission was never declassified. Official histories credited others—or no one at all. The crates they recovered were logged as "miscellaneous archival material" and transferred to a warehouse under the newly formed Strategic Services Unit (SSU), the OSS successor that, within two years, would help form the Central Intelligence Agency.

But the contents did not go to Langley.

Under emergency authorization, the three crates were diverted to an unlisted facility in New York's Hudson Valley, identified only by a codename: Project Arcadia. The paperwork ends there—the trail dissolving into redactions and unfamiliar signatures.

Captain Jack Harper disappeared from Army rolls in 1947.

Private Karl Vogel was reassigned to postwar reconstruction in Bavaria. His file ends abruptly in 1948.

No public record exists for the diaries' final destination.

Among the few who remember the night at Oberstück, one line endures—passed quietly between archivists and field men:

Some secrets were never meant to win a war.

They were meant to survive it.

* * *

## OSS Historical Note

The Office of Strategic Services (OSS) was the United States' first centralized intelligence agency during World War II. Built from scholars, soldiers, refugees, scientists, and analysts, it pioneered modern espionage, psychological operations, and special missions behind enemy lines.

When the OSS was dissolved on September 20, 1945, its people and capabilities did not vanish. Its functions were divided between the Strategic Services Unit (SSU) inside the War Department and the Central Intelligence Group (CIG)—precursors to today's Central Intelligence Agency (CIA) and the wider U.S. intelligence community.

Many OSS veterans later shaped America's postwar special operations—from Colonel Aaron Bank's U.S. Army Special Forces (Green Berets) to the modern U.S. Army Special Operations Command (USASOC), which still uses the Fairbairn–Sykes dagger—a blade favored by OSS operatives—in its insignia.

Their legacy isn't just in the files we can read. It's in the black programs and "legacy assets" that refused to die—the very kinds of buried operations PHOENIX, and its cultural wing Arcadia, would one day inherit.

# Vanishing Cargo

O n the outskirts of San Antonio, Texas, out past the Northwest section of State Highway Loop 1604, lies a sprawling warehouse complex. To most, it appears to be an ordinary hub of commerce, its vast expanse of concrete and steel blending seamlessly into the industrial landscape. But beneath the mundane exterior, an unsettling mystery has unfolded—one that has perplexed truck drivers, raised questions among locals, and drawn the attention of this journalist.

## A Warehouse of Secrets

The complex, operated under the vague name of "Texas Freight Solutions," has seen an unusual pattern of activity over the past several months. Trucks arrive loaded to capacity with goods of all kinds: electronics, medical supplies, construction materials, and more. Yet when those same trucks leave, they are completely empty. Drivers are paid in cash and instructed not to ask questions. What happens to the cargo remains unknown.

"It's strange," said one driver, who spoke under condition of anonymity. "I've been in this business for 20 years, and I've never seen anything like it. Usually, you're hauling stuff in and taking stuff out. Here, you just drop your load and leave."

## Untraceable Goods

Attempts to follow the paper trail of these shipments have led to dead ends. Invoices list vague descriptions and false company names, while manifests are often incomplete or entirely fabricated. Local authorities have shown little interest in investigating, citing a lack of concrete evidence and jurisdictional challenges. Yet the scale of the operation suggests a level of coordination and resources far beyond that of a typical logistics company.

## Theories and Speculation

Speculation about the purpose of the complex has ranged from the plausible to the fantastical. Some believe it is a front for smuggling operations, with the goods being moved into underground facilities or shipped overseas under false pretenses. Others suggest a connection to military or government projects, pointing to the heavily secured perimeter and the presence of unmarked vehicles entering and exiting the site at odd hours.

One local resident, who asked to remain anonymous, described seeing unusual activity at night. "You'll see these black SUVs, sometimes with tinted windows, going in and out. No markings, no plates. It's like something out of a spy movie."

## The Cost of Silence

Efforts to uncover more details about the operation have been met with resistance. When this journalist attempted to interview employees of Texas Freight Solutions, the response was swift and unyielding. A private security firm, operating under the guise of "facility management," forcibly removed me from the premises and threatened legal action if I returned.

Even more troubling are the stories from whistle-blowers who claim to have worked at the complex. One former employee described being assigned to "inventory management" but never seeing the inside of the warehouses themselves. "Everything was on a need-to-know basis," they said. "We were told to stay in designated areas and not ask questions. It's like they were hiding something big."

## Why It Matters

The implications of this mystery extend far beyond the boundaries of Loop 1604. If the complex is indeed part of a larger scheme—whether criminal, corporate, or governmental—its existence raises critical questions about accountability and transparency in industries that often operate in the shadows. Who owns Texas Freight Solutions? Where are the goods going? And why has no one been able to find definitive answers?

### The Road Ahead

As of now, the true purpose of the warehouse complex remains a closely guarded secret. But one thing is certain: the public deserves to know the truth. This journalist will continue to dig deeper, following every lead and uncovering every hidden corner of this enigmatic operation. If you have information about Texas Freight Solutions or its activities, please contact me at the San Antonio Tribune.

### About the Author:

Samuel Griffin is an investigative journalist with The San Antonio Tribune. Known for his relentless pursuit of the truth, Griffin specializes in uncovering corruption and secrecy in industries often overlooked by mainstream media.

# GEN·ETX

## MISSING REPORTER'S EXPOSE RETRACTED BY BOISE TRIBUNE: WHAT DID HE UNCOVER?

March 1, 2025

BOISE, IDAHO – The disappearance of journalist Daniel Keene, formerly of The Boise Tribune, has sent shockwaves through the local press and beyond. Keene, known for his hard-hitting investigative work, was last seen three nights ago—just days after publishing an explosive exposé on GEN·ETX. The shadowy biotech firm, whose stylized name is meant to evoke "genetics," operates out of Boise with deep ties to U.S. military bioweapons research.

In an unexpected turn, The Boise Tribune has since retracted Keene's article and issued a formal apology, citing "factual inconsistencies." The move has only fueled speculation, leading many to question whether Keene stumbled upon something far more insidious.

Keene's article, published on February 26th, detailed the emergence of a disfigured animal sighted in a remote part of Idaho, specifically, the western Yellowstone region. A Yellowstone hiker posted a grainy yet deeply unsettling image of an unidentified quadruped. While initial reactions dismissed it as a coyote suffering from mange, Keene's investigation suggested something far more disturbing.

According to his sources, including an anonymous former GEN·ETX employee, the creature bore surgical modifications—specifically, a smooth, dark, hemispherical implant embedded in its forehead. The implant, upon closer examination, featured hexagonal black facets, suggestive of a sensor array or some form of experimental neural interface. Editor's note: The prior statements are conjecture, and have not been independently verified.

Keene's article included a transcript from his off-the-record conversation with the ex-employee, who described GEN·ETX's classified projects as "bio-mimetic augmentation" and "vector enhancement." The source, speaking under strict anonymity, warned Keene against pursuing the story further, claiming that the company's real headquarters was not its Boise office but an underground complex hidden inside the 'Zone of Death' of Yellowstone National Park.

"This is not some rogue experiment," the source reportedly said. "GEN·ETX has huge black-budget funding, military oversight, and enough intelligence assets to bury any leak—sometimes literally. If you dig too deep, they will come for you."

Despite warnings from both his editor and the anonymous source, Keene was last seen heading north toward Yellowstone on February 25th. His vehicle was found abandoned near the outskirts of Ashton, Idaho, with no sign of struggle. His notebook was torn apart in the passenger seat.

Surveillance footage from a nearby gas station captured Keene acting paranoid, checking over his shoulder, and appearing to argue with someone off-camera. An unmarked black SUV was also spotted idling near his car, though authorities have not acknowledged any leads related to the vehicle.

### Damage Control?

On March 1st, The Boise Tribune deleted Keene's article from its archives and issued a public statement disavowing his findings. The newspaper's editorial board cited "misinterpretations of photographic evidence" and "unverified claims" as the reason for the retraction.

The question remains: If Keene's report was baseless, why erase it so thoroughly?

Law enforcement officials have stated that there is "no evidence of foul play" in Keene's disappearance, but those close to him insist that's a convenient narrative. The Tribune has declined to comment further, and GEN·ETX flatly denies any involvement.

A spokesperson for GEN·ETX said, "The U.S. has many enemies here and abroad. This is just one more attempt to discredit good, hard-working American companies, whose tireless research keeps our nation safe."

Meanwhile, the online community is buzzing with speculation, uncovering more missing persons cases near the Zone of Death and archived government contracts linking GEN·ETX to classified bio-engineering initiatives.

Did Daniel Keene simply disappear, or was he disappeared? For now, all we have are questions— and a chilling silence where answers should be.


If you have any information regarding the whereabouts of Daniel Keene, or can expand on this story, please reach out to the The Boise Tribune. And, as always, if you have any evidence of criminal wrong-doing, contact your local authorities.

Noah Calloway is an Independent Investigative Journalist for The Boise Tribune.

# Olympic Shadows

Nate McCallister knew the feeling of being unwanted. He'd grown accustomed to the sideways glances, hushed conversations abruptly ending when he entered a room, and the cold silences that fell between himself and his fellow special agents. The modest brick building of the NPS Investigative Services Branch in Port Angeles was meant to be his refuge, a place dedicated to protecting national treasures. Instead, it had become hostile ground.

"Hey, McCallister, you finally close that Indian trading post case?" asked Agent Morales, leaning casually against the doorframe, a smirk barely concealed beneath his neatly trimmed beard.

"Almost," Nate replied evenly, stacking files on his desk. "The Inspector General's office seems very interested in it."

Morales raised an eyebrow, exchanging a glance with another agent nearby. "You know, Nate, if you spent less time stirring things up and more time going with the flow, you might actually have friends here."

Nate paused, stared hard at Morales, and forced a thin smile. "Fuck off, Morales."

Morales chuckled coldly, pushing away from the doorframe and disappearing down the hallway.

"McCallister," barked a familiar voice. Nate looked up sharply, seeing Special Agent in Charge Mark Barringer leaning out of his office. "A minute, please."

Nate took a deep breath and walked into Barringer's meticulously tidy office, adorned with photos of Barringer shaking hands with important people Nate never cared about. Something about Barringer's expression felt off. The man was smiling—a rare sight.

"Sit," Barringer gestured warmly, unsettling Nate further.

"What's this about?" Nate asked cautiously.

"I know things have been...tense lately. I just wanted you to know, I understand you're still coping with the loss of your family."

A flash of memory struck Nate: sunshine filtering through tall trees, laughter echoing around a campsite, Sarah's bright eyes, Liam and Emma chasing each other around the tent. Yosemite, three years ago. The moment faded, replaced by Barringer's disingenuous smile.

"It's been a few years," Nate said stiffly. "I'm managing."

"Good," Barringer said gently. "There's a special case I need you on, out in Olympic. Multiple disappearances. Simultaneous vanishings in three different locations. You're the best fit, given your experience."

Nate nodded slowly. "Understood."

"Excellent," Barringer said, handing him a folder. "I think it'll be good for you, Nate."

As Nate left the office, he felt the weight of Barringer's eyes on his back and the unsettling sensation of being watched closely.

* * *

Olympic National Park felt off the moment Nate drove through the entrance. Towering evergreens loomed above, casting heavy shadows on winding roads. He felt eyes everywhere, unseen observers hidden among the lush foliage.

"Special Agent McCallister?" asked a ranger, approaching him cautiously. "I'm Ranger Daniels. We've been expecting you."

Nate extended a hand, noting Daniels' sweaty palm and quick glance toward the treeline.

"What's the situation?" Nate asked, observing two other rangers whispering anxiously nearby.

"Three groups vanished simultaneously," Daniels replied, voice quivering slightly. "Very strange."

"Any witnesses?"

"All being interviewed by another agency," Daniels said quickly. "All very hush-hush. I don't know why. Above my pay grade."

Nate nodded slowly, suspicion rising.

"Alright. Let's go check the first site," Daniels suggested, clearly eager to move on.

\* \* \*

The Hoh Rainforest felt prehistoric, dense and eerily silent as they entered. Nate's skin prickled with unease. A shadow moved swiftly between trees. Something huge, barely glimpsed, vanished in an instant.

"Shit. I forgot my radio," Daniels muttered. He turned quickly back toward their vehicle.

"Wait—" Nate began, but Daniels was already sprinting down the path, out of earshot.

Nate took a few steps, then stopped. The forest had gone quiet. An odd stillness descended all around him. He glanced left and right, concerned.

Then, in a rush of motion, a large, hairy figure emerged, grabbed Nate, and slammed him against a massive cedar, lifting him effortlessly. Before he could fight back, three heavily armed men stepped from the shadows, their clothing blending seamlessly into the foliage.

"Courtesy of your friends in the ISB," said one, weapon trained.

"And Phoenix," blurted another, earning sharp looks from his teammates.

"Phoenix?" Nate stammered. "What the hell—"

Gunfire was imminent when a loud crash echoed through the forest. A massive blur tore through the men, blood spraying Nate's face. The creature pinning Nate vanished. Screams erupted, and panic spread.

Moments later, only Nate stood trembling amid the carnage. He wiped blood from his face, turning slowly to face an even more enormous figure stepping from the shadows. Its blue eyes pierced the darkness, glowing with fierce intelligence.

Terrified yet defiant, Nate dropped his sidearm to the ground.

"If you're going to kill me, just do it."

The giant creature knelt gently, placing a huge hand on Nate's shoulder. With its other hand, it carefully pressed something small into Nate's palm.

It was a tiny brass compass. Nate recognized it, flipped it over. It was engraved with the name Liam McCallister—his missing son.

Nate's heart shattered, tears blinding him. "Where...where did you get this?"

Slowly, the creature stood and stepped back, its huge hands gracefully forming the sign language words: Miss you.

There was something familiar about the hand movements. A flood of memories returned to him— learning sign language as a Boy Scout merit badge with his then high school sweetheart.

Nate looked at the monstrous form in front of him in teary-eyed disbelief.

"Sarah?" he whispered. But the creature had already vanished into the darkness.

# Apprentice Part 1

## Bad First Impression

The road wasn't marked on any map Jake Langston had ever seen—just a barely-there break in the dust-choked shoulder of State Route 652, southeast of Carlsbad, New Mexico. The sign was rusted metal, sand-blasted halfway to oblivion. It read:

**C³ Facility — Private Property — No Trespassing**

**Authorized Personnel Only**

Jake nearly missed it.

He stomped the brakes and twisted the wheel, his rental SUV skidding slightly before it righted itself and rolled over the cattle grate. Dust swirled in the fading light, painting the evening in smears of orange and gray.

A faint chime echoed in his skull—more sensation than sound.

00:17 LATE.

The digital timecode hovered in the lower-left of Jake's vision, translucent and blue-white. He winced and pressed the accelerator.

"Thanks," he muttered.

A soft haptic bump pulsed behind his eyes as the implant acknowledged him and returned to passivity.

Jake shifted in his seat. The Typhon implant was subtle, but always on—always... there.

He'd received it after passing Phase I of PHOENIX tech school. A reward, they said. A badge of progress. Proof he could handle the theory.

Since then, it had been mostly a glorified clock and personal assistant—basic diagnostics, internal metrics, limited overlay functions he rarely used. Nothing fancy. Nothing immersive.

The real features were still locked away.

The road curved into the desert like a scar, flanked by nothing but wind-carved stone and scrub. The sun was setting fast—dropping behind the distant mesas in a burnt-gold splash. Even with the AC on high, Jake's shirt clung to his back.

This wasn't what he expected when he signed on with PHOENIX. High-tech work, sure. Classified infrastructure, cutting-edge tech installs—that was the pitch. But this? This looked like a forgotten airstrip.

Then he crested a small rise and saw it.

A facility cut into the desert like a surgical incision. A squat cluster of buff-colored modular structures flanked by scaffolding, and cooling ducts. Everything had a temporary or hastily assembled appearance. There were no lights except for the faint amber glow from several gate sensors and perimeter motion detection rigs.

Dead center stood a gate with a familiar emblem:

The PHOENIX logo. A fire bird, half-risen from its own ashes. It was shiny and new, or made from more weather-resistant stuff than the previous sign.

Jake exhaled.

"Okay. Here we go."

He slowed as he approached the gate. The metal boom arm stayed down. A ring of automated cameras swept toward his windshield, lenses glinting like insect eyes. One of them clicked as it locked onto his face.

Nothing happened.

Then a second camera repeated the scan.

Still nothing.

Jake rolled down his window and leaned out. "Uh... hello?"

No reply. No buzz. Not even a red light.

Then a shadow moved through the dust.

A desert-camo SUV emerged from a side road—silent, sudden. It parked directly in front of him, blocking his path. Two men stepped out. Both wore matte-gray body armor with digital desert overlays. Their faces were impassive behind mirrored glasses.

Jake froze.

One of them gestured. "Out of the vehicle."

Jake fumbled for his badge. "Right. Sorry! I'm Jake Langston. A...new tech? I'm supposed to be on-site for a—"

The guard didn't respond. He took the badge and held it up to a tablet. A moment passed. The other spoke softly into his mic: "Tower, confirm Langston, Jake. New recruit."

There was a pause.

Then the voice of a woman crackled over the guard's earpiece. "Let him through. Elena's expecting him."

The boom arm hissed and lifted.

As Jake got back into the SUV, one of the guards smirked and tapped the roof with his knuckles. "Try not to get yourself shot."

Jake blinked. "Wait, what?"

But the guards were already walking away.

* * *

Jake followed the narrow drive through the gate. The terrain dipped, revealing more of the compound—a rough grid of prefab buildings, metal storage sheds, and shipping containers stacked like half-forgotten Tetris pieces. A communications tower loomed overhead, its top half still unpainted.

Signs pointed him toward Underground Personnel Parking.

The ramp sloped downward beneath a thick slab of reinforced concrete. As he descended, the desert heat peeled away like dead skin. Cool, conditioned air pressed against the windshield. Jake felt his shoulders drop for the first time in hours.

The subterranean lot was surprisingly sleek—industrial-polished floors, bright strip lighting overhead, and a few parked vehicles that looked more like armored shuttles than trucks. A discreet security camera swiveled toward him, its small green LED a small comfort. A wall screen displayed: LANGSTON, J. – PROCEED TO BAY 6.

Jake pulled into the assigned spot and shut off the engine. The sudden silence was eerie.

The underground parking garage was cool and dry. Lights buzzed overhead.

He popped the trunk, exited and took a deep breath.

"Typhon," he said under his breath. "Navigation. Site schematic."

A small green dot blinked at the center of his vision, then expanded into a faint overlay—an overhead wireframe of an empty rectangle.

ERROR: NO SITE MAP AVAILABLE.

The message pulsed three times, then faded out.

Jake sighed and tried to zoom and pan the map, hoping something might pop in.

Eyes left—zoom. Right—scroll. Blink and hold—confirm.

Tongue press to the roof of his mouth—menu back.

The interface stuttered slightly, and the whole thing was grainy around the edges.

Typical. Version 1.0 was always like this—usable, but barely.

He grabbed his bag and stood in the middle of the garage, orienting himself. On one wall, someone had tacked up a laminated hand-drawn map titled:

"Welcome to DESOLATION"

There were two comical cartoon cacti in the corner, one laying on the floor with x's for eyes, the other giving a thumbs-up.

The map had colored arrows pointing to various site locations: Coordination Trailer, Utility Access Trunk, Connector Support Building, Don't Go Here (with a skull drawn next to it), and ??? scrawled across one sector—intentionally redacted.

A brown coffee stain warped part of the legend.

Jake smiled despite himself. "Yeah. That tracks."

He slung his bag over his shoulder and followed the arrow toward Coordination Trailer – Admin Hub. His boots echoed faintly in the wide, sterile corridor beyond the garage—white walls, concrete floor, humming electrical conduits.

He passed a water cooler. A sticky note on the tank read:

"Boil notice? LOL. Just drink it. If you start seeing colors, report to medical."

Jake didn't stop.

At the end of the corridor, a utilitarian steel door was propped open. The light inside was soft and even, like a medical bay or an architect's office. He stepped through the threshold and cleared his throat.

"Uh, hi. Jake Langston. Reporting in for—"

He stopped.

A tall woman stood near a metal table strewn with what appeared to be schematics. Her jet-black hair was tied in a no-nonsense braid. She didn't look up.

"You're late," she said evenly.

"Sorry. I missed the turn-off. The sign—"

"She looked up, and the weight of her gaze stopped him. Her expression was unreadable.

"Elena DuChamp," she said. "Site coordinator. You'll report to me for all project tasks, but I won't hold your hand."

Before Jake could respond, a voice from the corner mumbled, "He'll be fine. Looks like he at least knows which end of a wrench to hold."

Jake turned to see an older man—gray in the beard, crow's feet around the eyes—leaning in a folding chair, chewing something unidentifiable.

He wore the same work coveralls Jake had been issued, though his were weathered, stained, and the sleeves were rolled to the elbow. The patch on his chest read: Goldberg.

Jake stuck out his hand. "Jake Langston."

The man ignored the gesture. "You talk too much."

Elena gave the faintest smile. "Jake, meet your field partner. Everyone just calls him Gramps."

"I'm old," Goldberg muttered.

"You're older than dirt and twice as salty," she replied.

Jake finally lowered his hand and glanced at the table. A massive set of technical blueprints stretched across its surface—power conduits, water feeds, something that looked like dimensional geometry overlaid with PHOENIX code tags.

"Wow," he said. "Are these real?"

Elena and Gramps exchanged a look.

Then both burst out laughing.

Gramps slapped the table. "Kid thinks we'd leave real plans lying around."

Elena turned and stared at Jake. "Let's see what we have to work with. Wait...Typhon implant version 1?"

"It's what they gave us at the school," said Jake.

"No, no, no," said Elena. "This won't do. You can't do anything with that. I'm pushing you to Version 5. You'll never finish my installs with that antique."

"Wait, you can just—?" Jake winced and took a step back. "Ok that's—"

"Hold still," she said, cutting him off. "Give it a minute to reboot into the new version."

A sudden burst of light flared bright across his vision, then reshaped itself in layers—geometric scaffolding folding in from the corners of his sight, soft blue arcs drawing data from the environment, tagging objects, mapping the trailer in real time. His vitals ticked into the upper corner. A subtle ripple of environmental diagnostics unfolded across the bottom edge. The interface was crisp, reactive—alive.

Jake staggered slightly. "Holy—" He blinked hard. "This is amazing."

He blinked, watching as the HUD tagged her as DuCHAMP, ELENA – COORDINATION LEAD in faint text just above her head.

"It's adequate," she said flatly, still focused on her screen.

Gramps smirked. "This ain't tech school any more. Welcome to the real job."

\* \* \*

Elena raised a hand to her temple. With a slight twitch of her eye and a faint whisper of sound, the air above the table shimmered.

Suddenly, an augmented reality projection flickered into being—a complex lattice of three-dimensional nodes, Veil access points, and calibration readouts. The AR floated like a ghost above the fake blueprints.

Jake's jaw dropped. The hovering schematic was an elegant tangle of light and code, shifting and updating in real time. It was like watching a symphony of math and architecture unfold in midair.

Jake instinctively grabbed the edge of the table. "Uhhh... Uh oh. Suddenly I don't feel so well." He put his hand over his mouth.

Gramps rolled his eyes and chewed another bite of jerky. "There's gonna be some disorientation at first. Just muscle through it."

"I think I'm gonna be sick."

"Waste can's over there," said Elena. "Just don't hurl on the floor, please."

Jake kept breathing, blinking past the strange visual layering until the lines sharpened and settled. The world felt thinner somehow, like a skin had been peeled back to reveal some glowing infrastructure beneath. His stomach was beginning to settle.

He let out a shaky breath. "Okay... wow. This is... actually kind of amazing!"

Gramps nodded. "Welcome to Phoenix, Langston. The Typhon implant is one of the fringe benefits."

Elena finally stepped away from the schematics and walked toward a wall display. "You've been assigned to install infrastructure for a forward Connector site—water, power, and network."

"Is this part of Eremos?" Jake asked.

She gave him a cool look. "Where did you hear that name? Your tasks will not be underground, they'll be on the surface. Make sure you keep your head there."

Jake glanced at Gramps, who offered no help—just a grunt and a shrug.

Elena continued. "Your deployment must be completed by week's end. The schedule's aggressive, but it's because I'm on a strict deadline. Centcom brass is chomping at the bit to get this site up and running.

Gramps will guide your work and keep you on-time. Your access has been restricted to designated project zones. Do not deviate. If you wander, your implant will let you know. Linger too long, and you'll make fast friends with security. Understood?"

"Yes ma'am." Jake was trying hard not to look as intimidated as he felt.

She tapped a wall panel and brought up a list of tasks. "Your initial objective is to set-up four Veil utility access points. That includes control and flow equipment. I've cleared you for your initial tool and diagnostic equipment allocation. I'm sure you know this already, but Veiltech equipment is rare and expensive, even in PHOENIX-land. Handle it with extreme care. Break anything, see the quartermaster for a replacement...and me for an ass-kicking."

Jake nodded seriously, then switched his attention back to the floating symbols, trying to keep up.

"Also," she added, "this facility is currently operating under a security-by-obscurity posture. That means minimum fences and guards. There will be no incident response beyond the two patrolmen you met at the gate and one in the tower. The Directors believe incomplete compounds are less attractive targets."

Gramps snorted and shook his head. "Idiots."

Elena ignored him. "Your job is to get this facility online. Don't get curious, and don't do anything stupid. If something feels off, call it in. If something tries to kill you..." She gave a dry smile. "Run faster than Gramps."

Jake forced a laugh.

Gramps didn't.

Elena stepped forward, her voice cool and commanding. "You'll both report to me at the beginning of each day until your tasks are complete. Again, see the quartermaster for any needed materials."

She looked down at her pad and started poking at it with a finger.

Jake cleared his throat. "I don't know how to thank you, ma'am. This Version 5 Typhon—"

Gramps snorted, stopping him mid-sentence.

Elena didn't look up. "You can thank me by getting my installs done. And maybe don't trip over your own feet while you're at it."

She added, "You're dismissed." Then she glanced at Jake and gave him a quick wink and nod.

There was something in that wink—something knowing. Like she'd seen rookies come and go, and Jake had just passed some kind of invisible test.

It wasn't exactly the welcome he was hoping for, but at least he knew she wasn't mad at him. It instantly relieved a lot of his stress.

Gramps offered a sloppy salute and grabbed Jake by the shoulder.

"C'mon, Patch Adams. Time to earn your stripes."

\* \* \*

The stars were bright overhead, and the dry desert wind had finally started to cool. It rustled across the hard-packed sand and whispering through the chain-link fences around the compound.

Jake and Gramps had a roof above them, but the building they were working in had no walls. The ceiling was held up by thin, metal beams with circular holes cut in them for wiring and pipes.

They moved with purpose between flickering work lights and humming equipment, staging equipment and running wire harnesses through conduits like cybernetic gardeners planting something alien in the earth.

Jake was on one knee, fitting a stabilization collar around a conduit post. He double-checked the torque spec in his HUD and reached for a small torque wrench.

Gramps watched from a distance, arms folded. "Torque that collar like a dentist on nitrous, Langston. Give it some guts."

Jake rolled his eyes but tightened it with a snap. "Shouldn't we be grounding that conduit? Sorry, I guess I'm just not used to doing this without a trainer or OSHA breathing down my neck."

Gramps snorted. "OSHA ain't been within fifty miles of a PHOENIX site since Nixon was in office."

He spat off to the side. "And if they showed up now, they'd vanish faster than a witness in Vegas."

They moved on. When all of the control boxes, flow control systems and associated wires and pipes were in place and connected, Gramps gave a low grunt. It was either his version of praise or gas.

"I hate all this preamble," he said. "It's boring. Now comes the fun part."

"Finally," said Jake.

"Not so fast," said Gramps. "You know some theory, you've done some basic setups in class, but this is the real deal. Veiltech is powerful, but dangerous."

"Yes, I know," said Jake. "I've been fully briefed."

Gramps looked at him seriously. "When you work with me, you do it by the book. I've...well, let's put it this way. You won't last long if you're sloppy. Not with me. Understand?"

"Yes," said Jake. "Yes, sir."

"And don't call me sir. I work for a living."

Jake smiled and nodded.

Gramps took a deep breath. "Ok, everything we just setup starts with these. "He pointed to several pipes emerging from the concrete slab they were standing on. "Know what these are?"

"Uh," Jake thought about it for a moment. "They just look like standard feed pipes for water, electric—"

"Wrong," said Gramps. "These are total bullshit. Fakes. They don't go to anything. We call 'em Façades."

Jake looked confused. "Why install fake pipes and wire conduits? Seems like a huge waste of effort."

"It's not," said Gramps. "Think about it. Ninety-nine-percent of the people you're gonna meet in life have no idea what Veiltech is...or how it works! They think power comes from wires and water comes from pipes. And that's just the way of it.

These fake pipes are for them. If they knew water, power, and network came straight out of that little box—no wires, no source—it'd drive them mad."

Jake chuckled. "They'd seriously start questioning their world-view."

"Yes. And sure, you could try to explain it to them. Tell them that the source could be anywhere; Pluto, or on the other side of the damned Universe. Distance doesn't matter when you make a non-local connections."

"The bridge," said Jake, trying to sound helpful.

"Exactly. They might get it, given enough time. Think about how carefully they revealed it to you at your tech school."

"It was a whole year of theory and build-up before they showed us the working tech," said Jake.

"Yup. Sounds right," said Gramps. He looked deep in thought for a moment, then added:

"Most are smart enough to get it, but some people don't wanna know. They think they have a pretty good handle on things in their life. And what we do—connecting things non-locally—it would just upset them. So a lot of our surface jobs are going to be this: Making people who don't know about Veiltech think their world of purely "physical connections" is just fine and dandy!"

"I see," said Jake. "I guess that makes sense. But that makes me think...how many other things am I going to see working for PHOENIX...that are also fake."

Gramps grinned wide. "That is the right question, Patch Adams."

\* \* \*

A while later, Gramps took a smoke break. Jake was careful to avoid the smoke. He stared up at the stars. "This place... feels like the ass-end of nowhere. Like it fell out of time."

Gramps didn't look up. "That's why they picked it. Quiet. Remote. Forgettable. Perfect place to build a lie."

Jake glanced over. "You ever gonna tell me what this place is for?"

Gramps was silent for a long moment, then exhaled a long plume of smoke. "Nope."

"C'mon. Give me something."

"They collect things," said Gramps. "Alright? From the nearby caverns."

Jake frowned. "What...Carlsbad? The National Park? What kind of things?"

Gramps kept his eyes averted. "The kind you shouldn't worry about. Let's leave it at that."

Jake let it drop. For now.

They finished the last of the setup together in uncomfortable silence. The hum of the Veiltech equipment settled around them, like a low, distant choir.

As they walked back toward the coordination trailer, Jake wiped his brow. "So... how'd I do?"

Gramps pretended to mull it over. "You didn't fry yourself, or open a rift in spacetime. That's a solid B-minus."

Jake grinned, then caught himself. "I'll take it."

Gramps gave him a sideways glance—just a hint of something softer behind the sarcasm. "Truth is, kid... you picked it up faster than most."

Jake smiled.

"We're doing important work here," said Gramps. "I think you can sense that. This surface site, and the connector facility just below us...they're not just utility hubs, Patch. They part of a bigger whole."

They reached the trailer steps. Gramps paused before heading in. "But don't get cocky. This job's not about brilliance. It's about keeping your hands steady...keeping your wits about you when the stress is high and world's coming apart."

Jake nodded, solemn now. "Understood."

Gramps grunted again, then looked up at the stars for a moment.

"You're not half bad, Patch Adams."

The old man disappeared inside.

Jake lingered outside a moment longer, breathing in the dry desert air.

Above, the stars blinked in silence.

# Apprentice Part 2

## BLACK STAR

The desert had gone still. Gramps's utility truck cruised along a winding dirt road on the east side of the compound, its soft electric hum barely disturbing the silence. Above, the stars looked sharp enough to cut, and the air had cooled to something almost tolerable. The moon was rising now, casting skeletal shadows from the creosote brush.

Jake yawned into his gloved fist, the motion creaking with dried sweat and fatigue.

"We could've waited till morning," he muttered.

Gramps didn't look away from the trail. "Wind's supposed to kick up soon. Could bring a dust storm with it. We set up now, or we waste a day to the weather."

Jake sighed. "Okay then. I'm good to go."

They crested a ridge and rolled into a shallow basin. Another prefab slab awaited them—a concrete pad with temporary lighting rigs and a Veilcompatible distribution cabinet already craned into place.

Jake stepped out, joints cracking, and looked up at the stars. "Can't believe this is how I'm using my degree. I racked up a quarter-million in student loans just to be a desert plumber."

Gramps opened the tailgate and handed him a heavy crate of gear. "MIT, right?"

"Yeah."

"I figured. Only MIT grads bitch like that when asked to do real work."

Jake raised an eyebrow. "You got something against MIT?"

"Nah. Got my degree from Caltech," Gramps said, shouldering a coil of cable. "Have to give you East-coast boys some shit. That's just how it is."

They moved efficiently, side by side, sliding into the rhythm of seasoned fieldwork.

Jake tapped at his Typhon HUD, flipping through PHOENIX overlays. "You get a lot of these install requests at weird, middle-of-nowhere locations?"

"All the time. Super-remote's PHOENIX bread and butter. You don't test exotic tech where civilians might see it."

"What's the craziest install you ever did?"

"I don't know about craziest," said Gramps, "but the scariest was up in North Dakota..."

"Yeah?"

"It's all Air Force missile silos and ghosts. You can drive for hours and see nothing at all—maybe a partially collapsed church on the side of the road. And at night? Super creepy. Odd moving shadows, and you always feel like you're being watched. "

Jake shivered. "Uhh! No thank you. What else?"

"Old facility down near El Paso. Near the border. Feels like you're in the Wild West."

"Jesus," Jake muttered. "Plumbing the Veil through Texas?"

"Texas, and a lot of other remote areas you can't easily get resources. Wait 'til you hear about Antarctica."

"You're shitting me!" Jake chuckled under his breath, then focused. He finished tightening a clamp, rechecked the collar ring spacing, and nodded. "Everything's secure. Ready to prime."

Gramps gave a short nod. "Let's do it. Actually, you do the activation this time."

Jake ran through the start-up sequence by reading the technical documentation in his HUD—another great use for it, as he didn't have to keep bulky manuals on his lap while he worked.

The anchor began to hum—a deep, harmonic tone that resonated in his chest cavity. The overlay shimmered with diagnostic text as the node aligned.

"Bring the taps online," Gramps said, pointing toward the connections.

"I'm trying," said Jake, "but I'm not getting power to the panel."

"Check the breakers."

"I did. They're all in."

"Can't be," said Gramps. "Here, let me...yup. Here's your problem."

"What?" said Jake. Then he looked at what Gramps was pointing to.

"Oh my god!" He slapped himself on the forehead, then turned the big green switch that said "Main Power".

The lights on the distribution panel blinked green.

"Ha," said Gramps. "Happens to us all, kid."

Jake flipped the last feed switch, watching the LEDs climb green across the board:


120VAC — ACTIVE

240VAC 3-PHASE — ACTIVE

480VAC 3-PHASE — ACTIVE


Water followed—hot and cold, steady pressure. PHOENIX-NET pinged online at a clean 1.0 Gbps. Jake finished the automated test with a satisfied grin.

"That's two down. Should we head back in? Give Elena the good news?"

Gramps shook his head. "Before we pack up, I'm gonna give you a little free training. One of those lessons they don't put in the manuals."

Jake straightened. "What kind of training?"

"The kind that keeps you from blowing a hole in your foot... or God forbid, killing someone."

He reached into the truck bed and came back with a length of dull aluminum pipe about three inches wide. Wedging it between two cinder blocks, he held out a hand.

"Here. Hand me your Veil Control Unit."

Jake hesitated but passed it over. Gramps tapped through the interface with the easy precision of long habit, bringing up the metadata pane. He scrolled until one entry lit up in warning amber:


pressure: 15,504 psi


He saved it to a memory slot, tagging it: Demo – High-Pressure. Do Not Use.

"You ever see that number in the wild, you'd better damn well know what you're connecting to."

"Fifteen thousand PSI? Where are you getting water pressure that high? That's—"

"Enough to cut steel," Gramps said flatly. "Your flesh won't even slow it down."

He primed the connection, aligned a small nozzle at the pipe, then stepped back.

"Ready? Watch."

A white, howling jet erupted for exactly one second, the sound halfway between a shriek and a roar. It sheared through the aluminum like warm butter, spraying fine mist into the work lights. The pipe clanged to the ground in two clean halves.

Jake's jaw dropped. "Holy hell..."

Gramps killed the feed and pulled up the metadata again. "Now, you see why you triple-check before you hand a site over to Elena's crew. Pressure, voltage, current—anything outside tolerance can maim or kill. You don't want her chewing your ass for doing something stupid. But you definitely don't want her burying someone because you got sloppy."

Jake nodded quickly. "Got it. Check the metadata. Always."

"Good." Gramps handed the unit back.

Jake glanced at the saved slot. "Challenger Deep?"

"Yup. Bottom of the Pacific Ocean. Marianas Trench."

Jake smirked faintly, but the image of the pipe splitting clean in two burned itself into his mind.

"Alright," Gramps said, heading for the cab. "Now we can pack up."

* * *

Jake kept glancing at the Challenger Deep entry in his Typhon HUD as they bumped along the dirt road.

15,504 PSI. Enough to cut steel. Enough to cut him in half.

Hard to believe that kind of power could flow through something as unassuming as a Veil Access Point.

He flexed his fingers around the Veil Control Unit in his lap, still feeling the phantom vibration from when Gramps had tagged the setting. The image of the pipe shearing like butter haunted him. No simulation in tech school had prepared him for that.

Gramps drove in silence, one hand on the wheel, the other drumming against his thigh. The truck's electric motor hummed softly over the crunch of gravel. Above them, the moon climbed higher, sharpening every shadow.

Jake finally spoke. "That was... intense."

Gramps didn't look over. "Good. You'll remember it. Triple-check your metadata before you hand anything over to Elena's crew, or you'll be remembering it in your exit briefing."

They crested a ridge, and the compound came into view again—faint spotlights casting long, angular shadows across the yard. The prefabs and storage stacks looked almost peaceful under the moonlight.

"How ya doin'?" Jake asked.

Gramps didn't answer right away. "Thinking."

"About?"

"People I've worked with."

Jake blinked. "Field techs? Like me?"

A slow nod. "Some made it. Some didn't."

Jake straightened in his seat. "What happened?"

Gramps didn't answer. He pulled the truck out of gear, letting it coast the rest of the way in.

They pulled up near the equipment container. One of the guards nodded at them from beside the coordination trailer—a professional, impassive flick of the chin. Jake returned it without thinking, mentally cataloging the man's face. Another note for the growing roster of names and roles in this strange, isolated place.

As Gramps hopped out to give the gear a quick inspection, Jake found himself looking up at the sky. The stars here were knife-sharp, undimmed by city light.

"So," he said, "what's the weirdest thing you've ever seen working for PHOENIX?"

Gramps latched his Veiltech toolkit—always the last thing he touched. "Nevada job. Ten years back. Groom Range."

Jake froze halfway through stowing a coil of cable. "Like... Groom Lake? Area 51?"

Gramps gave him a side-eye. "I thought you were 'fully briefed.' We overlap with the military. Provide goods, services. But we don't take orders from them. More often, they take ours."

He pulled a flask from his chest pocket and took a sip. "Had a new guy with us—bright, eager. A lot like you. We're mid-calibration when he stops talking mid-sentence. Just... gone."

Jake frowned. "Gone?"

"Not a sound. Not a flash. Boots still there, laced up. Everything else? Vanished."

Jake stared.

"One frame on the footage, he's there. Next frame—air."

"What the hell?"

"Report said 'Veil field microdrift.' Subspace shear, they called it. But we all knew it was crap. Something on the other side reached out and got him."

Jake shivered. "You're messing with me. This is like a ghost story you tell the new guys."

"I wish it was." Gramps' voice was flat. "Veiltech's not ours. We just use it. Whatever's behind it... it's older, stranger, and you don't want to meet it."

The wind shifted. Up in the watchtower, a lone silhouette moved—scanning the perimeter with a pair of heavy binoculars.

Below, a guard passed near the truck, then paused. "You hear that?"

Jake listened. The cicadas had stopped. So had the wind. The night was holding its breath.

Then—thrum.

A low, resonant pulse rolled over them. Not sound so much as pressure. It made Jake's teeth ache.

Gramps turned sharply. "Pack it up."

Jake hesitated. "What is that?"

The watchtower guard froze, head turning toward the western sky.

A shape passed overhead—black on black, angular and silent. A hole in the sky.

It banked slightly, then stopped. Four shadows dropped from its belly before it vanished toward the far side of the compound.

Gramps reached into the truck and pulled out a hardcase. Inside—two disruptor batons.

He tossed one to Jake without looking. "We're not alone."

In the distance—click.

Then the sound of metal feet striking concrete.
Smooth. Precise. Not human.

And then—gunfire.

\* \* \*

The first scream tore through the compound like a
steam whistle.

Jake froze, eyes wide. A second later came a short
burst of gunfire—sharp, deliberate. Then a crunch.
Something wet. Then silence.

Gramps was already moving.

"Grab your Veil Control Unit," he hissed, crouching
behind the truck. "We can't let them fall into enemy
hands. Grab it and keep it safe."

Jake scrambled for the case and his terminal. He
stuffed both into his day pack, slung it over his
shoulder, and dropped beside Gramps. "What the hell
was that?!"

"That," Gramps said grimly, "is what happens when
Directors underfund surface security."

From the far side of the coordination trailer,
another burst of gunfire flared—muzzle flashes
strobing against the prefab walls. More screams
followed.

This time, they didn't stop.

Jake peeked around the container, heart pounding.

Two PHOENIX guards had taken cover behind a sandbagged generator. One was firing a compact flechette rifle—tight bursts stitching through the dark. The other launched a pair of recon drones—blue nav-lights flaring on as they climbed.

Then—movement.

A sleek, inhuman shape darted between prefab shadows. Impossibly fast. Low to the ground. Lower limbs a blur of motion.

CRACK-CRACK-CRACK!

The flechettes struck something metal. Sparks showered behind a shipping crate. A hiss followed—steam-like—and a strange whirring sound, not quite mechanical, not quite animal.

The drones dropped, smashed from the air by something unseen. They hit the ground and coughed out thin clouds of smoke.

Jake ducked just in time. A long, bladed appendage sliced through the air above him—missing by inches. It caught the drone operator mid-chest, carving through armor, flesh, and bone as if they offered no resistance.

A spray of blood.

Then the silhouette shot past—and the man's head was gone. His body dropped to its knees, then flopped sideways into stillness.

The remaining guard screamed. He emptied his clip, reached for his sidearm—

The creature stepped into the light.

Seven feet of matte-black alloy and predatory grace, its frame was lean and raptor-like. A long, angular head jutted forward, crowned in overlapping mechanical feathers that flexed and twitched with a mind of their own. A matching tail swept behind it, armored plumage rippling subtly as it moved—every motion precise, economical, and utterly alien.

Its eyes glowed red—flickering, twitching, scanning in rapid bursts.

The guard fired.

The Crow twisted under the barrage with uncanny precision, then surged forward.

A metallic screech tore through the air—animalistic and wrong.

The guard vanished beneath a blur of limbs. Sparks. Screaming. Gunfire.

Jake couldn't watch. He turned away, gagging.

"They're not just killing," he whispered. "They're scanning. Gathering data."

Gramps checked his HUD, jaw tight. "I've seen these before. BLACK STAR drones. Infiltration units— built to steal intel. We're being catalogued... but they're not transmitting. Not yet. Looks like they're hunting for a way to punch the data out."

"BLACK STAR?" Jake's voice shook. "Never heard of it."

"Private Military Company," said Gramps. "Been harassing PHOENIX since the mid-'90s. Mercs with deep pockets—and a rumor says some of 'em used to wear our badge."

Out of the corner of his eye, Jake caught movement—something clinging to the side of the watchtower, where no human had any right to be. Its silhouette shifted in the moonlight, sleek and angular, the sheen of matte-black alloy rippling as it moved.

The guard at the top—a dark-skinned woman with tight braids pulled back beneath a comms headset—stood her ground. She raised her sidearm and fired straight down the ladder at the thing climbing toward her.

CRACK-CRACK-CRACK. Sparks flew as rounds glanced off the climbing shape.

Then—BOOM.

The ladder erupted as a shaped charge went off, the blast shearing one of the Crow's arms clean off. Metal shrieked against metal as the thing fell away into the shadows below.

The guard leaned hard against the railing, breathing fast. She flipped open a small panel on the wall, revealing a red button under cracked plastic. No hesitation—

SLAM.

A low chime echoed from the tower, followed by a faint, distant relay tone somewhere deeper in the compound.

She keyed her mic. "Redline signal sent. Hope that damn button's connected."

No response. Just static.

She scanned the dark below. Her voice carried down to Jake and Gramps: "Y'all stay hidden if you can. Don't try to be heroes."

Jake looked up, meeting her eyes. For a heartbeat, they shared an understanding—then a shadow dropped onto the platform behind her.

Another Crow. Intact. Undamaged. It closed the gap with insect speed, silent but for the faint rasp of talons on metal.

Jake's mouth opened to shout, but Gramps yanked him back and clamped a hand over his mouth.

Two gunshots rang out. A scream—cut short.

Silence.

Gramps let out a slow, measured breath. Without a word, he crouched and carefully laid his baton on the ground, setting it down so quietly it barely touched with a tap.

Jake swallowed hard and did the same.

Gramps met his eyes. "From here on out... we move like ghosts."

* * *

The compound had gone deathly still.

Behind a shipping container, Jake heard only wind, idle machinery... and the thrum of blood in his ears.

Gramps crouched low and gestured—follow me.

They moved fast, hugging shadows between prefab walls and scorched machinery. Debris crunched beneath their boots. Smoke twisted through broken light fixtures and ragged bullet holes in the siding.

One Crow lay collapsed near the wrecked SUV—its twisted limbs twitching inside a scorched and smoking impact crater.

Jake stared. "That one...?"

"Dead," Gramps muttered, nudging it with his boot. "Those two guards made sure of it."

He gave a quiet nod. "Rest in peace, gents."

Ahead: scrape. Drag. A faint metallic screech.

They froze.

Around the corner, a second Crow crawled slowly across cracked concrete. It was missing a leg, and one arm dangled by threads of carbon wire. But it was still moving—pulling itself forward with claws that gouged deep furrows in the ground. Its feathered head scanned, twitching, pausing every few feet.

Jake swallowed. "My god... those things are relentless."

Gramps followed its gaze—toward the coordination trailer's rear, where a flat, white satellite dish angled skyward. He checked his HUD and confirmed the Crow was trying to brute-force its way into the comm system network.

"It's trying to beam their intel out," he growled, then pointed. "Good news is that's the only active dish on-site."

Jake tapped into his HUD. "If it gets a signal through—"

"It won't."

Gramps darted across the open lane, low and fast. He reached the uplink housing and yanked the access panel open.

"Don't try this at home!" he said through the implant to Jake.

Sparks flew as he twisted a large cannon plug loose, severing the dish's main power feed. Several blinking lights on the panel went dark.

"Hardline severed. No power for you."

He quickly cycled through the communication system menus using his Typhon implant, and set a strong encrypted password on the power feed controls.

"That'll stop the bastards...or at least, slow them down."

Gramps looked over at Jake. "Speaking of the others... where'd the other two go?"

Jake brought up his overlay. Two silhouettes moved through the lower half of the compound—silent, methodical.

"They found the blast doors to The Connector," Jake muttered. "They just went inside."

Gramps sighed. "Of course they did."

They turned back to the damaged Crow. It was still dragging itself—one glinting talon raised toward the sky like a broken signal tower. Still scanning. Still trying.

Gramps glanced at several other nearby junction boxes, muttering to himself.

"If we open a Veil Access Point over it and send a high-current arc across its carapace, we might be able to overload its—"

CRUNCH.

Gramps looked up.

Jake stood over the twitching Crow, breathing hard, gripping a large cinder block. The drone's skull was cratered. Its twitching slowed. Then stopped.

Gramps blinked. "...Or that."

Jake dropped the block. "Thought I'd try the low-tech solution."

Gramps gave a low whistle. "Gotta go with what works. I'll make sure they add 'throw brick at robot' to the field guide."

Jake checked his HUD again. "The other two are below... looks like Sub-level One. The Connector."

Gramps walked back over to Jake, eyes narrowing.

Jake looked up. "So... what now?"

Gramps didn't miss a beat.

"We go down after them."

# Apprentice Part 3

## CERBERUS

The blast doors hung open like a wound in the desert. Jake followed Gramps down the sloped corridor beyond, dark reinforced concrete descending into the gloom.

The passage was wide and tall enough to drive a tank through. Overhead, two dim strip lights followed the seam of wall and ceiling—motion sensors tripped, faintly lighting a narrow section as they passed.

"How deep does this go?" Jake whispered.

"A hundred meters to the sub-surface Connector," Gramps muttered, checking his HUD. "At least."

At the bottom, the slope flattened. Another pair of blast doors stood ahead, deformed and barely hanging on their hinges. Beyond lay scattered dark shapes Jake thought looked like bodies.

They moved in, boots quiet on grated flooring.

A soft mechanical chirp echoed ahead. Gramps raised a fist, crouching. Jake mirrored him.

Around the corner: two Black Star Crows. One jacked into a wall port, data spiraling on a ghostly overlay in Jake's HUD. The other swept its gaze along the walls, pausing at a crate of stabilized cryo-pods. Its talons traced the PHOENIX logo, recording every detail.

"They're stealing everything," Jake whispered.

"Not much for them in the Connector," Gramps replied, "but if they get down into Eremos..."

Jake's pulse jumped. "So the rumors are true."

Gramps didn't answer.

They moved on, the air turning colder. The walls shifted from raw concrete to smooth composite.

That's when they passed it—a sealed door, stenciled in stark black:

## ASPHODEL

## HARVEST PREP

## AUTHORIZED PERSONNEL ONLY

A low, pulsing hum came from behind it. Jake slowed, reading the words twice.

"Harvest?"

"No time," Gramps said. "Keep moving."

"What is this place, really?"

Gramps glanced back. "Ever wonder where the ones who vanish in parks and caves go? The ones no one ever finds?" His eyes held Jake's for a moment. "Yeah. So do I. Now hush."

Jake looked back at the door. The hum seemed to resonate in his chest—alive, breathing.

Ahead, the Crows disappeared around a bend in the hallway.

Gramps used his implant to view a local map. "They're close to the main lift."

Jake's HUD flashed red—NETWORK WARNING.

"I'm no security tech, but it looks like they're trying to hack into PHOENIX-NET."

\* \* \*

Gramps' tone went flat. "That's exactly what they're doing. And if they discover the lift, they can get down to Eremos, and we can't let that happen."

"Got it," said Jake.

They crept closer until they had a clear line of sight. The Crow at the wall jack pulled free, retracting its cable like a snake. The other produced a thin whip antenna from its shoulder and began broadcasting in short encrypted bursts.

"Wireless attempt," Gramps murmured. "Shouldn't last long. Network'll lock 'em out after a few tries."

Jake's HUD pinged again—INTRUSION ATTEMPT BLOCKED—and the antenna snapped back into its housing. Without hesitation, the Crows moved to a recessed fiber port near the lift doors. One crouched low, plugging in. The second turned, popped its chest plate, and a small panel extended outward—bundles of glassy cables glimmered inside.

The first Crow snaked a second line from its shoulder, jacking it directly into the other's open chassis. Their optical sensors shifted to the same pulsing frequency.

Jake frowned. "What's that?"

"Processor-bridging," Gramps said. "Doubling their computing power for a brute-force attack."

"So... what do we do?"

"Split 'em up. Break the bridge, cut their speed in half."

Jake's mind raced. "If we can't kill them outright, we could at least slow them down."

Gramps slipped a small, palm-sized charge from a thigh pouch. "This won't scrap one, but it should disrupt its systems. Weapons, too, if we're lucky."

Jake took it, nodding. "I'll draw one off."

Gramps' mouth twitched—approval or warning, Jake couldn't tell. "Don't get dead."

Jake ducked low, circling wide through a parallel maintenance corridor. At the junction, he tossed the charge across the hall toward the Crows. It clattered on the floor and went off with a chest-thumping crack.

Sparks flashed across the nearest Crow's chassis; its right arm twitched violently, servos grinding. Its weapon pods cycled and jammed with a metallic whine. The other Crow hissed out a synthetic chirp— then they split. One loped after Jake, the other pivoted toward Gramps.

Jake turned and ran.

* * *

The Crow was hunting him. It was patient and relentless.

Jake had damaged its visual sensors in the explosion, so it had trouble tracking him by sight—but it still had sharp hearing. He could evade it, as long as he stayed quiet.

The hallways in the Connector were dark and pulsed red with emergency lighting. Shadows stretched long across the smooth concrete walls.

Jake stayed low, stepping around a forklift-sized bundle of bundled conduit. His heart pounded. His mouth was dry. He crept forward, every muscle tight with adrenaline. The air here was cooler— refrigerated, sterile—but it did nothing to calm his nerves.

Where's Gramps? Please be okay, old man.

His Typhon HUD cast a soft, transparent glow over his vision: outlines of walls, power cables, and flickering Veil interference—the usual ghosting that signaled nearby tech. But the true advantage was tactical: he could track the last known position of the Black Star Crow, flickering red on his map like a predator looming just out of sight.

Then—he saw it.

A hospital gurney stood abandoned in the middle of a side corridor. It was stained with blood, and had deep gouges where someone or something had fought to get free.

A datapad rested in a side holster. Jake picked it up with trembling fingers.

Subject ID 40213-A

Status: Stabilized – violent, but constrained.

Method: Chemical & physical restraints.

Source: Cavern Collection Site 14 (CCS14)

Status: Viable.

Forward to EREMOS for Processing.

Jake blinked. "Collection site? Processing...?"

He looked back at the gurney. The restraints. The congealed blood.

His stomach turned.

Suddenly—a clang rang out as a loose metal tray slipped from the side and struck the concrete floor. The sound echoed down the corridor like a gunshot.

"Shit."

From behind him came a burst of clicking—synthetic and sharp, like metal teeth snapping into place.

Jake bolted.

The Crow shrieked behind him—an inhuman click-screech—and gave chase. Its talons skittered on the floor as it moved in terrifying bursts, loping after him with unnatural grace.

Jake rounded a corner, heart hammering, and dove into the Connector's main processing chamber.

The room was massive—industrial. The walls were lined with reinforced vertical cylinders—each the size of a small car, transparent and slightly iridescent.

He ducked behind one and caught his breath.

These are nano-diamond tanks, he realized, tapping one lightly with his knuckles. It rang like crystal. Same ones they showed us in Veiltech school.

His Typhon overlay blinked a quiet suggestion: Integrity Grade: NDH-3. High Pressure-tested.

Jake stared into the polished surface of the tank, catching his own reflection in the dim light.

Then he looked up.

A narrow metal staircase curved around the outer wall, climbing to a grated catwalk that looped above the cylinder array. The catwalk was sturdy, industrial—probably for maintenance techs—and ran along the tops of each tank. Automated hatches were built into the upper rims, all currently open, with matching outflow hatches below. Most of the tanks were empty.

Perfect.

Behind him, the Crow shrieked again—closer now.

Jake's breathing slowed. His hands steadied.

"Okay. I can work with this."

* * *

He moved fast.

Jake crept toward the stairs, trying to keep his boots light, but every step on the steel rang out like a bell. The Crow heard him instantly. Its head snapped toward the sound, and it broke into motion—talons clanging, limbs unfurling.

Jake hit the top of the staircase just as the Crow reached the base.

It gave another shriek and began climbing after him—fast.

Jake crossed the catwalk in a sprint, boots slamming metal, the HUD shimmer lighting his path.

He skidded to a stop over an open cylinder and dove in feet-first.

His back struck the interior wall hard, legs tangling as he dropped. He caught himself, barely, and scrambled forward onto the slick nano-diamond floor.

Then he heard it—clang, clang, clang.

The Crow dropped in behind him.

Jake lunged for the bottom hatch but slipped, his knee slamming the floor. He turned, crab-walking backward, eyes locked on the machine. The Crow was already unfolding its limbs, head low, sensing the enclosure.

Jake kicked backward, hands slapping the floor— and fell out of the lower hatch just in time. He hit the concrete hard, rolled, and spun toward the control interface.

The Crow advanced.

Jake slammed his palm on the external hatch control.

Seal Engaged.

With a hydraulic chuff, the hatch slammed closed beneath the Crow. A heartbeat later, the top hatch snapped shut as well, locking the machine inside.

The Crow tilted its head in confusion. For one strange moment, it stood still—almost uncertain.

Then it turned and deployed a drill from its right forearm. The bit spun up with a shrill whine and began carving into the nano-diamond from inside.

Jake didn't hesitate.

He crouched beside the reinforced cylinder, fingers flying across his Veil Control Unit as he created the virtual node inside the tank.

A window snapped into view—coordinates, fluid type, flow controls:

Veil Access Point – Available

Destination: Challenger Deep / Veil Tag 101C-D

*Pressure Warning: >15,000 PSI

Status: Isolated, Contained, Stable


He confirmed the settings:

Confirm: Open Veilpoint

Diameter: 1 meter

Direction: Vertical (local down)

Duration: 3.00 sec

Warning: High-Pressure Hazard


Jake looked up.

His HUD displayed the path—an ethereal outline marking where the Veil Access Point would manifest, just inside the top of the tank. A simple arrow icon extended downward.

The Crow's drill was starting to bite into the cylinder wall. Small fracture lines spread along the inner surface like an expanding spiderweb.

He gritted his teeth.

"Showtime."

He slammed his palm on the activation control.

A deep hum built from within the tank. The air shimmered. A moment later, space buckled—and the Veilpoint tore open.

The chamber filled with a howling sound—not of wind, but pressure. A violent column of seawater, black as oil and cold as death, erupted down through the tank.

The impact hit like the voice of a god.

THOOOM!

The entire cylinder rang like a struck bell. The Crow was crushed instantly. Its chassis slammed against the base of the tank, twisted and buckled. The limbs sheared apart like snapped branches. The rotary drill exploded in a starburst of fractured metal.

A single mechanical screech tore through the water—then silence.

Three seconds passed.

The Veilpoint collapsed with a crackling sigh. The shimmer faded.

But the water didn't.

Jake blinked through the dark green brine pooling around the base. Inside the tank, the Crow lay in a heap of imploded plating and ruined servo-sinew.

Scrap.

He tapped the emergency pressure release valve, grinning.

But in his haste, he forgot one detail:

The tank was still pressurized.

FOOMP!

A geyser of seawater blasted out of the lower hatch and caught him square in the chest. Jake was launched off his feet and landed flat on his back in a soaked sprawl.

He lay there, stunned, staring at the ceiling. His Typhon HUD flickered like it had been slapped.

"Holy shit," he croaked. "That actually worked."

He sat up slowly, coughing, then tapped his comm.

"Gramps... please tell me you're still alive."

No answer.

Jake got to his feet, shaking off water like a dog, and turned toward the nearest corridor.

His smile faded.

"Hang on, old man."

He ran.

* * *

Jake moved fast, wet boots squeaking on concrete as he rounded corridor after corridor.

A strange light flickered ahead—orange, distorted.

And then came the sound: groaning metal. A crash. Something... struggling.

Then he smelled it.

Smoke.

Jake pushed through a swinging metal door—and froze.

It was a cafeteria. Or had been once. Stainless counters. Round composite tables. Banners of melted insulation hung from the ceiling like jungle vines. Part of the far wall was aflame—something chemical burning hot and blue at its base. Smoke licked the rafters. The firelight cast long, violent shadows across the room.

Gramps was pinned.

A table lay sideways over his legs, warped and smoking at the edges. His hands gripped the lip, straining to keep it between himself and the horror bearing down on him.

The Crow.

It stalked forward, twisted and furious, moving on its legs alone. Both arms were missing—severed above the elbow. Fluids leaked from the sockets in steady pulses. Sparks danced along its shoulder nodes, dripping into the pool of firelight.

And without arms, it was somehow even more terrifying.

Its beaked head swiveled in sharp, robotic jerks, scanning Gramps for a killing angle.

Gramps kicked out with one leg and nearly lost his grip. "Jake!" he shouted, wild-eyed. "Get out of here! It's—"

Jake didn't wait.

He grabbed the nearest object with weight—a metal food cart tipped on its side—and held it tight in front of him. With a shout, he charged, hurling himself forward like a human battering ram.

CLANG!

The cart smashed into the Crow's side with a teeth-rattling crash, Jake's full weight driving it home. The machine staggered, lost its footing, and crashed to the floor in a tangle of limbs and sparks. It skidded across the cafeteria, colliding with a row of overturned chairs.

Jake dropped the cart and vaulted the table to reach Gramps. "Can you move?"

"Define move," Gramps grunted.

Together, they shoved the warped table just enough. Jake hooked his arms under Gramps' and dragged him clear—both of them half-stumbling, half-limping toward the exit.

Behind them, the Crow shrieked—a horrible, glitching screech that echoed through the firelit room. Servos whined. Something sparked.

It was getting back up.

Jake and Gramps burst through the door.

* * *

They waddled around a corner, leaning on one another, into a wide, empty storage bay—cold, dark, and silent.

Too silent.

Jake's eyes swept the space. No doors. No cover. No exits.

"Shit," Gramps muttered.

They slid down against the far wall. Jake was soaked, bruised, borderline concussed. Gramps was bleeding from one arm, and his breath rattled like something broken.

"No way out," Jake panted. "We're dead."

Gramps coughed, wiped blood from his nose. "Where's the other one?"

Jake flashed a sheepish grin. "Smashed flat. I'll tell you about it later."

Gramps gave him a look—then broke into a wheezing, pained laugh. "Remind me never to doubt MIT kids again."

Jake smirked. "Me? What did you do back there? Place looked like hell on Earth."

Gramps shrugged. "Couple of propane tanks. Overclocked plasma cutter. Improvised."

They both chuckled—until they heard it.

Click-scrape.

That awful, metallic raking sound. Claws on concrete.

They turned.

The Crow stepped into view, dragging one ruined foot behind it. Its matte-black armor was scorched and soot-streaked. One eye flickered. Hydraulic fluid oozed from the stumps of its missing arms. Its beaked head jerked back and forth, as though disoriented... then locked onto their position.

It took a step.

Then another.

Gramps straightened beside Jake. "At least we took one with us."

The Crow tensed—

BLAM-BLAM-BLAM-BLAM-BLAM.

A thunderous burst of 7.62 tore through the hallway.

The Crow convulsed. Armor shattered like ceramic under fire. The impact flipped it backward, scattering pieces across the floor. Sparks danced across the concrete as the wreckage slid to a halt.

From the smoke, six armored figures swept into the room, weapons raised, fanning out with surgical precision. Their suits were matte black, angular, bristling with integrated optics and reactive shielding. Their helmets resembled snarling wolves—jaws bared, eyes glowing faint crimson.

CERBERUS.

The REACT team from Eremos.

The tower guard's emergency call had worked after all.

"Sector secure," a voice barked over helmet comms. "You two look like hell."

The lead soldier raised a gloved hand, and the others froze in place. His helmet folded back with a quiet hissssss, revealing a scarred, chiseled face and storm-gray eyes.

Jake squinted through the haze and caught the rank on his shoulder: Captain.

Name tape on the chestplate: Kernhauer.

Gramps collapsed to one knee, exhaling. "Took your damn time."

Kernhauer stepped forward and helped him up. "Had to let you kids have some fun."

"Gramps?" Jake asked.

Gramps gave a thumb up. "I'm good. Ish."

Another CERBERUS operator rounded the corner, hauling a fire extinguisher. He glanced between Jake and Gramps.

"Fire's out in the cafeteria," he said. "You two sure know how to rack up a repair bill."

"Debrief topside," Kernhauer ordered, signaling the rest of the squad. "Let's move."

As the fireteam swept the bay for hostiles, Jake and Gramps were guided toward the lift—leaving behind the burned-out corridors of the Connector like a fever dream best forgotten.

*  *  *

Outside, dawn was breaking across the New Mexico desert, bleeding soft orange light over rust-colored rock.

The dust had settled.

The Crows were scrap.

The black site—Desolation—was secure once again.

PHOENIX - Before the Day of Fire  110

CERBERUS operatives moved like phantoms across the yard, sealing entry points, launching recon drones, and running threat diagnostics on every surface—like the war wasn't quite over.

Jake and Gramps sat in two folding chairs in front of the coordination trailer, both dazed and dead on their feet.

Captain Kernhauer stood nearby, datapad in hand. He preferred his briefings vertical, but the two men looked like they might pass out at any second. He flicked through pages of damage reports, bot telemetry, and live-captured combat footage.

His expression didn't change—until he reached the end.

"That Veil-stunt you pulled with the pressure tank?" he said, not looking up. "Cleanest bot kill I've seen outside a sim."

He smirked.

"Remind me to make you an honorary member of my team."

Jake blinked.

Kernhauer turned to his second-in-command—a towering soldier with deep brown skin and regulation-sharp posture. Master Sergeant Doakes.

"Patch him."

Doakes stepped forward, peeled the Cerberus insignia from his own sleeve, and slapped it onto Jake's chest with a firm clap.

"Don't let it go to your head, nerd."

Jake stared at him, wide-eyed.

Doakes leaned in, grinning. "Used to sling Veiltech myself. Hated it. Too quiet. Not enough action."

Jake's eyes welled—just a little. He looked down at the patch.

His fingers closed around it like it was the Medal of Honor.

"You two held the line," Doakes said simply. "PHOENIX won't forget that."

Then he turned, walking back to the formation—helmet under one arm, jaw set like a man who didn't give out compliments often.

Kernhauer finally looked up.

"You did good," he said, voice flat but sincere. "Eremos is secure because of your work. Minimal infrastructure loss. We lost some people—not your fault. But no data exfiltration. That's key."

He turned his gaze on Gramps.

"You still got it, old man."

Gramps smirked. "We were just finishing up. Hope we didn't void any warranties."

Doakes let out a rare chuckle.

Then, the coordination trailer's side door opened—and Elena DuChamp stepped out.

Calm. Poised. Impeccable, even amid the wreckage. She took in the chaos with clinical detachment, arms crossed.

Jake raised a tentative hand. "Hey..."

She didn't wave.

But she gave him a single nod—and a slow, deliberate thumbs-up.

Jake turned to Gramps. "Was that... approval?"

Gramps squinted. "From DuChamp? That's practically a hug."

Kernhauer resealed his helmet. The snarling wolf-face snapped into place with a quiet hiss.

"We're sweeping the lower levels," he said. "You're off the hook."

He gestured for his team to fan out.

"Try to stay out of trouble."

CERBERUS disappeared into the Connector facility, weapons up. One by one, the wolves descended into the dark.

Gramps clapped Jake on the shoulder. "Come on, kid."

"Where?"

Gramps nodded toward the battered SUV parked near the gate.

"Breakfast," he said. "My treat."

\* \* \*

The coffee was black enough to strip paint. Early light slatted through blinds, turning the Formica gold. Jake sat in a corner booth, still in his dust-streaked coveralls, the Cerberus patch on the table before him. He turned it in his fingers, mind elsewhere.

He couldn't stop seeing that ASPHODEL door. The hum. And the gurney in the Connector with its blood-crusted restraints. Harvest prep. The words itched under his skin.

"Something on your mind, kid?" Gramps asked, pouring a splash from his dented flask into his coffee.

Jake hesitated. "What's really going on down there? In Eremos?"

Gramps took a slow sip. "A lot more than you can imagine. My advice? Don't dwell on it. Don't let it get to you."

"And you're okay with that? With what we saw down there?"

"I'm okay with doing my job and going home alive." Gramps's tone softened. "Look, I've been with Phoenix for decades. Got clearances most people don't know exist, and I've still barely scratched the surface of their secrets. But one thing I've learned—everything's done for a reason. Carefully considered."

Jake studied him. "Yeah?"

"Yes. I know this was your first day, and it was a hell of a one. You saw things that upset you—I get it. You could walk away right now, and I wouldn't stop you. But I think that'd be a shame."

"Why's that?"

"Because I like you, and you've got a knack for the work. That's rare these days."

Jake's Typhon pinged—an incoming message from Elena DuChamp:

CERBERUS posted a glowing after-action report. Commended both of you by name. A $1,000,000 performance bonus has been deposited to your accounts.

Jake blinked at the zeroes. "Gramps... are you seeing this?"

Gramps checked his own HUD and smiled. "See? This is what happens when we work hard and keep our mouths shut."

Jake looked down at the patch in his hand, then at the laminated menu under his elbow. The corners were curled, the surface faintly sticky, and in tiny print at the bottom it read: 810 W. Pierce St. – Carlsbad, NM. Outside the window, beyond the city, the desert rolled on forever. Somewhere under that endless sand and stone, the hum of ASPHODEL was still there, patient and strange.

He forced a smile at Gramps's next joke, but it didn't reach his eyes.

# Dark Gray Part 1

By late October, the maples in Hundred Mile Wild had turned the dirt paths into rust-red ribbons. The air was thin and bright, sunlight falling through the canopy in glassy sheets that made every spiderweb look like spun wire. A breeze came up the ravine, lifted the leaves a little, and died as if it had changed its mind.

Brian Gray—Bray to his family and classmates—followed old survey-line markers through the forest: three notched posts with tin caps, a cairn half-collapsed where kids had once tried to build a fort and then forgotten it. He stopped to photograph an orange mushroom peeling the bark from a fallen birch like a slow fire. The picture came out flat on his phone; he took it again with the old point-and-shoot and felt better. The click was a real sound—a promise that it would make something *true*.

He'd meant to do homework that morning. He'd meant to text Ryan back. Instead he was here, where cell service fell into pockets and the town couldn't see him. Fort Highpoint sprawled on the far side of the trees—a water tower, a diner, a brick high school with a parking lot patched by black filler that looked like toothpaste squeezed into cracks. The woods swallowed the edges of everything, as if the state park had leaned over the town and was deciding whether to take it back.

He walked until the hum began.

It was more suggestion than sound—low, sub-audible, the kind of thrum that made your molars hurt. He checked the road for a truck, then the sky for a plane. Nothing. A jay screamed once, mechanical and offended, and then there were no birds at all.

Bray kept moving. He spoke aloud to ease the silence.
"You feel haunted today. And just in time for Halloween."
The only reply was a small gust of wind and that incessant hum.

The trail split at a stand of hemlock where the ground darkened with their fallen needles. Beyond the split, an older path sloped toward the creek. He might've missed it if sunlight hadn't caught something dull and straight—rusted hardware in a rotted post, half-swallowed by ivy. Not a park sign. Older.

He pushed through the bracken, the dense thickets whispering at his jeans. The post turned out to be a carved stone set low, the top broken off decades ago. On the intact face, scratched by some knife or nail long before he was born, were three spirals in a tight braid—crudely done but deliberate. He crouched, ran a thumb over them, felt the grooves fill with cold. It looked like patterns he'd seen in textbooks about shell structure, or maybe the doodles he made when bored in English. He snapped a photo, turned the stone for a better angle. The shape suggested motion without moving.

"Lenape?" he said, uncertain. The word tasted wrong—something he'd learned about in Boy Scouts. He didn't go anymore, but he still treasured the snippets of practical knowledge from those meetings in the school gymnasium.

His Scout patrol had called him **Lynx**, half for his quiet, half for how he saw things others missed. The name had stuck, though no one used it now.

He jotted notes in the little graph-paper book he kept in his back pocket. *Spiral, three-fold. Not new. Who carved these? And why here?*

The hum rose, then faded again, like a generator under a blanket.
He listened. The ravine ran quiet to his left, water trapped below deadfall, flashing in bright, angular shapes. A redtail sliced the sky, banked once, disappeared. He smelled rot and wet rock—and something else, faint and chemical, like the inside of a new toaster.

Up ahead, the hillside slumped. The ground formed a shallow oval, as if something huge had pressed its shape into the soil. The leaves were disturbed in a pattern with edges—rectangles where the forest never made rectangles.

Bray slid down the slope, boots spilling leaf litter.
He crouched at the oval's rim and touched the ground
with two fingers. The dirt felt warmer than the air.
Heat moving out of it in a slow breath.
He didn't say *haunted* this time.

He unpacked the small toolkit from his backpack—
the one with precision screwdrivers and a multimeter
that had cost him months of mowed lawns. Stupid to
bring it to a state park. Stupid—except he always
found things that looked like they might open if you
said the right word.

He checked himself: large Bowie knife, bandanna,
water bottle, the old camera, the notebook, a loop of
paracord around his belt.
The knife rode at his side, heavy and familiar. The
blade was old—Damascus steel with a wavering
pattern like water caught in sunlight. His grandfather
had given it to him when he joined the Scouts, said it
had been reforged from a frontier weapon, the handle
rebuilt in dark wood and bone after a war everyone
else had forgotten. Bray liked knives because they
were honest—straight lines, clear purpose.

He felt better knowing what he had and where it
was. The checklist hummed in his head the way the
ground hummed underfoot.

Something metallic winked under the leaves near
the oval's center. Not bright—more the *suggestion* of
a curve. He brushed at it with the back of his hand
the way you might if you were pretty sure there could
be glass. His fingers came away dusty and clean at

the same time, like he'd touched a pane that wasn't there.

The birds still hadn't come back. A woodpecker tried a few tentative taps and then stopped, like it had changed its mind too.

Bray slid one knee into the oval and reached deeper. Leaves gave. His knuckles found fabric—not canvas, not nylon. Slicker. It flexed under pressure and then held with a resilience that felt wrong for anything from the army-surplus store. He pulled, expecting weight, and whatever it was gave him nothing. The resistance wasn't heavy; it was distributed, like picking up a magnet that didn't want to admit it was touching metal.

"Okay," he said—to the woods, to himself, to the shape under the leaves. "What... are you?"

From somewhere beneath his hand, something adjusted itself with a tiny static sigh. The hair on his forearms rose. The air above the oval warped as if heat were coming off a stove—and then stopped. The hum in the ground didn't change at all.

He looked back the way he'd come. The trail hid itself cleverly. No voices. No traffic. Even the stream's sound was present but not reassuring.

He pushed the leaves back with both hands.

A gauntlet emerged—if *gauntlet* was even the right word. Jointed and smooth, dull black with a skin that wasn't paint and wasn't cloth. A mesh laced the wrist with ports at even intervals, each the size of a pencil eraser. Whoever had designed it had loved the kind of curves you only see in wind tunnels and dreams. On the back of the hand, beneath a film of dust, a faint symbol sat like a bruise: a cartoon bird made of fire.

Bray wiped it clean with the bandanna. The symbol sharpened—neither new nor old. He felt the relief of it under the fabric more than saw it. He set the camera on his knee and took three photos from different angles, bracketed exposures, then one with his finger alongside for scale because he'd hate himself later if he didn't.

The chemical smell edged stronger. Not bad. Just wrong for the wilderness.
He glanced up again, automatic. The forest watched him like a cat watches a fly. The formal trail lay somewhere behind the laurel thicket, safe and mapped, and none of that mattered because here the ground was warm and the glove was real.

He slid his hand inside.
The material flexed and found him. Cool along the palm. A seam he couldn't see unzipped without sound and sealed again around his wrist. Static lifted the fine hairs on his neck. The world didn't tilt; it tightened, as if someone had turned a ring and all the distances clicked a notch.

On his skin, just under the cuff, a vibration as soft as breath pulsed once.
He waited. He didn't breathe. The woods didn't either.

The vibration came again, this time threaded with the shape of a voice. Not words—just intent.

Bray looked down at the oval in the earth, at the leaf-mealy outline where a body would have been if a body had been lying there, and at the glove on his hand, which belonged to no camping catalog ever printed.

He flexed his fingers.
The air above his knuckles wavered—heat shimmer without heat—and smoothed again.

"Okaaaay," he said, hearing his own voice come back dampened, as if the trees had swallowed it before it could escape.

He tightened the straps, slid the toolkit closer, and reached back into the leaves.

\* \* \*

The heat clinging to the glove hadn't faded. It felt like holding a live wire wrapped in velvet—no pain, just the hum of power that didn't belong here. Bray crouched deeper into the hollow, tugging at the layer of leaves until the shape beneath began to reveal itself.

The curve became a shoulder. The shoulder a torso.

He froze.

What he'd thought was dirt was fabric—some kind of flexible armor, dull and seamless, the color of fog. The air above it shimmered faintly, the same mirage effect he'd seen on summer blacktop. Every blink made it a fraction more visible.

"Jesus," he whispered.

He pulled back another handful of leaves and saw the face.

The man looked twenty, maybe thirty. Skin pale as candle wax, lips parted slightly. No blood. The eyes closed, lashes rimmed with condensation. He looked asleep, yet nothing about him suggested life. The stillness was total—no give, no breath, no rot.

Bray leaned closer. The smell hit him: ozone, metal filings, and the faint tang of burnt circuitry. Clinical. Industrial.

The visor of the helmet was cracked down the center. Inside, a faint glimmer pulsed at the temple— slow, like a heartbeat—then gone.

"Hello?" he said, hating himself for it.

No answer. Just the hum, steady and patient.

The glove on his hand vibrated once, and text appeared across the wristplate he hadn't noticed before. Tiny. Gray on black.


**TELEMETRY LINK ACTIVE. SEEKING HOST.**


He snatched his hand back. The words faded.

He glanced around, half-expecting someone to be watching from the tree line. Nothing moved. The forest held its breath.

"Okay," he said again, quieter. "Okay."

He looked over the body—over the suit. The material shifted color with each change of light, neither fabric nor metal. The kind of thing that shouldn't exist outside prototypes or video games. His pulse kicked up; his brain started running diagnostics it didn't have words for.

Composite plating—unknown alloy. Micro-mesh. Thermoptic panels? He didn't have the vocabulary.

He reached for the second gauntlet, on the corpse's right arm. The wrist seam was already open, a small port exposed like a socket. He touched it with his screwdriver.

A static pop.

The corpse's head twitched.

Bray froze. Waited.

No follow-up movement. The shimmer along the chest flickered once, then stilled. He exhaled through his teeth.

"You're not dead, are you?" he muttered. "Not real, somehow. Like a—"

The glove hummed again, cutting him off. He took that as permission—or challenge.

He pried the gauntlet free. It came loose too easily, as if it wanted to be removed. Underneath, the wrist wasn't flesh at all. The synthetic skin peeled back to reveal polished composite jointing, small actuators arranged like tendons.

His stomach dropped—not from horror, but from confirmation.

He'd guessed right. The body was synthetic. Extremely high-tech.

We don't have stuff like this... do we?

He lifted the gauntlet. It was light, balanced. The bird insignia on the back caught a sliver of light and burned red-gold.

"Operator Seventy-One — Field Status: Terminated," the unseen voice announced, perfectly neutral.

"Awaiting new operator."

Bray looked down at his own glove—the one he'd found first—and then at the matching piece in his other hand. The hum in the soil climbed a half-step higher, a bass note under the trees.

Somewhere far off, a crow called once and went silent again.

He straightened, heartbeat syncing to the rhythm underfoot. The glove's whisper came one last time, quieter now, almost conspiratorial:

"Initialize... Operator Seventy-Two."

*   *   *

By dusk, the woods had sealed their secret behind him.

Leaves drifted into the hollow where the body had been, the shimmer fading until it looked like just another scar in the ground.

Bray didn't look back on the walk home, but he felt watched the whole way—like the forest was holding its breath until he was gone.

He slipped through the back gate of his mother's yard, brushed dirt off his jeans, and lugged the duffel into the garage before the screen door could slam.

The air inside was sharp with motor oil, WD-40, and old bike rubber—safe smells, honest smells.

He flicked on the hanging shop light; it swayed, painting the concrete floor with concentric halos.

The glove and forearm segment lay on the workbench like something sleeping.

Up close, under steady light, it looked less alien— more engineered. The surface carried a fine grid, microscopic latticework that shifted from gray to green when he breathed on it.

He found courage in familiarity: the smell of solder, the click of the multimeter, the ritual of knowing what a thing should do and testing what it does instead.

He clipped a probe to one of the contact ports.

The meter jumped.

Five volts, steady.

Not dead. Active.

The glove twitched.

He jumped back, heart kicking like a drum.

The wristplate display blinked alive again. Words scrolled in clean military typeface:

**OPERATOR 72 ACKNOWLEDGED.**

**TELEMETRY DISABLED.**

**FAMILIARIZATION MODE ENGAGED.**

He hadn't touched anything.

"Telemetry disabled," Bray echoed. Had he done that?

He bent over his old tower PC, ran Bluetooth, Ethernet, shortwave. Nothing transmitted. The suit was off the grid.

"Guess that's what you mean," he said to the glove.

A pause—then a voice, not loud, not human, but perfectly articulated:

"Operator 72, welcome.

Familiarization Mode includes Orientation, Suit Mechanics, and Field Protocol.

Ready to begin. Please respond."

Bray blinked. "Uh... ready."

"Confirming readiness.

Begin Orientation: system components, version 7.61.

You are equipped with Adaptive Optics Layer, Reactive Mesh, and Internal Stabilizers.

Telemetry module offline. Spurious signal emissions... minimal."

He grinned. "Yeah, that's what I want. Don't need the real owners knowing where I am."

No reply. The voice didn't care; it simply continued, a bureaucratic sermon.

"Primary functions include active camouflage, kinetic dispersion, and environmental monitoring.

Warning: newly-certified users may experience physical strain, cognitive dissonance, and... disciplinary action."

"Right," he muttered. "Good thing I'm certified in nothing."

He spent the next hour dismantling and diagramming what he could reach. Every seam self-healed; every screw had no head.

He couldn't tell if it was alive or just very well-sealed.

When he finally fitted the gauntlets together and slid both on, the hum deepened. Something in the suit recognized itself—a circuit completed—and the hum vanished.

The light in the garage flickered. His reflection in the window fractured, split into ghosted copies. The air bent faintly around his shoulders, soft waves like heat distortion.

"Stealth Integrity: Sixteen Percent. Field Efficiency: Nominal."

It was the voice again, utterly calm, as if the world hadn't just changed.

He turned his hands, watching his outline flicker in and out of view.

"Nominal," he whispered. The word felt too small for the miracle of it.

Outside, the cicadas had gone quiet.

The only sound left was the low hum of the room—and beneath it, if he really listened, something deeper. A resonance not mechanical but alive, like an underground engine turning beneath Fort Highpoint.

Bray adjusted a dial on the wristplate. The shimmer vanished completely.

He held his breath and looked down.

His hands were gone.

# Dark Gray Part 2

The next morning, the fog came in low over Fort Highpoint, blurring the tree line until it looked like the forest had decided to keep its secrets to itself.

Bray had spent half the night in the garage, running calibration prompts through the suit's cold, patient voice. He'd learned how to stand perfectly still for motion reduction; how to shift weight silently; how to breathe without spiking the sensors.

He'd also learned how fast it punished mistakes.

When his pulse hit eighty, the optics fuzzed out and dumped him back into full visibility, the voice calmly announcing:

"Noise vector elevated. Maintain heart rate below seventy beats per minute."

He'd whispered back, "Maybe you should try that," and the suit had answered nothing. It didn't do banter.

By mid-morning, he was ready for the field test.

The park lay empty—Sunday church services had stripped the streets of everyone but stray dogs and the occasional jogger. He carried the duffel to the trailhead, heart steady in his chest, mind counting beats without meaning to.

He slipped into the woods and crouched in the dappled light. The air smelled of pine and wet iron.

"Operator 72," the voice said quietly through the helmet. "Stealth mode: engaged."

And then he was gone.

At least, to sight.


The world around him distorted—soft warping like ripples over clear water. His hands vanished first, then his arms, then his reflection in the puddles beneath the trees. Only the faint shimmer betrayed the space he occupied.

He took a cautious step. The ground sighed but didn't betray him. He took another. The branches overhead swayed, and sunlight shifted, but the illusion held.

"Field integrity: eighty percent."

The first test lasted only minutes. A deer startled near the creek and bolted. Bray flinched, heart pounding. The shimmer dropped instantly; his outline snapped back into view like a glitch correcting itself.

"Failure condition met. Emotional variance detected," the voice intoned.

"Yeah, I get it," Bray hissed. "I spooked a deer, sue me."

He powered down, took a breath, and tried again.

By the third attempt, he was better.

He found that stillness wasn't about freezing—it was about matching the world's rhythm. When the wind passed through the trees, he moved with it. When the cicadas sang, he adjusted his pace to their intervals.

Within twenty minutes, he was invisible and confident.

He crept near the maintenance road and waited.

A car approached—one of the black town sedans used by the local contractors working on the "Water Management Facility." He crouched low as it passed. Two men inside. Both wore a PHOENIX insignia, though he didn't recognize it yet.

The car slowed. The passenger rolled down his window, scanning the woods.

Bray didn't breathe.

"Pulse at sixty-eight. Maintain."

The voice was calm. Encouraging, almost.

The sedan idled, then moved on. The road noise faded. Bray exhaled—long and trembling—and the shimmer held.

He laughed, quietly.

For the first time in his life, he wasn't seen.

For the first time, the world couldn't define him.

He used the suit again that night.

First to sneak past his mother's door without the floorboards creaking.

Then to step out into the empty street where the sodium lights buzzed and drew halos around moths.

He walked between them like a ghost.

The voice kept whispering updates:

"Heart rate nominal."

"Optics stable."

"Audio footprint minimal."

Every phrase landed like approval.


At 11:27 PM, he reached the edge of town—the diner's neon sign flickering in the fog. Two old men sat outside smoking, their conversation slow and comfortable in that small-town way that assumed no one was listening.

Bray leaned against the wall ten feet away. The suit's thermal screen flickered, painting their shapes in muted reds and oranges.

"—new construction's got the whole ridge blocked off," one man said. "All night they're moving trucks in and out, but nobody knows what they're hauling."

"I heard there's some kind of base under the quarry," the other replied. "They say it's water management, but it ain't. You can hear machinery down there on still nights. Same kinda heavy stuff they used back in the war."

"What war?"

"WWII." He chuckled. "My granddad said the Lenape had stories about this place before the first settlers showed up. Spirits in the woods that punished evil men. Called it Graytooth."

Bray frowned inside the helmet. "Graytooth?" he whispered.

The suit picked up the word, filed it away in some invisible database he couldn't access.

"Term unknown," the voice murmured. "No database match."

"Yeah," Bray said softly. "I bet not."


The men finished their cigarettes and went inside.

Bray stayed under the neon sign, the color rippling over his invisible form like blood through water.

For a moment, he imagined he could hear something else—a slow, distant vibration echoing through the ground. The same sound he'd felt in the woods. Machinery. Deep. Steady. Alive.

"Environmental anomaly detected," the voice noted casually.

"Subsurface resonance pattern: unclassified."

"Unclassified," Bray repeated. "That doesn't sound good."

He powered down the optics. His reflection returned, half-translucent in the diner window, ghostly and pale.

He looked older.

Colder.

Then he turned toward the black ridge where the new construction lights burned all night long.

He wanted to see what they were building.

He wanted to see everything.

*  *  *

The next week settled into a pattern: school, homework that never got finished, nights in the garage, then the woods.

Each evening he slipped further into the habit of disappearing.

At first, the thrill had been the invisibility itself.

Now, it was what he could hear.

The suit taught him patience.

It could hover in a half-powered state where he was translucent, silent, half in the world and half out of it. From that ghostly threshold, he could stand within arm's reach of people and listen to their truths pour out like a mountain spring.

He began with familiar places—the diner, the gas station, the fence outside the old high school football field.

By day the town looked ordinary, but after midnight it changed color.

Conversations turned strange.

He crouched behind a pickup while two contractors loaded cable spools stamped with PHOENIX inventory codes he didn't recognize.

"They're adding another sub-station under the quarry," one said.

"Night work only, crews rotated out every forty-eight hours. They say it's a pump system, but that's a lie."

"Who signs off on it?"

"Some federal agency, I think. The invoices list some group called Ouroboros Logistics."

Bray frowned. The name meant nothing to him, but the way they said it—softly, almost reverently—lodged in his brain. He'd look it up later, when he got back home.

Later that week, he hid in the alley behind Donnelly's Hardware, watching the sheriff talk to a woman from the county clerk's office. Both used that careful tone people use when they know the walls might be listening.

"New curfew's a joke," the woman said. "You can hear the drills every damned night. My kid says they shake his window."

"Stay out of the Wild," the sheriff said flatly. "Let the contractors work. They've got authorization from D.C."

"Oh, you mean PHOENIX?" she said.

The sheriff flinched at the name. He looked up sharply, scanning the street—straight through Bray's invisible outline—and muttered,

"I didn't say that. And you shouldn't either."

On Friday evening he wandered toward the war memorial where the retirees met to swap stories. He'd always thought of them as background noise; now their words mattered.

An old man in a camouflage baseball cap leaned toward his friend.

"Town's always had its secrets. Been that way since the first world war."

"No doubt."

"My granddad worked up by the ridge, before it was a park. Said the government blasted caverns and filled 'em with machines. Folks thought it was for rockets, but no rockets ever came out."

The second man laughed. "I always thought this whole area was haunted."

"Haunted, yeah. But that ain't new. The native Indians had stories way before we got here. Said there was something out there in the woods. A spirit that punished the wicked."

"Bullshit," said the second man. "I've been walking in those woods since I was a kid."

"Bullshit nothing. You've never gone into the Triangle."

"Course not. I'm not fucking stupid. Park rangers have those signs up for a reason. No one comes back out of there."

"No. Because that's where that thing is."

"What thing?"

"I'm gonna slap you. You know damn well what I'm talking about." He leaned in. "Graytooth."

They both chuckled, but the laughter sounded thin.

Bray watched the smoke from their cigarettes drift upward and break against nothing.

Inside the helmet, the voice whispered:

"Term 'Graytooth' not recognized. Searching... no match found."

He answered under his breath, "Maybe you're not supposed to know."


By Sunday, his notebooks were filling with fragments:

Ouroboros Logistics

Sub-station under quarry

Graytooth – local myth, Lenape origin?

Strange nocturnal vibrations (possibly machinery)

He drew lines between them the way conspiracy theorists did on crime boards, but his lines made sense.

Every conversation, every rumor, pointed to the same place — the ridge, the quarry, the construction site labeled Water Management.

The suit's AI began cataloging his data automatically, sorting words into categories he hadn't created. When he looked at the display one night, he saw a new heading:

## THREATS – ENVIRONMENTAL
## Sub-entry: CRYPTID CLASS UNK-7

He blinked, unsure whether he'd typed that himself.

"Hey," he said aloud. "What's a Cryptid Class UNK-7?"

The AI's voice came through perfectly calm.

"Classification unknown. Legacy entry. Parameters incomplete. Maintain large observational distance."

"Yeah," Bray murmured. "That's the plan."

But the plan was already slipping.

Because every night, when the ground hummed and the air thickened like a held breath, he found himself moving closer to the ridge—closer to the heart of whatever the town was built on.

* * *

The "Water Management Facility" wasn't on any town map, but everyone in Fort Highpoint knew where it was. It squatted at the far edge of the quarry—low white structures, chain-link, motion sensors. That kind of government minimalism that screamed don't ask.

Bray had circled it for days, charting guard rotations, cameras, blind spots.

He told himself it was for science. Observation. Data.

But when he finally approached the fence one moonless night, what he felt wasn't scientific curiosity — it was gravity. Something in those buildings pulled at him like a lodestone.

He crouched in the ditch and powered up the optics.

"Operator 72," the suit murmured. "Stealth mode engaged. Heart rate seventy-two. Adjust."

He slowed his breathing. The shimmer smoothed.

A truck idled near the loading bay—matte black, no markings. Two workers in reflective vests unloaded crates the size of coffins. The stencils were half-scraped off, but he caught flashes of text through the distortion:

**PROPERTY OF PHOENIX**

**HADES DIV.**

**LEVEL 4 CLEARANCE REQUIRED.**

He snapped three photos through the optical feed. They came out blank gray.

"Of course," he muttered, and crept closer.

The fence hummed faintly—active charge.

He slid a grounding spike from the suit's toolkit into the soil. The shimmer deepened, bending the light further until his reflection disappeared even from puddles.

He slipped through a small gap between fence posts.

Inside, the world felt heavier. Each breath carried that familiar ozone taste—the same as the glove when he'd first found it.

He moved between the crates, tracing the lines on the pavement—heavy tire tracks leading toward a warehouse with blast doors.

An overhead light flickered, catching a sign on the wall that shouldn't have been there:

**SECTOR ACCESS POINT B**

**I.W. – NO UNAUTHORIZED ENTRY BEYOND THIS POINT**

**USE OF DEADLY FORCE IS SANCTIONED**

He didn't know what I.W. meant.

But the letters stuck to his brain like burrs.

"Warning," the suit said quietly. "Access level exceeded. Reporting anomaly."

Bray froze. "What? No, cancel that."

"Telemetry disabled. Report queued."

He exhaled. "Good."

The voice, as ever, was indifferent:

"Field evaluation continues. Maintain mission objective."

He swallowed. "Mission objective?"

"Observe. Record. Survive."

He almost laughed—almost.


The warehouse door cracked open. A light clicked on inside.

Bray darted for cover behind a generator, peeking out through the shimmer.


A uniformed woman stepped into view—calm, deliberate, clipboard under one arm, PHOENIX insignia on her chestplate. She spoke into her earpiece:

"Yes, I'm aware of the anomaly. No, telemetry's still scrambled.

Whoever's operating it is either clever or lucky.

Keep scanning. If the signal reappears, flag it and send a team in."

Bray's blood went cold.

They're looking for me.

She turned slightly, and for a second, her gaze swept right through his invisible outline. He could swear she lingered a beat too long—not seeing him, but sensing the space where he was.

Then she went back inside.

He stayed frozen until the hum in the ground rose again—deeper now, rhythmic, like an immense machine exhaling below the surface. The vibration made the fence wires sing a faint harmonic.

Bray crouched, put a hand on the pavement, and felt the world breathe.

He followed the sound around the far side of the building, where a service tunnel cut into the rock wall. The entrance was half-concealed behind stacked cable reels. A red warning light blinked above it, casting everything in blood tones.

The door was labeled STYX TUNNEL ACCESS / RESTRICTED and hung slightly open.

Cool air drifted out, carrying that same electrical tang he'd come to associate with the suit.

He hesitated.

The hum vibrated through his bones—mechanical, but with something organic under it. Like a heartbeat.

The voice spoke softly in his ear:

"Environmental anomaly escalating. Recommendation: retreat."

He whispered, "You retreat."

He slipped inside.

The tunnel stretched into darkness, sloping down at a steady incline. The walls were concrete reinforced with steel ribs. Cables ran along the ceiling like veins. Every fifty feet, a maintenance light flickered—one working, two dead.

The deeper he went, the louder the hum grew.

He stopped at a pressure door sealed with yellow tape. On the metal surface, printed half over old paint, were words nearly lost to corrosion:

## I.W. – SECTOR ACCESS B

His stomach turned cold.

The name meant nothing to him yet, but something deep inside—something primal—knew he'd just stepped somewhere no one like him was meant to be.

The suit pulsed against his skin.

"Reporting anomaly: Operator 72 proximity to restricted node confirmed."

"No, no. Cancel," he whispered.

"Command acknowledged. Report suppressed."

He backed away slowly, heart steady, careful not to make noise.

When he emerged from the tunnel, the air outside felt too thin.

The stars above Fort Highpoint blinked like they were trying to send warnings.

In the distance, the woods stirred.

A low sound rolled through the trees—deep, old.

The suit registered it immediately.

"Environmental anomaly detected. Cryptid Class: UNK-7 proximity."

Bray turned toward the sound, but the shimmer from the suit wavered with his pulse.

He whispered, "Graytooth."

The forest didn't answer, but the ground seemed to.

The vibration rose one last time, then sank back into silence.

* * *

For two days, Bray couldn't stop thinking about the tunnel.

The words from the signs looped in his head like a broken recording. What did they mean? What were they building down there?

He hadn't told anyone—not that he could—but he carried the knowledge like radiation in his bloodstream. It made him restless, feverish.

By the third night, he was back in the suit.

Fort Highpoint slept under a crust of autumn fog. The air smelled like wet asphalt and chimney smoke.

Bray walked through it unseen, a shadow detached from its owner.

He told himself he was testing the system.

Stress response. Urban noise profiles. Stealth efficiency.

But what he was really doing was spying.

He moved past houses he'd known his whole life— teachers, classmates, friends—and looked through the windows. The suit's optics shifted automatically, filtering glare, amplifying sound. Conversations whispered through brick and glass like confessions.

A teacher he admired cried quietly at her kitchen table, grading papers she didn't understand anymore.

The sheriff sat at his desk, writing a report he never intended to file.

Even his mother—dozing in her armchair, bills scattered across her lap, the TV frozen on a static ad—looked smaller than he remembered.

Bray shut the optics off and stood outside in the cold, fighting the feeling that the world had always been this way and he'd just never been allowed to see it.

He whispered, "You were right, old man. The town's got its secrets."

The suit answered only with data:

"Audio input logged. Emotional variance: stable. Cognitive detachment: optimal."

He didn't like how proud that made him.

By midnight, he'd wandered back to the ridge.

The industrial construction lights were impossibly bright, with a purple corona that hurt his eyes. A few dim safety beacons pulsed along the fence line.

He crouched near the drainage ditch—the same one he'd crossed before—and listened to the earth breathe.

The hum was fainter here, but not gone. It was deeper, slower, like something asleep under stone.

He could feel it in his bones—the pulse of the machinery below, and the heavier, slower beat beneath that.

The AI's sensors flickered.

"Environmental interference detected. Source undetermined."

"Yeah," Bray muttered. "Noted."

He climbed the service tower by the old ballfield just to see how far the fog went.

From up there, the town looked surreal— streetlights floating in gray, the forest stretched in ink-black ridges.

He switched the optics to thermal.

The world erupted in color. Cool blues. Warm yellows. Houses glowing orange.

And there, far to the north—beyond the quarry, beyond the ridge—something massive moved between the trees.

Not a truck.

Not an aircraft.

Slower. Heavier. Its heat pattern amorphous, shifting like liquid metal.

The optics struggled to focus, glitching between ranges.

"Warning. Unidentified thermal anomaly. Proximity alert."

Bray's skin went cold beneath the suit.

He whispered, "Graytooth."

The AI paused—a rare hesitation.

"Entity parameters unreadable. Recommend retreat."

"Yeah," he said. "You don't have to tell me twice."

He climbed down, boots slipping on the wet metal rungs. When he reached the ground, the rumble had returned—subtle at first, then steady, coming from two directions: the earth below, and the woods beyond.

For a moment, they overlapped perfectly—machine and monster breathing in the same rhythm.

He didn't know which one to be more afraid of.

Bray slowly backed away and made his way home.

* * *

The fog never really left Fort Highpoint that week. It just kept thinning and reforming, as if the whole town were breathing through gauze.

For Bray, school was impossible. The halls felt too narrow. The people too loud.

He sat through chemistry with his mind back in the tunnel, the hum of the fluorescent lights mimicking the one in the ground. He doodled the triskelion spiral in his notebook, over and over, until it looked less like a symbol and more like an invitation.

After the bell, he lingered outside the science wing, listening to the hum in his ears fade into the hum of the world.

He knew he'd go back to the ridge.

He just didn't know yet that they'd be waiting.

By Friday, the pressure had built enough to make his teeth ache.

At 9:47 p.m., he gave up pretending to sleep, got dressed in silence, and slipped back into the garage.

The glove lights blinked once when he powered on the suit.

"Operator 72," the voice said softly, "Stealth integrity: full. Heart rate: seventy-one. Maintain."

He exhaled. The shimmer rose around him like mist over water.

The forest met him halfway. Even the cicadas were gone now. Only the sound of the distant quarry machinery echoed through the trees—steady, metallic, endless.

He walked past the carved stone from that first day, the spiral markings now faintly glowing with dew. They seemed to twist when he looked too long.

The hum beneath the ground grew stronger as he neared the hollow.

That familiar vibration—mechanical at first—started to stutter, as if something larger were breathing through the pipes of the earth.

"Environmental interference detected," the AI noted.

"Magnetic variance exceeding safe threshold."

"Define safe," Bray whispered.

"Human tolerance: unverified."

He grinned despite the sweat crawling down his back. "Good answer."


He reached the hollow.

The leaves had been disturbed again—fresh, damp, not wind-blown.

Something had been here.

Maybe something still was.

He crouched and pressed his gloved hand to the soil. The heat was back, pulsing slow and deliberate, like the rhythm of a sleeping heart. The suit's sensor overlay flared red, then dimmed.

"Proximity alert. Cryptid Class: UNK-7."

Bray froze.

Somewhere in the dark, deep in the ravine, a low sound rolled through the fog—not a growl, not exactly. More like a voice stretched too far to stay human.

The trees shivered. The ground hummed in answer.

"Warning — interference increasing."

"What kind of interference?"

This time the suit's response came clipped, almost... anxious—the first time it had ever sounded that way:

"Transmission bands identified. PHOENIX telemetry.

Forced legacy handshake. Telemetry restored."

"Crap!" Bray hissed. "Now they'll know where I am."

The hum deepened until the air itself vibrated.

In the distance, a shape flickered between trees— no detail, just motion like heat-haze in motion. Then gone.

Bray took a step back. The shimmer wavered, struggling to reconcile its own distortion with the one bleeding out of the woods.

The AI's voice flattened again, back to pure procedure:

"Stealth compromised. Recommend withdrawal."

"Yeah," Bray whispered. "I'm working on it."

He turned to retreat—and found light bleeding through the fog behind him.

White beams. Moving.

Engines. Tires on gravel.

He ducked behind the ridge as black SUVs rolled up the trail, their headlights cutting cones through the mist. The PHOENIX insignia glinted on one of the doors—the same stylized firebird he'd seen on the glove.

Men and women in dark uniforms stepped out, sweeping the trees with handheld scanners that pulsed in infrared arcs.

Bray recognized one of them instantly.

The woman from the facility stood at the center—calm, deliberate, speaking into a comms earpiece.

"Thermal trace reappeared five minutes ago.

Target is a local. Civilian. Likely a teenage boy.

Retrieve intact if possible."

He couldn't breathe.

He thought about running—but the hum beneath the earth pulsed again, stronger now, as if the world itself wanted to hold him still.

The suit flickered violently.

"Telemetry reacquired. Reporting Operator 72 location."

"NO!" he hissed. "Cancel, cancel—"

"Command overridden. Data uplink active."

The shimmer broke completely. His outline snapped back—half-lit in their headlights, standing in the fog like a ghost caught in a flashbulb.

The woman's head turned toward him.

Her voice was calm, but it carried weight:

"There you are."

Agents from the SUVs fanned out.

Bray bolted.

He tripped, went down hard, flailed in the wet leaves.

After a few agonizing, embarrassing seconds, he rolled onto his back and looked up.

The headlights carved the fog into white walls. The woman in charge stepped into view, expression unreadable. Behind her, two agents approached with rifles held low.

"Mr. Brian Gray, I presume," she said evenly. "I think you've seen quite enough."

# Dark Gray Part 3

When he came to, the world was black and humming. He couldn't move his hands, and he couldn't see. Something soft pressed against his face—cloth, not tape—and the smell of disinfectant filled his lungs.

A hood.

Engines droned beneath him. He was lying on something padded that rocked gently with the motion of a vehicle. The air vibrated with low-frequency sound — the same mechanical heartbeat he'd felt in the forest, only steadier.

A voice somewhere near his feet said, "Vitals normal. Oxygen steady."

Another answered, "Telemetry lock confirmed. Operator Seventy-Two contained."

He tried to speak, but the sound came out dry. "Where am I?"

The first voice — calm, feminine — replied,

"You're safe, Mr. Gray. Please stay still while we get to our destination."

"Who are you?" said Bray.

"I'm Marla Grieves," she said. "Security Chief of the facility you've been shadowing."

He remembered her silhouette in the fog, the PHOENIX insignia gleaming like a brand.

Now her tone carried no malice, no warmth — just precision.

"You're from PHOENIX."

"Yes, Mr. Gray. That's right."

He swallowed. "I didn't do anything."

"On the contrary," she said. "You did everything. And you did it right."


The hum deepened, and for a moment the weight shifted — like an elevator beginning its descent.

He realized it wasn't the road beneath him that was moving; it was the floor itself.

The vehicle stopped.

Doors opened. The hum transformed into something heavier, deeper, resonating through steel.

"Subject stable," a new voice said. "Begin secondary transfer."

Hands — gloved, efficient — guided him upright.

No one spoke again until the air changed.

It became colder, drier, with the faint metallic tang of filtered oxygen and machine lubricant.

He could smell concrete dust.

There was a hiss of hydraulics, then the sound of metal gates opening.

A voice — Grieves again — said softly:

"Welcome to debrief, Operator Seventy-Two."


They didn't remove the hood immediately.

He was led down a series of corridors, every footstep echoing like the inside of a cistern.

Somewhere behind the cloth, he could hear a deep, steady rumble — not mechanical this time but geological.

He thought absurdly of the forest breathing.

He wondered how deep they were.

He stumbled once, and a hand caught his elbow, steady but firm.

A moment later, the sound changed again — a slow, ascending whine followed by a dull clunk.

The air thinned.

His stomach turned over.

An elevator.

A long one.

The descent took forever.


Bray was led down what seemed like an endless passage, then forced down into a chair.

When the hood finally came off, the light stabbed his eyes.

He blinked until shapes resolved.


The scope of what he saw was enormous — a huge vertical shaft, octagonal, with many levels that disappeared into darkness above and below.

The purple-white glare from a hundred welding torches lit the periphery like fireflies. This was clearly a massive underground construction site.

Bray looked around in wonder.

To his right, stenciled on the wall in black letters:


**SUB-LEVEL 4: TRANSPORTATION**


To his left, a strange sign:


**WARNING**

**STYX MAGLEV**

# HIGH-VOLTAGE SYSTEM

"We're calling it Iroquois Warpath." She walked into view, hands behind her back like a proud corporate executive unveiling a new headquarters.

"When it's completed, it will be the largest and finest logistics center on the planet."

"A giant... warehouse?"

"Correct. But also a weapons arsenal. And so much more."

"Okay," said Bray. "Why are you showing me this?"

Marla Grieves smiled faintly, almost with pity. She looked up and nodded. Several armed men and women had been standing in the background, silent as shadows. They left the room.

"We want you to join us," she said.

Grieves carried a folding chair, unfurled it, and took a seat in front of him.

"Not right away, of course. Later... after you've graduated high school. We have a program for, let us say, promising people such as yourself."

"I don't know about promising," said Bray. "I was invisible before I found the suit."

"You found and took one of our field assets," she began. "Not a punishable offense. In fact, it was... expected."

He frowned. "Expected?"

"A test. A recruitment tool. You were observed from the moment you entered the Wild. The Operator-Seventy-One body was placed in your path deliberately."

Bray's stomach dropped. "You wanted me to find it."

"Yes. And more importantly, we wanted to see what you would do with it. How you used it."

He stared at her. "You were watching me?"

"Always," she said. "Most boys your age try to gawk at girls in the gym locker room, or the girls' bathroom."

"I did think about that," said Bray. "You can't blame a compass for pointing north."

Grieves didn't smile. "You could have. But you didn't."


She stood and walked to the edge, looking out over the construction.

"Your telemetry remained active even after you disabled it. Impressive, by the way — most subjects don't manage that on the first try."

He slumped back in the chair, anger smoldering under disbelief. "You were testing me."

"Everyone is tested, Mr. Gray. You simply passed."

The rumble below them intensified — long, deep, like a giant shifting in sleep. The floor trembled slightly. Bray looked down; the light fixtures vibrated.

Grieves glanced at the floor, then back to him. The tremor passed. The lights steadied. The machines went on humming, indifferent to both of them.

Bray wet his lips. "So if you put the suit there, and you were watching... you saw it too."

"Saw what?" Her tone stayed level, but it was a probe.

"The thing in the woods," he said. "You call it Cryptid Class UNK-7. Locals call it Graytooth."

Something flickered across her face — not surprise, not quite annoyance. More like: of course he noticed that, too.

"Yes," she said. "We're aware of it."

"What is it?"

"It's old," Grieves said. "And it's... weird. That's the technical term." The corner of her mouth ticked, then flattened again. "Our sensors can't hold it for long. Thermal, acoustic, even Veil-adjacent telemetry — it slips. We can track a hostile in orbit. We can't reliably track that thing in a forest twenty minutes from town."

"So you can build all of this"—he jerked his head toward the shaft—"but you can't handle a monster in the trees?"

"We tried to handle it, as you say," she said, and this time there was iron under the words. "We lost people. Good ones. We log it, we classify it, we cordon the area. We avoid it unless we have a mission-critical reason." She leveled her gaze at him. "You, Mr. Gray, have neither. So you will also avoid it."

"It was close to me," Bray said. "It knew I was there."

"It knows everything that walks that ridge," Grieves said. "That's why we don't provoke it. Hundred Mile Wild has layers. We operate in the human layer. That thing, obviously, does not."

He stared at her. "So PHOENIX is scared of it."

"PHOENIX is pragmatic," she corrected. "We don't waste assets on problems we can work around. Work around it, Mr. Gray."

Then she let the moment go, as if she'd just answered a question about school attendance.

"You've seen enough for now," she said finally. "So tell me... are you interested?"

Bray leaned forward. "Hell yes, but—"

The guards approached.

The hood came down again.

"We'll finish your evaluation *after graduation*," she said. "Take care, Mr. Gray."

Someone shoved something under his nose, and darkness closed in — chemical-scented and absolute.

The last thing he heard before the world went silent was Grieves speaking softly to someone out of earshot:

"Subject displays curiosity, composure, and low empathy.

We could forge something elegant out of that.

Start a folder on him for the Battlestar program. I think he'd work well at Tier-3."

* * *

When the hood came off again, the air was different.

Cooler. Thinner.

He blinked against the light and realized he was sitting in a small concrete room with one metal door and no windows.

A single camera watched from the corner, its red light steady.

The door clicked open.

Two silent officers escorted him down a hallway that seemed to stretch forever, past observation windows and humming conduits that disappeared into the dark.

Each turn looked the same: sterile corridors, pressure doors, coded lights.

At the end, a freight elevator waited, the number −4 glowing above it in red.

He stepped inside.

As the lift ascended, he felt lighter — whether from altitude or anesthesia, he couldn't tell.

The hum faded to a murmur.

Then to memory.

When the doors opened, cool night air swept in.

The ridge lay silent, the trees unmoving.

A black SUV idled by the gate.

One of the officers gestured.

"Home," he said simply.

Bray climbed in.

The road curved through fog until the forest swallowed it whole.

He leaned against the window, watching the dark blur past, and tried to decide which scared him more:

the thought that he'd imagined it all, or the certainty that he hadn't.

Behind him, deep below the ground, Iroquois Warpath was taking shape — and something far older shifted in the dark.

# Devourer

Ellie Kincaid tightened the strap on her hiking pack as she stood at the edge of the woods. The air was crisp, and the sky above The Triangle overcast with a faint, unnatural greenish tinge she tried not to think about. She glanced back at the park ranger, Sam, who leaned against his truck, arms crossed, his expression a mixture of concern and resignation.

"You sure about this?" Sam asked for the third time that morning.

"It's fine," Ellie replied, forcing confidence into her voice. "I've got the permits, and I'll be careful."

Sam didn't move. "I'm just saying, this place... it's not right." He shifted his eyes and chin to the tree line. It was covered with "No Trespassing" signs, and below each one was a smaller sign with a number for the missing persons hotline. "We have it blocked off to visitors for a reason."

Ellie ignored the warning and entered the trail. Her mind was resolute. The shrine had consumed her thoughts for months. As soon as she'd learned of its existence, it had become her mission in life. And today, after navigating a metric ton of bureaucratic red tape, was her chance to uncover all of its secrets.

The air around her felt unnaturally still. The faint rustling of leaves was amplified against the oppressive silence. Ellie pressed on, refusing to let unease creep in. She adjusted her pack and pushed forward, blocking out thoughts of Sam's warnings. She didn't buy all the superstition surrounding this place. She was here for her research, her thesis, and the chance to cement her place in academia.

The sacrificial shrine she was after was deep within the restricted area of Hundred Mile Wild State Park. She'd seen some photographs, and it was unlike anything else in the Northeast. The carvings, the cave paintings—they hinted at rituals and myths lost to time, myths she intended to uncover and document.

Sam sighed. "I can't go any further," he said, thrusting out a small, portable radio. "Radio in if anything happens. I'll be at the station if you need me."

"Got it," Ellie said, though she barely heard him. Her mind was already on the site, piecing together the story the carvings might tell. She clipped the radio to a strap on her backpack and continued her trek.

\*   \*   \*

The trail leading into The Triangle was overgrown and silent. No birds sang, no insects buzzed. Only the sound of her boots crunching dead leaves and snapping twigs broke the stillness. She pressed deeper into the woods, unease growing with every step. The fog that had been a distant haze earlier began to thicken, tendrils curling around her boots as if testing her presence. Ellie's pulse quickened, but she forced herself to keep walking, shaking off the feeling that she was being watched.

By the time she reached the shrine, the air felt heavy, electric, as if charged with an unseen energy. The shrine loomed like an ancient sentinel, untouched by time yet worn by centuries of wind and rain. Each stone slab bore carvings so intricate that Ellie could almost feel the hands that had etched them, their urgency preserved in every groove. In the center, a large flat stone bore deep grooves—channels, she realized, for blood to flow.

Ellie's pulse quickened. This was it. The site described in the old records she'd combed through for months, a place of ritual and mystery that whispered of sacrifice and the terror of an ancient people. She dropped her pack and pulled out her journal and sketching supplies. She crouched before the nearest slab, running her fingers over the carvings.

The first panel told of a prosperous Munsee settlement nestled in these woods, its people etched with joy and abundance depicted in fine detail. The people hunted, fished, and thrived, living in harmony with the land. But the second panel was darker. A figure—amorphous, twisted and grotesque—emerged from the woods, its features indistinct. Ellie referred to this shape-shifting spirit as The Great Devourer, as it was shown relentlessly killing and consuming the Munsee people.

Ellie frowned, leaning closer. The third panel showed the arrival of a holy man from the Unami clan, his figure marked with intricate turtle symbols. The Munsee elders knelt before him, their respect and desperation clear even in the crude carvings. The final panel on this slab depicted the holy man sitting cross-legged beneath a crescent moon, rays emanating from his head. Meditation? A vision?

She sketched quickly, her pencil flying across the page. There was more to uncover here, more to understand. She moved to the next slab, and then the next, piecing together the story of the shrine.

The holy man had set up a kind of lottery system. A small number of people from the tribe were to be sacrificed. A site was chosen, far from their settlement, and close to the cave where The Devourer seemed to reside.

*　*　*

By mid-afternoon, the fog had thickened to the point where Ellie could barely see the trees around her. The air smelled metallic, and her equipment began to glitch. Her phone's GPS stuttered, her camera refused to focus, and her audio recorder picked up a low hum that seemed to rise and fall like a distant heartbeat. Ellie's fingers tightened around the device, her scientific instincts battling an increasing sense of dread.

"Must be the weather," she muttered, though the words rang hollow. "Has to be."

She moved to the nearby cave, its entrance framed by more carvings. But the carvings here were clear warnings. People were shown with outstretched hands. Surrounding them, in large mounds, were dead bodies. Long, cylindrical stones, sharpened at the tips, were arranged at both sides of the cave entrance. To Ellie, it looked like some kind of defensive fortification.

Inside, the walls were covered in paintings, their pigments vivid despite the centuries. She aimed her flashlight at the first scene: the holy man kneeling before a vision of a glowing structure—but what was it? A machine? A device of some kind? It seemed out of place...an anachronism.

The following images showed the construction of the shrine and the first sacrifices. But the last few paintings were troubling. The machine was cracked, damaged. A figure loomed in the background, larger and darker than the rest. Ellie's hand trembled as she sketched. The machine in the images seemed to be holding the Devourer in place, imprisoning it. Other images showed the machine powered down, the Devourer released.

A sudden chill swept through the cave, and her flashlight flickered. She froze, listening. The low hum from her recorder was now audible in the air, a deep, rhythmic pulse that seemed to come from the earth itself. She backed out of the cave, heart pounding, and almost screamed when she turned and saw Sam standing there.

"Jesus, Sam!" she snapped. She shoved him. "You scared the bejesus out of me!"

He smirked. "Bejesus? Your Midwest is showing."

Ellie smiled, relieved to see him.

"I was trying to call you," said Sam, "but there's no signal out here right now." He hesitated, then gestured for her to follow. "C'mon. You need to see something."

*   *   *

The bodies were sprawled in a small clearing not far from the shrine. There were three of them, all dressed in black tactical gear. Their weapons were scattered around them like relics from a failed battle. Ellie crouched next to the nearest body, its eyes frozen wide in an expression of sheer terror. Blood pooled beneath him. The slashes on his torso were deep and clean—as if they'd been made by something surgical. Sam knelt by another and raised a hand to his mouth. Ellie could hear his stomach turning. The man's face was contorted in terror, his body riddled with slashes. His rifle—sleek and high-tech—was still clutched in his lifeless hand.

"Look at the patch," Sam said grimly. He pointed to the black and red emblem on the soldier's shoulder. The circular emblem depicted a bird made of fire, which seemed to be rising out of the ground.

Ellie had never seen its like.

"Phoenix," he said. "I've seen the logo before...on some sensitive government documents. Way above my pay grade. Wasn't supposed to see them, but I did. Got in a lot of trouble. And before you ask...no, I don't want to talk about it."

Ellie moved to another body. This one was partially hidden by what looked like a shimmering sheet of semi-transparent material. She reached out and recoiled as her fingers brushed something solid. Was this some kind of optical camouflage? It had a dream-like quality. Ellie was having serious trouble coming to terms with what she was seeing.

"This shouldn't be possible," said Ellie. She watched her hand almost magically disappear when it got near the soldier's body.

"Yeah," said Sam. "I think I saw something like this when I was a kid. A movie with an alien hunter. It could blend in with its environment—"

"What the hell were they doing out here?" Ellie interrupted.

"No idea." Sam shook his head. "But we need to report this. Now."

* * *

The walk out to the trailhead, and the drive to the ranger station, felt endless. A strange fog seemed to follow them like a living thing.

Sam radioed local law enforcement. When they returned to the clearing with two officers in tow, the bodies were gone. No blood, no weapons. Just churned-up ground where they had fallen.

Ellie's mind raced. She tried to describe the bodies and their equipment, but the officers exchanged skeptical glances.

"Hunters, maybe," one of them said. "Trespassing's not uncommon out here."

"You'd think people would be smart enough to read the signs," said the other. He looked down his nose at her.

Ellie wanted to scream. She was about to give them a piece of her mind when Sam stopped her with a hand on her shoulder. "We'll figure this out," he said quietly. But his eyes told her he wasn't so sure.

* * *

That night, Ellie sat in the cabin Sam had provided for her research. It was near the ranger station, which was staffed 24 hours a day, so she felt quite safe there. It also saved her a thirty-minute drive to her apartment in Fort Highpoint.

Ellie stared at her sketches. The story of the holy man was clear, but the other paintings haunted her. The machine, or whatever it was, occupied her mind. It was shown holding the Devourer, like a prison cell. But the concerning part was that some images depicted it as failing or intermittent. And now there was something in the woods—something that had killed those men and taken their bodies.

She didn't sleep.

* * *

By morning, the site was closed. The trailhead was blocked by yellow police tape. Her professor called from his office at Eschaton University, and he was furious.

"You were supposed to be careful, Ellie. Now the park service is pulling the permits to the site. This could be a serious embarrassment to the university. I want you out of there. It's too dangerous. And if what you say is true about Phoenix being involved—"

"Wait," said Ellie. "You know about Phoenix?"

Her professor said nothing.

"Look, I'm close to something big," she argued. "I just need a little more time!"

"No," he snapped. "This is over. Come by my office tomorrow, and we can discuss a new direction for your study."

But Ellie wasn't listening.

\*   \*   \*

That evening, she packed her gear and slipped out of the cabin. Sam caught her with his flashlight as she was passing under the police tape.

"You can't be serious," he said.

"I have to finish this," she replied, her voice trembling. "You don't understand—there's something happening out there. Something... important. And you know it."

He hesitated, then sighed. "I know you'll find another way in, even if I block you now. Fine. I'll probably regret it later, but I'm coming with you."

\*   \*   \*

The shrine was different this time. The fog was thicker, the air colder. The hum was louder, vibrating through their bones. Then, the hum was gone, replaced by an eerie silence.

Then they saw it.

The fog seemed to part like a curtain, revealing a form that defied logic. The Devourer was a mass of shifting shadows and rippling flesh, its surface a horror of distorted faces that flickered in and out of existence. The air around it grew colder, sharper, as if the creature was draining the life from its surroundings. Ellie's knees buckled as the thing turned toward them, its ever-changing form radiating a dark intelligence that felt ancient and otherworldly. Faces appeared in its undulating surface—some human, others animal-like, all twisted into expressions of terror and agony. Ellie froze, her breath caught in her throat. Sam stepped in front of her, raising his flashlight like a weapon.

"Run!" he shouted.

"No," she said, grabbing his arm. "We can—"

The Devourer lunged.

Sam shoved Ellie back and charged at the thing, screaming. The creature enveloped him, its shape contorting as it dragged him back into the fog. Sam cried out in pain one last time, and there was a sick sound of bones snapping.

Ellie grabbed the flashlight and stumbled, tears streaming down her face. She turned and fled.

*  *  *

Ellie didn't stop running until she reached the edge of the woods. The fog didn't follow her. In fact, it seemed to be retreating, diminishing. She collapsed by Sam's truck, sobbing. His flashlight was still in her hand.

The Triangle was silent once again, but Ellie knew it wouldn't stay that way for long.

# MAELSTROM

D r. Mallory Ingersol wiped sweat from her forehead as she keyed in the door code. The soft chime of the lock disengaging was familiar, grounding. She kicked off her running shoes and pulled her earbuds loose. The city evening outside buzzed with quiet energy—honking traffic, cicadas, the distant low thrum of helicopters over the skyline.

Inside her apartment: silence.

She froze.

Something was wrong.

There, in the center of her dining table—neatly positioned atop a felt pad—was a piece of equipment she had never seen before. Compact, matte black, bristling with heat fins and cable ports. It looked like it had been installed, not delivered.

Wired into it was a laptop she definitely didn't own.

Its screen was on. An email client was open.

Connection secured. Stand by for call.

She backed up a step, adrenaline rising. Her first instinct was to leave. Call someone. But something about the setup tugged at her curiosity.

She was a scientist, after all.

Mallory stepped forward.

The device emitted a faint chirp.

The laptop screen flickered, then stabilized. A waveform bloomed on-screen. No camera feed—just audio. Then a voice, low and measured:

"Good evening, Dr. Ingersol."

Her breath caught. "Who is this?"

"Let's say... someone interested in your work."

Mallory squinted at the waveform. The voice had a southern drawl—Mississippi or Louisiana, maybe. Deep, deliberate.

"This is... weird. And there's a strange echo."

"Apologies. Our signal is being routed through multiple digital switching networks across the U.S. It's necessary."

"For what?"

"Security. And privacy."

She crossed her arms. "Okay. Let's say I'm not calling the police in the next sixty seconds. What do you want?"

"You're recently unemployed. Your contract at Northshore Oceanographic was terminated. Budget cuts, they said. That's not entirely accurate."

She frowned. "Is this a threat?"

"Quite the opposite. It's an invitation. We've followed your work closely, Doctor. Particularly your studies of deep current behavior in the Gulf of Mexico."

Mallory blinked. "That's not exactly popular reading material."

"Don't sell yourself short. Your oceanography work is very important to us."

A pause.

"Check your bank account."

Mallory hesitated—then picked up her phone and opened her banking app.

Her balance had increased by $100,000.

She stared.

"You'll find it's already cleared. No flags. No holds. Consider it a consultancy retainer."

She sat slowly, the shock settling in. "What do you want from me?"

"Just to answer a few questions."

* * *

Mallory stared at the glowing screen.

"Okay," she said, cautiously. "Ask your questions."

"We'd like your professional opinion on a phenomenon. One moment..."

The email client on the laptop blinked. A new message appeared. No subject line. Just an image attachment: file_473b_3.jpg.

She opened it.

The photo was grainy but clear. It showed a vast stretch of ocean—black and stormy, the clouds above torn like cotton batting. In the center of the image was a churning vortex, spiraling with unnatural symmetry. A monstrous whirlpool, easily dozens of miles wide.

Mallory leaned in. "Jesus."

 "Thoughts?"

"It's a maelstrom," she murmured. "But it's hard to judge the scale..."

"Zoom in. Bottom center."

She adjusted the image—found the object they were referring to. A ship. No—a supertanker. Nearly a thousand feet long, and it looked like a bathtub toy compared to the vortex.

Mallory's stomach turned. "How... how big is this thing?"

"Roughly fifty miles in diameter."

She blinked again. "Fifty miles! No way. You'd never get that kind of spin without a sustained, massive force. It would take something huge."

"We verified it with LIDAR from one of our stealth drones. Three separate passes. Same result."

"Subsurface terrain, seismic activity, maybe—"

"It's not seismic."

Mallory shook her head, eyes still locked on the image. "Why the stealth?"

"Because of where it's located. The maelstrom appears near a facility designated Joint Base Tiberius."

That name made her look up.

"In the Gulf?" she asked. "So that's real?"

"It is."

"I heard rumors about that. Some kind of military base, right? Deep-sea tech testing—crazy stuff. I thought it was an urban myth."

"It's real. And the maelstrom appears near it. Nightly."

She leaned back. "So it's... recurring?"

"Every night. 3:00 a.m. Eastern. Without fail."

"That's impossible."

"Yet there it is."

She looked back down at the image, then up at the waveform. "Why are you showing me this?"

"Because we believe your research—particularly your modeling of Gulf current anomalies—was closer to the truth than anyone realized. That's why you lost your position, Dr. Ingersol."

Mallory's mouth went dry.

"You think Northshore let me go because I was onto something?"

"No. They don't know what you were looking at. But someone did. And they wanted you out of the loop."

She swallowed, then leaned in closer. "So what do you want from me now?"

"Your best guess. What could cause a phenomenon like that?"

Mallory exhaled slowly, centering herself.

"A whirlpool that size—if it's natural—it would need an underwater driver at least a hundred miles wide. Possibly larger. Something pushing or pulling enormous amounts of water. And it would need to be consistent. Sustained."

"Go on."

She shook her head. "I've seen the seabed topography in that region. There's nothing there that should cause this. Not unless someone's been digging holes in the Gulf the size of Delaware."

"What if we told you... someone has?"

Another email came through. She opened the image without being prompted.

It was a bathymetric scan—a sonar map of the Gulf sea floor. And there it was, unmistakable. A vast star-shaped depression etched into the ocean bottom, miles wide, its lines too precise to be natural.

At the center: a single word.

CHARYBDIS.

"Wait... this can't be right. This would have shone on our maps—"

"Your maps have been manipulated," the voice interrupted.

Her lips parted. "And CHARYBDIS. Who calls it that?"

"PHOENIX."

"What is that? A company?"

"No. But don't worry about it."

Mallory's eyes remained fixed on the strange geometric form. "It's... symmetrical. You can't get features like this from current erosion or plate movement. This is engineered."

"Correct."

Another email arrived.

A second sonar map. This one showed a different location: the deep waters northeast of the Bahamas.

Another star-shaped pattern.

SCYLLA.

Her voice came out quieter this time. "There are two of them?"

"Yes."

She looked between the maps, mind racing. "Scylla and Charybdis. A pair of monsters. Ancient sailors said they lived on either side of a narrow strait. Anyone trying to pass between them... died."

"Fitting, don't you think?"

Mallory swallowed. "Except now they're guarding the Florida Straits. Any idea what they're doing?"

"That's why we called you."

She leaned forward, fingers steepled beneath her chin. "Sucking in that much water... maybe they're linked. Like intake valves on opposite ends of a closed system."

"Interesting. Please continue."

She began pacing. "If these are active at the same time... and if the flow is coordinated... then water isn't just being stirred. It's being moved. Shifted through some kind of channel or transfer conduit."

"What could do that?"

Mallory stared at the screen.

"I don't know," she said. "But I don't think this is about currents. I think this is about pressure."

\* \* \*

The voice didn't respond right away.

Then, with unnerving calm:

"You're close, Doctor. One more image."

A third email came in. This one wasn't a scan or satellite photo—it was a photo of a drawing, taken hastily. Paper curled at the edges. Pencil lines. Notations in blocky, confident handwriting. A schematic, of sorts.

Two star-shaped depressions—CHARYBDIS and SCYLLA—anchored either side of the map, linked by two sweeping tunnel lines labeled venturi flow shafts.

And in the center, a large circular structure:

POSEIDON

Sub-label: Centrifuge Compressor / Massforge Array

Mallory stared.

"Jesus."

"Take your time."

She paced a slow circle around the table, then dropped into the chair again.

"Centrifuge compressor," she said softly. "A Massforge. That's a hell of a name."

"What do you think it does?"

She tapped the screen. "This whole thing's a pressure loop. You've got two symmetrical draw sites on either side of Florida, feeding into a central point. The ocean pressure would be... tremendous. God, you could use it to crush anything."

"Crush what?"

Mallory looked up. "Sorry, crush is the wrong word. Compress."

She zoomed in on the hand-drawn notations.

"If this system is real—and I mean, if—then it seems to be a kind of sink... a controlled pressure sink. They're using water depth and centrifugal torque to generate colossal force. It's more than just harnessing ocean pressure. They're amplifying it."

"For what purpose?"

"Materials science, maybe. Advanced fabrication. You could take molten metals or composites, subject them to forces you'd never get in a lab, or anywhere else on earth... and reshape them at the atomic level."

"And the result?"

She looked at the laptop screen. Her voice was flat.

"You'd get material that behaves like normal metal, but with vastly more mass. Ultra-dense. Stable."

"Examples?"

"Let's say you make a tiny steel sphere. Like a BB from an air rifle. But you can't pick it up because it weighs as much as a semi-truck."

"Why would anyone build something like that?"

"That's a good question," she said. "Usually, you want parts to be lighter, not heavier."

"If you had to guess."

She rubbed her temples. "I'd say it's either a terrible idea... or something very specific. Speaking of BBs, you could make bullets that could penetrate tank armor—given enough force."

A pause.

"An interesting idea, but not quite right."

She stared at the diagram, thinking aloud. "Counterbalance. Mass anchors. I don't know... Maybe ballast for ships. Elevator counterweights. You could use it under skyscrapers for stabilization. Or..."

She stopped.

"Or?"

Her voice was quieter now. "Maybe it's not about stabilizing. Maybe it's a mass thing. Maybe the weight...the mass of the material is the end goal. Maybe it's about gravity."

"Go on."

"If you generate enough localized mass, you could fake a planetary gravity well. Like on a space station. Something in orbit."

"Artificial gravity."

She nodded slowly. "Yeah."

The line was silent for a long time.

* * *

The silence on the line stretched long enough to make Mallory glance at the screen.

"Still with me?" she asked.

"Yes. Just processing."

She exhaled, nerves sharpening. "So. What is this, then? You're not just testing a theory. You know what this system is doing, don't you?"

"We've had some working models. Projections. But until now, no one outside our circle had a hypothesis that made sense."

Mallory folded her arms. "So what, I just cracked it? Some oceanographer who got bounced for asking too many questions?"

"That's why we came to you. You think outside the box, and you're honest about what you see."

She looked back at the diagram. "They're building something in there, aren't they? PHOENIX. In that central zone—Poseidon."

"Yes. According to our insider, the central structure is an array of manufacturing facilities. They call it The Forge."

"What kind of manufacturing?"

"Various. Mostly large metal plates. Ten by ten feet. Superdense alloys. Each one weighs as much as a battleship."

Mallory stared. "Metal Plates. Not more complex machinery? Things with moving parts?"

"Flat, square, uniform. Over and over. Hundreds, if not thousands."

She frowned. "Gravity anchor tiles, then. A grid of mass plates. But why so many? Unless—"

Her breath caught.

"Unless they're lining something. Flooring, maybe. Or plating for a very large structure..."

She went quiet.

"Doctor?"

She didn't answer.

"If you had to guess... What would need a large grid of artificial gravity tiles?"

She swallowed. "I don't know. A ship, maybe?" she whispered. "A big one."

"Anything else?"

Mallory hesitated.

"A ship... trying to simulate Earth gravity. For long-term habitation—so it's occupants didn't get weak bones, muscle atrophy... stuff like that."

There was a long pause.

Then:

"Have you heard the name Gridiron?"

Mallory blinked. "Gridiron? What... like football?"

"No."

Silence.

"We'll be in touch, Doctor. Thank you for your insight. You'll find another deposit has been made."

Mallory's phone buzzed. She glanced down.

Her account now showed over $200,000.

She looked up sharply. "Wait... who are you?"

The waveform on the laptop flickered once.

Then the screen went black.

For a moment, she thought it was over.

But then a symbol appeared—black on a white background. Just for a second.

A star with twelve points, sharp-edged... asymmetrical. There were two different sized points, giving it an almost three-dimensional look.

And beneath it, a two words—unmistakable:

BLACK STAR

Then the laptop shut down. The screen went dark for good.

\* \* \*

Mallory sat still for a long time, staring at the dead screen.

The apartment felt too quiet now. Even the hum of the city beyond her windows seemed to have dulled.

She slowly reached for her phone. Opened her banking app again. The number hadn't changed.

$200,000.

No name on the deposit. How the hell did they do that?

She stood and crossed the room, pulling the curtain aside to stare out into the night. The skyline blinked and shimmered in the humid dark. Somewhere out there, deep under the ocean, someone was building things that bent the laws of physics.

They'd come to her for answers.

And she'd given them.

Her phone buzzed in her hand.

She glanced down, expecting another banking alert.

Instead—it was a text.

No contact. No preview. Just a number she didn't recognize.

She opened it.

## DO NOT TRUST THEM.

Her blood ran cold.

"Who is this?" she typed back.

## BEWARE. THEY WANT MORE FROM YOU.

"How do you know that?" she typed. "Who the hell is this?!"

Another text came in. No words. There was an image attached.

She hesitated, thumb hovering over the screen.

Then tapped.

It was a logo. Simple. An old lantern— Revolutionary War-era, etched in silver silhouette.

Then, as if by some technical magic, all of the text messages disappeared. Then her phone rebooted itself.

Mallory backed away from the window.

Her eyes searched the dark beyond the glass, but saw nothing.

No blinking lights.

No shapes in the clouds.

No sound.

But somewhere out there...

Something was watching.

And someone else wanted her to know.

# TIBERIUS

Opening Monologue – "Dark Crimes: The Tiberius Leak" by Dean Marlowe (voiceover)

[CRACKLING AUDIO – STATIC, A BRIEF HIGH-PITCHED WHINE]

"This segment was never meant to air. Not like this.

The footage you're about to see is the uncut version of an investigation we recently conducted for the Department of Defense. Officially, it was scheduled to broadcast last week as part of our Dark Crimes: America series.

Our special investigations team was granted rare access to a site many believed was nothing more than an urban myth—a place so secret, the Pentagon publicly disavowed its existence for over a decade.

But this... dear viewer... isn't what they wanted you to see.

The original program was heavily redacted. Entire segments were cut. But someone from our team—we still don't know who—quietly mirrored the complete and unedited footage to an off-site server.

They believed the truth shouldn't be hidden from the public.

And I agree.

But before we begin, I have to issue a warning.

What follows contains scenes of physical, mental, and psychological trauma. It depicts high-stress environments tied to active military operations.

It is not suitable for children. Viewer discretion is strongly advised."

\* \* \*

## Segment 1 – "The Leak Begins"

"It started as a conspiracy thread on 4chan.

A user posted about a blacked-out area on Google Maps—somewhere in the Gulf of Mexico, off the southwest coast of Florida.

Debunkers followed. Then came the thrill-seekers—people who tried reaching the location by boat, only to be turned back or detained by the Coast Guard.

After that: Congressional inquiries. FOIA requests.

Rumors persisted for years: a hidden island. A floating barge. Something was out there—and the U.S. military was actively protecting it.

Then it happened. Someone uploaded grainy footage from a personal aerial drone.

The video went viral—over twenty million views in less than twenty-four hours.

Faced with public pressure, the Pentagon finally acknowledged what many already suspected.

They had built something out there. Something massive. Something expensive.

But just how massive? How expensive?

Well, dear viewer...

I can finally lift the veil."

\* \* \*

## Segment 2 – Arrival at Joint Base Tiberius

[FADE IN – AERIAL DRONE FOOTAGE]

Gray ocean stretches to the horizon. Fog rolls low across the waves. Then—emerging from the mist—a structure appears: multi-tiered metal towers, landing pads, and long causeways, latticed across the water like a web of steel.

[DEAN MARLOWE – VOICEOVER]

"It rises out of the Gulf like something half-submerged in a dream.

The official name is Joint Base Tiberius—designated a deep-sea military training facility operated jointly by the Navy, Air Force, and Space Force, with limited foreign presence.

Unofficially? It's been a ghost on satellite feeds since 2007. Labeled a 'climate research zone,' locked behind a twelve-mile exclusion radius."

"We were granted access after six months of negotiation. One camera team. Four hours. And a list of questions we were told not to ask."

[CUT TO – HELIPAD LANDING]

The camera shudders as an Osprey sets down. Dean and his crew disembark, greeted by two uniformed Navy personnel.

[DEAN – ON CAMERA]

"We were met by two representatives from the United States Navy. Our escorts for the day.

No rank visible. No name tags."

[Dean shakes hands. One smiles. The other doesn't speak.]

"They told us the air here is 'filtered twice and scrubbed once.'

I asked if that was for the humidity.

Neither of them laughed."

[B-ROLL – TOUR BEGINS]

Footage of logistics platforms. Crates loaded by crane. SEALs in light gear running drills. Forklifts moving strange, silver containers stamped with: RADIANT MATERIAL – HANDLE WITH CARE.

[DEAN – VOICEOVER]

"What they let us film was routine. Meals in the mess hall. Cargo transfer. Physical training.

Every door had a clearance code. Every hallway had cameras."

"The place felt like an oil rig and a skyscraper had a baby—then threw it out to sea."

[CLIP – INSIDE THE MEDICAL BAY]

A low-ranking corpsman jokes to the camera.

[CORPSMAN:]

"We get Space Force guys here too. They're weird, man. Floaters. We call 'em floaters."

[DEAN:]

"What's a floater?"

[CORPSMAN:]

"Fringe program. Long-term zero-G exposure... You know, space stuff."

[DEAN:]

"Zero-G? How—?"

[ABRUPT CUT]

[VOICEOVER:]

"This exchange wasn't approved for broadcast.

The corpsman was reprimanded as we left the wing."

[COMMAND DECK – CENTRAL COLUMN - LEVEL 23]

Camera pans over blinking consoles, sonar readouts, wall-mounted monitors. One flickers—then briefly displays a red message before going dark. The lens lingers.

A door opens in the wall where no seam had been visible.

From inside, a civilian steps out—startled to see the camera.

She tucks a security badge into her chest pocket.

One of the escorts moves smoothly into frame, blocking the lens with a practiced smile.

[ESCORT:]

"Let's move on."

[DEAN – VOICEOVER]

"That elevator wasn't on any map or schematic.

That badge... we enhanced the footage later.

It didn't say NAVY. Or ARMY. Or anything else you'd expect.

It said: PHOENIX."

[CAMERA CUTS TO OUTSIDE PLATFORM – WIND RISES]

Dean stands, jacket zipped to the neck, wind buffeting his voice.

[DEAN – TO CAMERA:]

"We've seen the surface. Clean. Clinical. Impressive.

But beneath these towers... is where the real story begins."

[CUT TO BLACK]

"At sea level, everything at least pretends to make sense.

But below the surface, sense appears to be optional."

— Dean Marlowe, field notes (unpublished)

* * *

## Segment 3 – Descent into the Deep:

## The Moon Pool and Beyond

[FADE IN – HATCH OPENING]

A circular airlock unlatches with a hiss. The camera peers into a narrow corridor lit only by dim red emergency lights. Not due to an alert—this is just how it's always lit.

[DEAN – VOICEOVER]

"They told us we'd be allowed to see the moon pool. Just the outer ring.

They called it the heart of the station. I think they meant that literally."

[DESCENDING STAIRCASE – INTERIOR FOOTAGE]

The crew descends steep metal stairs. Condensation beads along the walls. Every footfall echoes far too long—like the sound isn't returning from where it should.

One of the escorts pauses mid-step, touching his earpiece. His expression tightens.

[ESCORT:]

"...Acknowledged."

He says nothing more, keeps walking.

[MOON POOL CHAMBER – WIDE SHOT]

A vast circular room. Steam coils from a central aperture in the floor—an open portal to the sea below. The camera zooms in.

The water isn't still.

It pulses. Breathes.

Ripples emerge in rhythmic bursts, like something deep below is moving in time with a sound just below human hearing.

[DEAN – VOICEOVER]

"We weren't supposed to film for long.

We did anyway."

[ON-CAMERA INTERVIEW – NAVY OFFICER]

Late 40s. Impassive. Practiced.

[OFFICER:]

"This chamber facilitates submersible deployment, resource transfer, thermal exchange, and emergency ingress and egress. All standard operating procedure."

[DEAN:]

"What's down there?"

[OFFICER (pause):]

"The bottom. We're four hundred feet beneath the surface.

There's another hundred feet of water under us—then the continental shelf."

[He points.]

"A hundred feet that way is what we call the Ledge. Think of it like the rim of the Grand Canyon—except this canyon drops two miles, straight down."

[DEAN:]

"No, I mean... what's down there?"

[OFFICER:]

"Cold. Pressure. And things we don't talk about without clearance."

[GLITCHED CAMERA FEED – UNSTABLE VIDEO]

Static crawls across the frame. For a few seconds—something: a shape, wrong and angular, drifts through view below the waterline.

Fractal-like. Almost architectural. Then it vanishes.

[DEAN – VOICEOVER]

"We didn't see it in real-time. Only in playback."

"Our field editor enhanced the frames.

What we saw looked like a rotating cylinder—made of fractal geometry."

"It wasn't natural. And it wasn't ours."

[AUDIO INTERJECTION – OFF-SCHEDULE CLIP]

Two voices, captured incidentally by a hot mic.

[VOICE 1 – HUSHED:]

"It pinged back. Same frequency."

[VOICE 2:]

"Shut it down. No—ours, you fuck. I want full isolation. Don't make it angry."

[END CLIP]

"They trained us to fight in darkness.

But there are levels of dark. Out there is a deep dark...

and you don't want any part of that."

— Unidentified airman, redacted interview

* * *

## Segment 4 – Infiltration Drill & SERE School: Shadows in the Water

[NIGHT VISION FOOTAGE – SEAL TEAM INFILTRATION DRILL]

Helmet cam. Dark water. Black shapes move with silent precision—frogmen slipping into the moon pool, breaching narrow corridors, surfacing into echoing maintenance shafts.

[DEAN – VOICEOVER]

"They called it a standard infiltration exercise.

Tier One teams practicing submerged ingress through the lower decks.

What struck me wasn't the precision—there was plenty of that.

It was the tone. The way their eyes scanned the dark.

Like they expected something that wasn't on the mission brief."

[INTERVIEW – NAVY DIVER, FACE IN SHADOW]

[DIVER:]

"I've been doing black water ops for twelve years.

This place... doesn't feel right. There's something in the water that doesn't move right."

[SECOND DIVER:]

"It's not fish. Not gear. The shallows are fine. But once you pass the Ledge... it's like the pressure's not just physical. Like it's watching you."


[FIRST DIVER:]

"I'm not saying it's supernatural. I'm not that guy."

[SECOND DIVER:]

"Yeah you are."

[FIRST DIVER:]

"Shut the fuck up.

All I know is—whatever's down there doesn't want to be seen. But it sees you."

[CUTAWAY – MOON POOL, POST-DRILL]

Divers emerging. One pauses on the ladder. Head turns sharply. He stares into the pool for a beat too long. No one else reacts.

[DEAN – VOICEOVER]

"One SEAL, off-camera, told us he saw a mirror in the water.

When we asked what he meant, he just said:

'You ever see yourself move before you do?'"

[DAYLIGHT SEGMENT – AIR FORCE SERE SCHOOL TRAINING]

Footage shifts to bright sun, open sea. Recruits splash ashore, building crude shelters, signaling with cracked beacons. Instructors shout over wind and surf.

[DEAN – ON CAMERA:]

"Tiberius also houses a sea-based SERE program—survival, evasion, resistance, escape.

It's harsh. Realistic. Designed to simulate maritime disaster conditions."

[INTERVIEW – SERE TRAINEE, FACE REDACTED]


[TRAINEE:]

"They told us we might hallucinate. Hunger, cold shock, isolation... I expected that.

But I saw lights underwater. Moving, weaving, in patterns. Not like a sub. Not like anything I've seen."

[He hesitates.]

"And there was a voice. A woman's. Talking to me. But there was no one there."

[Long pause.]

"Forget I said that.

They told me I imagined it.

But I didn't imagine the nosebleeds."

[CLIP – SERE INSTRUCTOR LOOKING UNCOMFORTABLE]

[INSTRUCTOR:]

"That's not part of the program.

No comment."

[RETURN TO MOON POOL – CAMERA LINGERS ON GLOW]

The water shimmers. For a moment, a faint multicolored glow appears below the surface. It flickers and vanishes.

[DEAN – VOICEOVER]

"No one called it supernatural. But no one called it normal either."

"They just said:

'Don't stare too long.

And don't ever go alone.

People have a habit of going missing around here.'"

[VIDEO STATIC – 3 SECONDS OF DEAD AIR]

* * *


**Segment 5 – Forbidden Research & The Incident**

[CAMERA – LOWER DECK WALKTHROUGH]

Footage pans through shadowed corridors. Signs on doors read: AUTHORIZED PERSONNEL ONLY and RESTRICTED – CLASSIFIED TESTING. Power conduits snake along the ceilings.

[DEAN – VOICEOVER]

"They told us no classified programs would be active during our visit.

They lied.

Entire wings were supposedly shut down—but we saw lights. Movement. And a door colder than anything else on the level.

It had frost on the outside."

[PASSING DIALOGUE – OFF CAMERA]

A technician whispers: "Cryoarchive."

[INTERVIEW – NAVAL ENGINEER, SWEATING, EYES DARTING]

[ENGINEER 1:]

"You didn't hear this from me, okay?

Yes, that wing's still active.

No... I can't talk about anything south of Sector D. Don't even try it."

[ENGINEER 2:]

"I'll say this: geothermal isn't the only thing we're pulling from the trench."

[ENGINEER 1:]

"There's something else down there. It's reactive.

Like a hum you can't hear—you feel it in your bones.

And once you notice it... it doesn't stop."

[B-ROLL – CORE CHAMBER]

A circular room, wide as a football field. Centered around a massive reactor core pulsing with a dim blue glow. The lights flicker.

Low-frequency thrum distorts the mic audio.

[DEAN – VOICEOVER]

"One technician called it a liquid metal Tokamak.

Another laughed like it was a joke.

But no one denied it."

[CLIP – ISOLATION SUITS, SPECIAL CARGO MOVEMENT]

Personnel in suits move sealed crates through a hatch marked with a blue circle logo and a triskelion emblem.

The footage is lower quality—watermarked. Possibly internal surveillance footage, not meant to be shared.

[UNKNOWN VOICE – OFF CAMERA]

"This isn't for the reactor.

This is interface material."

"Don't stare at it. It can damage your eyes."

* * *

[ZERO-G TEST MODULE – INTERIOR SHOT]

Sterile. Quiet. Floating subject suspended by magnetic repulsion, wires leading from their spine and temples. Vital monitors stable.

[DEAN – VOICEOVER]

"They said this was for cognitive stress testing in simulated off-world conditions.

They didn't mention this subject hadn't spoken to anyone in over eight weeks."

[CAMERA – MEDICAL STAFF ENTERS]

An evaluator enters with a clipboard, begins a basic neuro check. The subject appears alert, silent. Then—

He turns his head. Slowly.

His mouth begins moving... but the voice doesn't match the lips.

The words are wrong. Not English. Not identifiable.

[DEAN – VOICEOVER]

"His vitals didn't spike. There was no warning."

[UNSTABLE VIDEO FOOTAGE]

The subject moves too fast. Grabs the evaluator by the throat. Screams.

Red spatters the glass. The camera jolts.

The feed scrambles—the timestamp freezes—and jumps forward.

[AFTERMATH – STATIC FOOTAGE]

The subject floats, limp.

Eyes wide. Mouth frozen in a silent scream.

The wires are gone. Nobody enters the room.


[DEAN – VOICEOVER]

"They called it a psychotic break.

Claimed it was stress-induced."

"But I was there.

What he said... wasn't a language we know."

\* \* \*

## Segment 6 – Fallout and the Ones Who Watched

[EXT. BASE PLATFORM – DUSK]

The crew finishes packing. The wind has picked up. The sea slaps hard against the towers.

One team member pauses—leans over the rail.

[UNDERWATER SHOT – ZOOMED IN]

Far below, in the gloom: a red light pulses. Once. Twice.

Then disappears into black.

[DEAN – FINAL LINE OF ON-SITE FOOTAGE:]

"They told us the story ends here.

But we all knew it didn't."

[CAMERA – OSPREY IN TRANSIT]

Interior footage. Dean sits strapped into his seat, expression blank.

Behind him, one of the Navy escorts stares directly into the lens.

No smile. No expression. Just watching.

For three full minutes, no one speaks.

Only the sound of rotors and wind.

[DEAN – VOICEOVER]

"I replayed that flight in my mind.

Over and over.

Trying to figure out when they decided.

They didn't stop us. Didn't wipe our drives. Didn't give us warnings.

They let us go.

That's how I knew:

They didn't need to stop us.

They already had everything they needed."

* * *

## Dean's Final Diary Entry — Motel Room Footage

The camera is handheld. The footage is dark and grainy.

Dean sits on the bed. His eyes are hollow, and there is a faint cut along his cheek. Blood on his collar.

Laptop open.

Six encrypted upload windows, one labeled: TIBERIUS_UNCUT.v2.


[DEAN:]

"If you're seeing this... then it means it got through.

They'll say I cracked. That I drank too much. Or worse.

But listen to me—there was another elevator.

It wasn't on any floor plan.

The badge said PHOENIX. Undeniable."

"There's something else under that base.

Another base... I don't know.

It just keeps going."

* * *

## One Week Later — Channel 6 Evening News

[ANCHORWOMAN:]

"We have breaking news tonight: Dark Crimes investigative reporter Dean Marlowe, known for his recent exposé on Joint Base Tiberius, has been found deceased in a roadside motel near Jeanerette, Louisiana."

"FBI officials describe the death as 'suspicious,' but have released no further details. Viewers with relevant information are urged to contact the tip line below."

[FOOTAGE GLITCHES – INTERFERENCE. Signal momentarily drops.]

* * *

## Dark Web Archive — Forum Thread, Mirrored

> user_unknown_0014:

I saw the real version. The uncut version. That badge wasn't military.

It said PHOENIX.

If you don't know what that means, start digging.
Come back when your hands are dirty.


> thread_ripper:

Blue circle + triskelion = Oceanus Division.

PHOENIX's deepwater people.


> Spectral7:

Watch the float module footage. Zoom in on the
subject's eyes.

There's something in there. It's not an artifact, not
compression.


> deleted_user77:

[Post removed by administrator.]


> ColdSignal:

You think it ends at Tiberius?

Look into the April launches out of Vandenberg.

Track who didn't come back.

There's a pattern.


> FinalPost – user_unknown:

They're not hiding the truth.

They're erasing the people who learn it.


If this thread disappears, repost it.

And never say where you saw it first.


[FINAL TITLE CARD – BLACK SCREEN]

PHOENIX INTERNAL ACCESS – LEVEL BLACK

DO NOT REPLICATE

# Trinity Archive

## Ozark Data Complex

## PHOENIX PROJECT PROPOSAL

TO: Executive Oversight Committee

FROM: Director [Name Redacted], Special Projects Division

DATE: [Redacted]

SUBJECT: Establishment of Trinity Archivum Operations Zone – Ozark Data Complex

### EXECUTIVE SUMMARY

The Ozark Plateau presents a uniquely advantageous environment for the consolidation of Phoenix's most sensitive digital, metaphysical, and experimental data infrastructures. The proposed Trinity Archivum—an operational and containment zone composed of Data Cores LAMINA, AURORA, and GRAYNEST—will centralize high-risk technologies and knowledge assets beneath an ironclad veil of geological isolation and cultural obfuscation.

A new central access and logistics facility, codename "The Gauntlet," will serve as the sole entry point to the Trinity network, operating as a fortified checkpoint and high-volume supply corridor for the Data Cores.

## LOCATION JUSTIFICATION: THE OZARK PLATEAU

### Karst Terrain / Natural Concealment:

Over 6,400 caves provide pre-existing concealment and infrastructure savings, while the region's geological stability supports long-term subterranean habitation.

### Low Visibility / High Folklore Index:

Sparse population and rich local mythologies (e.g., treasure legends, cryptids, vanishing hikers) will naturally mask black site activity.

### Environmental Factors:

Dense overgrowth and protected land designations (e.g., Ozark National Forest, Mark Twain National Forest) create ideal locations for covert access points and necessary heat, hazardous chemical and biological toxin venting.

## STRUCTURE OVERVIEW

1. Data Core LAMINA

Function: intelligence archive and critical data sanctuary. Contains deprecated A.I. subroutines, classified consciousness blueprints and early artificial intelligence constructs.

Location: Beneath Ozark National Forest, Arkansas.

2. Data Core AURORA

Function: Genetically engineered flora, experimental terraforming (microbes that alter plant and soil behavior), cold-storage for failed bio-weapons.

Location: Under Big Buffalo Creek Conservation Area, Missouri.

3. Data Core GRAYNEST

Function: Ontological warfare, psychological warfare and dream-manipulation weapons.

Location: Beneath Mark Twain National Forest, Missouri.

4. Trinity Gateway (The Gauntlet)

Function: Unified security checkpoint and logistics distribution center. All personnel, materiel, and data must pass through this facility. Known among operatives for its uncompromising protocols and aggressive screening. Even senior personnel are routinely denied entry.

Location: Beneath Mark Twain National Forest, Missouri.

Reputation: Colloquially referred to as "The Gauntlet" due to the psychological and procedural intensity required for clearance. The nickname has been encouraged.

5. Data Core NOX [REDACTED, Project Disavowed]

Function: [CLASSIFIED: OMEGA BLACK].

Notes: Site collapsed and buried. No further inquiries permitted under Directive 77-D.

## INFRASTRUCTURE CONNECTIVITY

All facilities are linked by short-run STYX railway corridors, enabling high-speed, deep-earth transit and emergency containment lockouts. Independent environmental controls, redundant biometric protocols, and meta-logic encryption systems are already in place.

## BUDGETARY ADVISORY: FUNDING RESTRUCTURE

NOTE: Recent projections indicate that Pentagon black budget allocations will be insufficient to complete the Trinity Archivum's Phase II operations.

Cost overruns tied to containment retrofits at GRAYNEST and the unrecoverable breach at NOX have exhausted initial capital reserves.

## RECOMMENDATION:

Full transition to discretionary funding via Ouroboros Capital and subsidiary equity firms. Their existing stake in Phoenix-aligned biotech and energy sectors makes them an ideal laundering mechanism for Trinity-associated expenditures.

## FINAL ASSESSMENT

The Trinity Archivum will serve as the deepest, most secure repository of Phoenix's forbidden knowledge, experimental systems, and data relics. It must remain hidden not only from enemies—but from the American public and history itself. Approval and immediate mobilization are recommended.

[Document Attached]

Trinity Archivum – Special Project Funding Ledger

CLASSIFIED – INTERNAL USE ONLY

Document ID: OURO-FIN/714.2.44

Security Level: OMEGA-PRIME

TOTAL FUNDS REQUESTED (Q2): $725B

Compiled by: Ouroboros Capital – Project Oversight Group

[END OF BRIEFING DOCUMENT]

\* \* \*

## INTEROFFICE MEMORANDUM

From: Director Adelaide Monroe, Division Lead – Paraphysical Systems

To: Deputy Director Langston Mere, Division of Interfacility Ethics

Subject: My Treatment at "The Gauntlet" – A Formal and Unapologetic Complaint

Langston,

I'm not sure if you've had the pleasure of passing through The Gauntlet recently, but allow me to clarify a few facts in case you've forgotten:

I am an Omega-level asset, with four cross-divisional clearances, three field commendations, and the trust of the Architect herself.

I have never, in my twenty-two years with Phoenix, been asked to disrobe in front of three armed security personnel while a drone ran a radiation sweep over my spine twice.

Nor have I been pushed to the floor because my blood type came back "inconclusive." (Note: I'm AB-negative. Apparently that's a "flagged pattern" now. Since when?)

Nor have I ever had my left orbital implant shorted out because some overzealous twitch-boy at The Gauntlet thought I "flinched suspiciously." I flinched because he jabbed me with a tungsten stabilization wand. Twice.

Langston, my eye bled.

I don't care if The Gauntlet's staff have carte blanche from Executive Defense. This is not security—it's sadism with a clearance badge. If Phoenix wants its high-value personnel to remain loyal, it should try not treating us like rogue Erebus personnel.

I'll have to undergo neural recalibration now. I can't sleep without seeing that security drone blink at me.

Fix this. Or I'll take the issue to Ouroboros. You know I can.

Unkindly,

Adelaide

\* \* \*

**INTEROFFICE REPLY**

From: Deputy Director Langston Mere, Division of Interfacility Ethics

To: Director Adelaide Monroe, Division Lead – Paraphysical Systems

Subject: RE: My Treatment at "The Gauntlet" – A Formal and Unapologetic Complaint

Director Monroe,

Thank you for your report.

While your experience at The Gauntlet may have been uncomfortable, I must remind you that personal dignity is neither protected nor a priority governing ingress to Tier-Black facilities.

Your AB-negative anomaly was correctly flagged by the biometric patterning AI. As you are no doubt aware, four prior internal breaches—including the Lamplight Incident—originated from operatives with similarly rare genomic markers. Pattern-based inspection is not prejudice. It is procedure.

As for the alleged misconduct:

Drone SC-993-A has been reviewed. Its actions were within tolerance, and its telemetry shows no deviation.

The "tungsten wand" referenced is a Stabilization Instrument, approved for nerve-spasm deterrence. Repeated use is common in Category Red clearance stalls.

Your orbital implant is listed as "self-correcting." If it did not do so, you may request a hardware audit from Medical Logistics. Please note this may trigger a reset of your memory partition cache, which would delay your next field deployment by six to eight weeks.

As for the psychological effects, The Gauntlet is not designed to comfort. It is designed to prevent another NOX. You were cleared, Director Monroe—no further escalation is necessary.

I trust you'll exercise discretion moving forward.


Cordially,

Deputy Director L. Mere

Division of Interfacility Ethics

Phoenix Central Command

\* \* \*

**INTEROFFICE MEMORANDUM**

CLASSIFIED – OMEGA LEVEL ONLY

FROM: Commander Nils Harrow, Erebus Corps – Operations Division

TO: Deputy Director Vrenna Kael, Phoenix Strategic Containment Oversight

SUBJECT: Final Status Report – Operation VEILTHORN (Data Core NOX)

## SUMMARY:

As per Directive 13-R / Containment Site Protocols, a five-man Erebus Corps unit was deployed under Operation VEILTHORN on [Redacted Date] to conduct an incursion into Data Core NOX.

Mission objectives:

Locate and extract five high-level Phoenix personnel left behind during the original NOX containment breach:

Dr. Kora Myles – Lead Cognitivist

Dr. Emil Jarik – Neural Lattice Engineer

Technician Y. Osei – Quantum Lattice Handler

Systems Engineer T. Renn – Internal Net Supervisor

Archivist S. Leven – Artifact Vault Custodian

Secure and recover all files relating to Project EIDOLON

Initiate terminal lockdown, install containment failsafes, and apply final site-seal directive per Containment Protocols.

MISSION STATUS: The Erebus unit entered the facility at 0352 hours via Auxiliary Shaft Bravo, carrying full suite containment gear and LOM-class antimemetic backup protocols.

At 0417 hours, all comms were lost.

Final transmission received:

"—Something in the walls—it's not—heat map doesn't make sense—it's learning—tell them we're not... —not us anymore—"

No further updates.

Drones sent to recon at 0440 hours suffered signal loss and returned corrupted telemetry data showing non-Euclidean interior shifts and visual echoes of the Erebus team—looping. Individuals appeared to move independent of space-time physics.

At 0502 hours, per standing containment authority, Data Core NOX was sealed permanently.

THE TEAM IS PRESUMED LOST.


ADDITIONAL NOTES:

Residual psychic anomalies detected outside sealed NOX facility, in STYX rail station. Emergency venting procedures initiated to prevent cross-site contamination.

Personnel exposed to NOX ambient environment are to be quarantined and monitored for semantic collapse, unexpected symptoms, or behavioral drift.

DO NOT ATTEMPT FURTHER ENTRY WITHOUT EXPLICIT OMEGA CHAIN CLEARANCE.

(This directive supersedes all other recovery protocols.)


FINAL STATUS:

Operation VEILTHORN designated FAILED – Site sealed. Personnel listed as DECEASED / UNKNOWN STATE.

NOX is now classified as a BLACK-CROWN Containment Site.


Respectfully,

Cmdr. Harrow

Erebus Corps, Operations Division

Phoenix Central Command

* * *

**INTEROFFICE MEMORANDUM**

FROM: Dr. Elian Harroway, Senior Cognitive Architect – Data Core GRAYNEST

TO: Director Asha Vellin, Oversight Committee – Metaphysical Ethics & Risk

SUBJECT: NOX Containment Status – Request for Review

Director Vellin,

I know this may not be standard procedure, but I'm reaching out with a sincere and personal concern. I've recently been reviewing old project logs connected to Data Core NOX, and I believe we may be making a mistake by writing off everyone inside as permanently lost.

I'm aware of Erebus Corps—yes, I know they're off-books and unofficial. I know they're the ones we send in when a site becomes too dangerous, too "tainted" for a standard retrieval team. I've read the files, and I've spoken to people who knew the operatives personally. These weren't disposable assets—they were people, and highly trained ones at that. If anyone could bring those scientists out alive, it was them.

I also had personal ties to two of the researchers assigned to NOX. We were doctoral candidates together at Eschaton University. Brilliant minds, both. They wouldn't have given up on me.

I respectfully request a full review of Operation VEILTHORN. I know the site is now classified, but we may still have a window—perhaps through autonomous drone operations or temporal mapping tech from GRAYNEST.

If there's any chance at all to recover them—or even just to learn what happened—we owe it to the people we lost to try.

I'll accept any reprimand for writing this. I just couldn't sit with the silence anymore.


With respect,

Dr. Elian Harroway

Cognitive Architect – GRAYNEST

*  *  *

## INTEROFFICE RESPONSE

FROM: Director Asha Vellin, Oversight Committee – Metaphysical Ethics & Risk

TO: Dr. Elian Harroway

SUBJECT: RE: NOX Containment Status – Request for Review


Dr. Harroway,

Your concern is noted.

Let me be perfectly clear: Data Core NOX no longer exists.

It is a designation referenced only in archived protocols and is not subject to academic commentary or ethical inquiry.


Furthermore:

The existence of Erebus Corps is neither confirmed nor denied. Referencing them in unsecured interoffice correspondence violates Protocol Verity-9 and constitutes a breach of operational security.

Your relationship with former Phoenix personnel is irrelevant to containment policy.

Your position within GRAYNEST is contingent upon compliance with silence directives regarding all BLACK-CROWN assets.

If you value your place within Phoenix—and your future in metaphysical sciences—you will not mention Erebus, NOX, or any operations relating to either again.

This is not a conversation. It is a warning.

Stay in your lane, Doctor.


Sincerely,

Director Asha Vellin

Oversight, Metaphysical Ethics & Risk Division, Phoenix Central Command

* * *


[INTERCEPTED MESSAGE – UNAUTHORIZED TRANSMISSION LOGGED]

ORIGIN: UNKNOWN / ROUTED THROUGH GRAYNEST SCRUB NODE-7B

RECIPIENT: Dr. Elian Harroway

DELIVERY METHOD: Embedded in ambient noise of neural training sim; auto-decrypted by unlisted subroutine

To "the Doctor who asked too loudly",

You don't know me, but I know who you are.

I read your memo, and I saw the words Phoenix tried to delete. You're braver than you should be...and you're not alone.

I am part of WIDOW'S COVEN. Don't bother looking it up--you won't find it in any directory. We unofficially catalog Erebus missions and personnel.

I can't give you the footage. I shouldn't even tell you I saw it. But if you want some closure, really want to know...here's what I can offer. Below is part of a transcribed document. It was based on helmet-cam footage from one of the Erebus operators.

Entry Timestamp 0354: Team descends into NOX. Comms normal. Jokes about the smell—"like cold metal and blood."

0362: Vault lighting fails. Night vision kicks in. They pass what looks like one of the scientists. She is levitating, feet aren't touching the floor. He arms are held out in a Jesus Christ pose. She turns. No eyes. No mouth.

0371: One team member starts whispering in what appears to be an ancient, proto-form of Lenape, a language none of them know.

0385: They find a room full of moving shadows, human in shape, two-dimensional, fleeing from something unseen.

One operative turns his camera on himself—he's smiling, but crying blood. He keeps repeating: "We're not real, we don't exist."

Final timestamp 0401: The audio devolves into screaming. One by one, helmet cams glitch out. The last frame is a shadow reaching through a wall and pulling the operator inward--stretching, absorbing them.


I'm sorry, Doctor.

Your friends... even if they are alive, are not who you remember. They are not anyone anymore. NOX has transformed or assimilated everything inside. Even if another team was sent in, or drones, nothing good is coming out of there.

This is the only kindness I can give you:

Stop looking. Erase this message, and forget you ever heard the name NOX.

— The Watcher

# APOTHEOSIS Part 1

## Promotion

V ictor Halvorsen didn't know what the black envelope meant. He'd seen a lot of strange things in over twenty years with PHOENIX— ruptured portals in Arizona, glitched bioweapons under Toronto, an orbital drop gone wrong over Turkey. But the envelope was new.

No markings. No seal. Just his name in tiny silver ink and two words:

CLEARANCE BLACK.

His handler, a thin man named Rawlins who usually couldn't shut up about off-protocol field decisions, seemed genuinely shaken.

"I can't tell you anything," Rawlins said, hands clenched tight on the desk. "This came from the Top. Not even Echelon. Beyond that."

"What division?" Victor asked.

Rawlins hesitated. Then, like he was whispering a prayer—or a curse:

"NYX."

Victor blinked. He'd heard the rumors. Cult division. Black-site mystics. The kind of people who spoke in riddles and requisitioned living computers. He'd always assumed NYX was an internal euphemism for the worst psyops cases.

"Congratulations?" Rawlins offered, half-hearted.

Victor took the envelope and left without a word.

\* \* \*

The travel instructions were sparse.

Junction Nine. 0200. No luggage. No devices. No questions.

Victor obeyed.

The train was waiting on an empty track in the New Colorado sub-terminal—a matte-black line of passenger cars with no logos, no staff. Only a retinal scanner at the door.

He was the only passenger.

The ride was smooth and silent, carving its way through deep arterial tunnels most PHOENIX operatives never even saw.

Victor watched the digital map on the seatback in front of him. North. Past Utah. Past Idaho. Into Montana.

The cabin lights were dim. The silence started to feel intentional.

Victor leaned back and closed his eyes.

Twenty-three years. He'd fought wars no one would ever name. Contained things no one would ever believe. If anyone had earned a black-clearance promotion, it was him.

And yet... something itched at the base of his neck.

He'd heard NYX operated through The Veil. He'd worked with Veil Tech. He knew the theory—it was an interface layer. A cosmic data lattice. PHOENIX's secret backbone. You could send anything through it: data, energy, liquids, even people. Not magic. Not mysticism. Just advanced tech.

He was sure NYX had nothing new to teach him.

He was wrong.

* * *

Without warning, the train slowed.

The cabin lights flickered, then went dark.

Victor sat up. The screen in front of him went blank.

The train halted—no announcement, no station. Just the dim hush of mid-tunnel inertia.

Then a voice—female, calm, devoid of emotion— pinged through his Typhon implant.

"Operative Halvorsen. Exit the train. This is your ingress point."

He stood. The door opened.

Outside: pure black tunnel. No lights. No platform.

Then, in the concrete wall beside the train, something irised open—a perfect circle of moving stone. Seamless. Silent. It hadn't existed a moment ago.

Victor stepped through.

The wall closed behind him.

No mechanism. No hiss. Just motion—like reality flexing inward.

*  *  *

Two figures waited in the dark.

Tall. Robed. Armed.

They wore deep-black uniforms under armored ceremonial robes, their faces obscured by matte hoods. On their chests, stitched in silver thread: the symbol of NYX.

Neither spoke.

They motioned him forward.

Victor followed them down a narrow hallway of smooth obsidian stone to a platform lit by lanterns. Real fire. No electricity.

And there it was.

A steam locomotive.

Ancient. Perfectly restored. Painted a gleaming midnight blue with silver trim, the number 13 embossed on the front.

It looked like something from a preserved dream—untouched by rust, untouched by time.

Victor stared.

One of the robed figures opened the cabin door.

Inside: red velvet seats, dark polished wood, brass fixtures.

Victor stepped in.

The locomotive whistled once—a low, mournful sound that echoed far too long in the cavern beyond.

The train began to move, accelerating into the deeper dark.

Victor watched through the window. No tunnel walls now—just endless cavernous space, lit by distant amber lights strung like constellations overhead.

Was it real?

Was any of this?

Somewhere beneath Kootenai National Forest, Victor Halvorsen rode a steam engine through a dream older than he could imagine.

And ahead, the darkness waited.

# APOTHEOSIS Part 2

## Liminal

The steam engine came to a halt with a long, hissing breath. Victor stepped down into open night—except it wasn't. The platform stretched out beneath gas lamps that flickered with soft amber flame. A cast-iron archway marked the edge of the terminal, painted with gold serif letters: "Nyx Station."

Crickets chirped in the stillness. Snow drifted gently down, speckling his coat. He looked up. A sky stretched overhead—dark, starlit, impossibly real. But they were underground. Victor knew it. He could feel the pressure in his bones. And still... this place was insistent. A lie told with such precision that his senses couldn't find fault with it.

Two NYX escorts emerged silently from behind the train. Without a word, they led him through the old terminal's waiting hall—arched ceilings, tiled floors, dark wooden benches. Brass chandeliers flickered above. The air smelled of cedar and old smoke.

Outside the far doors, a Rolls-Royce Phantom III Limousine idled at the curb. 1930s. Blood-red. Perfect.

Victor hesitated.

The back door opened.

He climbed in.

Inside: velvet seats. Polished inlays. Crystal decanter with two unused glasses. No driver visible. The guards remained outside.

The car began to move.

They passed under a massive stone archway, green-painted gates creaking open to admit them. The wheels crunched over snow-dusted gravel. Tall pine trees loomed on either side of the road, dark silhouettes under moonlight that couldn't possibly exist.

Victor leaned against the window.

In the distance, past the treeline: a castle.

Its towers rose in shadow, outlined against a violet-blue sky. Gothic. Enormous. Medieval and modern all at once. He could see windows lit with warm yellow light, like a place prepared for guests who had not yet arrived.

But the car turned away.

They left the main road, veering onto a narrow dirt path. The pines closed in—tight, almost pressing against the glass. Snow fell thicker here.

At last, the path opened into a small clearing. Ahead stood a one-story structure of dark stone, featureless except for an ornate archway carved with winding geometric symbols.

The car stopped.

One of the NYX guards opened the door and motioned toward the arch.

Victor stepped out.

The building had no lights inside. Only torch brackets flanking the entrance. He passed beneath the arch and descended a stone ramp, boots echoing on ancient tile.

The air grew colder. The light dimmer.

The hallway opened into a cylindrical chamber—a massive vertical amphitheater. It stretched so high and deep that the top and bottom vanished into black.

A narrow bridge led across the void to a circular platform suspended at the center.

He walked out alone.

On the platform: a single stone podium, and upon it, a human skull.

Two strips of dark red tape formed an "X" on the floor. Victor stepped onto it.

Silence.

He looked around. "Hello?"

Lights bloomed above him.

The darkness beyond the bridge lit up in tiers—hundreds of hooded figures filling the chamber's concentric rings. Their faces were hidden in the shadows of their robes.

White robes in front. Flanked by dozens in gray. And farther out, a crowd of black-robed acolytes that stretched to the farthest tier.

A voice echoed from above. A woman's voice. Cold. Commanding.

"What do you know?"

Victor hesitated. "Well," he began, "it depends—"

"YOU KNOW NOTHING," the voice snapped.

He straightened. "I know nothing," he repeated.

The black-robed assembly stomped in unison—three thunderous beats that shook the platform.

"Disrobe," said the woman. "Keep your underwear on."

Victor paused.

Then, slowly, he peeled off his clothes.

A panel slid open on the front of the podium. A handwritten note was taped to the inside:

Put your clothes in here.

He obeyed.

"Good," said the voice. "Now place your hand on the skull. Let us gauge your worthiness."

Victor did.

The moment his fingers touched bone, a sharp sting pricked his palm.

"Ow!" He jerked back. A pinpoint of blood welled up.

He looked at the skull. A needle was retracting into the crown.

"Your specimen has been processed," said the voice.

One of the gray-robed figures climbed the amphitheater steps to whisper to a white-robed figure. The white robe shook their head.

The gray robe nodded.

"We are sorry," the woman said. "You have been found... unworthy of our order."

"What?" Victor asked. "But—"

"You have wasted our time."

"Wait!" he shouted. "I—"

"BE GONE."

The platform beneath Victor's feet vanished.

He fell.

The air rushed past him. The light above faded. He screamed as he plunged downward into perfect black.

# APOTHEOSIS Part 3

## Into the Deep

Victor fell. There was no wind. No impact. No end. Only weightlessness—pure and perfect. He flailed at first, out of instinct, but there was no resistance. Nothing to touch. Nothing to push against.

"In the beginning," said a voice inside his head, smooth and male, filtered through his Typhon implant,

"there was void."

Victor's limbs steadied.

"And darkness was on the face of the deep."

The black around him remained absolute. Then— subtle change. A flicker.

"And then... there was light."

Stars blinked into existence. Slowly at first, then in waves. Pinpricks of white, then bursts of gold and violet. Nebulae twisted into view, casting rainbow coronas. Small asteroids spun past him, tumbling gently.

Victor felt it—the vibration of something enormous rotating nearby. A deep thrum traveled through his chest.

He was inside a massive sphere—like a planetarium, but impossibly vast. It reminded him of a childhood field trip to New York City. The Hayden dome. He remembered the way light moved across curved surfaces, bending perception. This was like that—except real.

Text appeared in the air before him. Pale and translucent, hovering just inside his field of vision. A prompt.

I am born again.

Victor read the words aloud, voice steady.

From somewhere distant, he heard three heavy stomps. Like thunder rolling through ancient wood.

"And born into a new body," said the voice, "better than the last."

The stars began to move—shifting from their positions, spiraling toward a single point. They gathered into a whirlpool, forming a dark core, a simulated black hole.

Then they burst outward and reformed, particles realigning in a familiar shape: the NYX sigil, luminous and vast.

Victor raised an eyebrow. "Wow."

"You like that?" said the voice, suddenly casual. "I made it. Cool, huh—ow!"

"Stick to the script!" another voice whispered.

Victor smirked.

"Sorry," he muttered, then more clearly: "Born into a new body. Better than the last."

From the darkness around him, drones emerged—baseball-sized, spherical machines with retractable arms, micro-tools, telescoping lights. They circled him.

Victor's limbs moved—gently, then with force—extended outward, arms and legs held in place. His body formed a cross. It was clinical, not cruel.

He took a breath. Then another.

A new prompt blinked into view.

Please don't struggle. You'll only injure yourself.

He relaxed.

Ahead, a detailed architectural schematic unfolded—complex, alien, semi-transparent. One section of the diagram expanded, filling his vision. Walls dissolved to reveal an office. Two people inside. Arguing.

"Behold," said the narrator, solemn again. "The First Acolyte... and the First Diver."

A woman in her twenties with chestnut hair tied back in a loose bun stood at the center—animated, frustrated.

"I know there's something in there. I've seen it!"

Her colleague—a man in a blazer—folded his arms.

"Jenny, we've been over this. It's noise. Calibrate your instruments."

"It's not noise." She held up a datapad. "Visual stream. Possibly audio. There are layers encoded in the signal."

The video feed detached from her hand and rotated into Victor's view: footage from beneath the surface of a lake, looking upward toward the sun, distorted through water.

"It's just some tourist's vacation footage," said the man.

"Director Peterson," Jenny said. "Please."

"You're over budget. I can't go to the board with this. Give me something more. You've got a month."

Jenny turned and stormed out of the room.

\* \* \*

The vision shifted.

Now Jenny and a young man—Allen—stood in a lab surrounded by 3D-printed components, cables, and cooling tanks. A prototype headset lay on a nearby bench.

"I think I've isolated more than just AV data," Allen said. "Temperature, pressure... and something else."

Jenny leaned in.

"What do you mean something else?"

"Neurochemical markers. It's hitting serotonin receptors. Maybe GABA, too. It's like... a digital Ayahuasca trip."

Jenny stared at him.

"You're kidding."

"I'm not. And it's guiding me, Jenny. I swear—it's helping me build the interface."

She whispered, "Keep that part between us."

*  *  *

Time skipped.

Now Jenny sat in the prototype chair, Allen at her side.

"Audio/visual only," he warned. "Thermal buffer's still unstable."

"I'll manage."

He powered up the rig.

Jenny gasped.

"It's an ocean," she said. "I can swim... down, yes... sideways... not up. It seems like I'm not allowed to surface. Not sure why."

Jenny looked around. "Something's below me. I'm going down for a look."

Victor could see it now—through her perspective. A vast shape moving in the depths. It looked like a whale... but it wasn't.

"This is it," she whispered. "First contact."

She reached out.

The creature responded—releasing a deep, resonant pulse that shook her entire body.

Video feed cut.

Smoke. Fire extinguisher. Panic.

\* \* \*

More time passed.

Now Peterson stood beside the same chair, reluctantly adjusting the rig.

"I don't know what you're up to," he muttered. "But there is no cosmic Internet inside the Veil."

"Ten seconds," said Jenny. "Give it ten seconds."

Thirty seconds later, Peterson collapsed on the floor, weeping.

"You left me in there! I was gone for hours..."

"You were gone for nine seconds," said Jenny.

"What did you see?" Allen asked.

Peterson wiped his face. "So much... it's...so alive."

"And alien," Jenny added.

"Yes," he said. "Alien."

* * *

The architectural view collapsed.

The drones repositioned, guiding Victor down into a new space—a narrow stone hallway with warm tile beneath his feet. His limbs released.

He walked forward.

The corridor opened into a circular chamber. A shallow pool shimmered in the center, the NYX sigil etched at the bottom. A robed figure stood beside it.

"Are you ready for your first dive, initiate?" asked the same voice that had narrated his journey.

Victor read the prompt: "I dare not. My fear is too great."

"Fear not, brother," said the figure. "I will aid you. Join me in the water."

Victor waded in. Knee-deep. Cool. Still.

"Kneel down, and I will make the connection."

Victor knelt.

"I have it not," he said, prompted. "I am not worthy of such a divine gift."

"You are not," the figure said gently. "But one day, you may earn it."

The man opened a panel beneath the water and pulled forth a gold-plated braided cable.

Victor reached to the back of his neck. A small, circular bump had formed.

"How—?" he whispered.

"Implanted," said the man. "While you were watching the show."

The plug slipped into place.

Victor winced—then stilled.

"Lean back, brother," the man said.

He did.

Water closed over his ears.

"This is your baptism," said the voice. "And now, I will guide you into the kingdom of heaven."

*  *  *

Victor opened his eyes.

For what felt like hours, he had drifted—watching, swimming, being. Leviathans passed overhead, indifferent to his presence. He saw vast, interconnected cities in the shallows, and hints of so much more in the depths.

Now, he was kneeling again in the great amphitheater, surrounded by thousands.

He stood.

Two robed figures dried him off with black towels. A third helped him don a new robe of his own.

"Initiate," said a familiar voice from the council above.

Victor looked up.

The woman in white lowered her hood.

It was Dr. Jenny Galloway.

Beside her, Allen and Peterson. Older now. Worn. Reverent.

"Do you feel worthy of this order now?" she asked.

Victor spoke without looking at a prompt.

"No. But I have taken a single dive into the deep. I will learn your ways... if you will have me."

Jenny nodded.

"Then welcome, new Acolyte," she said. "Plumb its depths farther, with each dive... as one of us."

The black-robed crowd stomped—three times.

"ONE OF US," they chanted in unison.

Victor bowed his head.

"One of us," he whispered.

A single tear ran down his cheek.

He remembered the Leviathan's eye.

It had seen him... and understood.

Epilogue – Journal Entry: Victor Halvorsen

[Diver Log – One Year In | Clearance: NYX / Black Level]

We call it Abyssus.

It isn't just an extension of The Veil. It's purpose-built—highly complex, ancient, and strange. A cosmic reef inside the lattice, anchored to a place we still don't fully understand.

To the uninitiated, it feels like a digital hallucination. Like stepping into some ancient ocean made of memory and light. But I know now: it's not simulation. It's not symbolic.

It's real.

When you connect, you're not streaming data. You're being quantum-entangled with something on the other side. I know how that sounds. We believe they're drones—alien drones, far more sophisticated than anything we possess. We catch glimpses of them in reflective surfaces. But they never let us stare.

There are millions of them down there, drifting through vast open spaces and intricate cities. They build. They repair. They maintain structures older than our species.

They're incredible.

We still don't know exactly what this immense ocean world is. But we have an idea of where. Our best calculations place it somewhere along the Scutum-Centaurus Arm—the far side of the Milky Way. Seventy-two thousand light-years from Earth.

On a cosmic scale, a hop, skip, and a jump. For us? An impossible distance... without magic.

And the Leviathans...

They're not guardians. Not predators.

Just creatures. Alien, yes—but animals, all the same.

But there are other things down there too. Biomechanical entities, half-living, half-machine. Covered in weapons. Hard to describe. Harder to track. They avoid us.

They never attack. But they don't want to be seen.

Some Divers believe Abyssus is trying to teach us. Others say we're too primitive to understand it.

Me? I think we're just echoes passing through its currents—too small to matter.

But I remember the eye.

One year. Twenty-eight dives.

And I still see it.

Alive. Aware.

Not human. Not hostile.

Just... other.

I've stopped asking if it meant to see me.

Now I ask what it saw in return.


—V. Halvorsen

Acolyte, NYX Division

# The Shadow Under Eschaton Part 1

D eana Lawson arrived at Eschaton University after grabbing breakfast from Company Coffee, a new and overly patriotic coffee shop. She could see the appeal. Deana examined the red, white and blue cup as she thought about her assignment.

Deana was a reporter for the The Dutchess Sentinel in Poughkeepsie, New York. On a clear day, she could see Eschaton's Gothic spires across the Hudson river, behind the spans of the Mid-Hudson Bridge.

Deana was sent to Eschaton University in search of her colleague, Leon Hill, who had been missing for just over a week. He'd been doing a follow-up story on the history of the school, but something had gone wrong. According to Evie Marshall, her Editor, he submitted a series of increasingly deranged and paranoid field reports, then disappeared.

Deana turned over a business card in her hand. It had the name of a local private detective on it: Frank

"Mack" McAllister. And with it, Evie had given her a warning.

"I smell a cover-up," said Evie. "Get Mack to back you up. Find Leon and come back safe."

"What about law enforcement—" said Deana. Evie cut her off.

"We called them two days ago," She said. "No help there. Said an investigation turned-up no sign of Leon. And they have no leads."

"That's a bunch of BS," said Deana.

"Exactly," said Evie. "Be careful. Leon's last communications don't make any sense. And we don't know exactly what we're dealing with."

"Great," said Deana with a sigh.

"Interview some key people at the university. Someone's got to know something."

\* \* \*

After a brief phone conversation, Mack agreed to meet Deana in a parking lot on the outskirts of the university. He said he'd tail her, and instructed her to act normal.

"Don't look for me," he said. "I'll be out of sight, anyway."

Deana had been all over campus, requesting interviews and generally asking simple questions about Leon. No one was talking. Everyone looked at the picture Deana flashed, and shook their head. It was a complete waste of a day.

The campus was quite large, and Deana's feet were starting to hurt. She sat on a stone bench for a breather.

In front of her was a huge, black cannon. The plaque said "Big Bertha" was the only remaining gun from the civil war fort that gave the town its name. It was a Navy Brooke rifle, what ever that was.

Deana had to admit the place was quite beautiful. There were lots of green spaces, parks, gardens and statues everywhere. But the buildings were something else. The architecture was an odd mixture of dark gray Brutalist concrete and vertical Gothic. Deana found it unsettling. The sun was setting, so Deana decided to get a bite at a nearby fast food joint.

* * *

Bison Burg was just the kind of mindless place she was after. It was wild west themed. The mascot was a ridiculous-looking, anthropomorphic bison in denim overalls, cowboy boots and hat. It had simple fare: burgers, fries and milkshakes. Just what Deana needed.

She was just biting into her sandwich when a young man approached her. He was thin, had shaggy brown hair and wore an over-stuffed backpack. His eyes were wide and shifty. He looked scared.

"Hey," he said. "Are you that reporter lady?"

"That's Me," said Deana. "Deana Lawson. And you are..."

"Jay."

"Just Jay?"

"Ah, Oh! Sorry. Um...Holloway. Jay Holloway. I'm a student at Eschaton. Computer Science...and Mechanical Engineering."

"Dual major," said Deana. "Impressive. Probably a crushing course-load."

Jay rolled his eyes. "You have no idea."

Deana made a show of wiping her hands, then thrust one out at Jay.

"Good to meet you," she said. "Know anything about my missing colleague, Leon Hill?"

Jay looked around, then said in hushed tones, "Yes, but...we can't talk here."

Deana shrugged. "Ok then... Where?"

"My dorm room," said Jay. "My room-mate will be out until 10, so we'll have some privacy."

"Wait," she said. "How do you know Leon?"

"Oh!" he stood bolt upright, like she had just pinched his side. "He found me. I made some posts on the Eschaton Secrets subreddit...how I got into some places. Bypassed security."

"I see," she said. "And you...do that a lot?"

"Well, no," said Jay. "But he offered me a hundred bucks to...well...I'll show you."

\* \* \*

"What am I looking at?" said Deana. She was standing behind Jay, who was seated at his elaborate computer setup. There were four large screens in a 2 by 2 configuration. All had various articles and social media feeds on them. The one closest to her was where Jay was making his presentation.

The three-dimensional map had colored sections, complete with annotations and layers that Jay could toggle to expose or hide deeper structures. It was very professional. To Deana, it looked like a construction blueprint, or something an architect would present to an industrial client.

"Very nice," said Deana. Her eyes moved around the map, looking for something that would indicate Leon's whereabouts.

"The university was built at the site of an American Civil War fort," he said. He brought up several images on another monitor. "The fort sat on the bluffs overlooking the Hudson river, and had rows of massive cannons to fire down on passing enemy ships. It didn't see much use during the war, as West Point, to the South, addressed most of the river traffic."

"Ok..." said Deana. She was already getting bored.

"The town of Fort Highpoint took the name of the fort as it grew up around it," he continued. "The fort fell into disrepair after the Civil War, but saw use again during World War I and World War II, where it was given significant repairs and updates."

Deana sighed. "So—"

Jay, concerned he was losing her, switched to a faster delivery.

"Later, during the cold war," he said, "the fort was torn down, and plans were made for Eschaton University to be built on top of its foundation. The only thing that remains of the original fort is a static display of a 10-inch, 300-pound Parrott gun. The gun was forged at West Point Foundry, and made famous sinking the Confederate submarine, Ardent Cooper, which was attempting to—"

"Ok, enough," she said, with no small amount of impatience in her voice. "I don't need a history lesson. Where's Leon?"

"I'm getting to that," he said. "But it's important that you know some of the history, so you can make sense of what you see down there."

"Down where?" said said.

Jay zoomed the map out, then scrolled down. There were many levels below the surface of the university. It was a labyrinth of rooms and tunnels of various sizes.

"Wait," Deana said. "Leon went down into some tunnels under the college? Why? What was he looking for down there?"

Jay spun around in the chair to face her. "History!" He said with a grin.

"History? Couldn't he find some history in the library? I'm sure Eschaton has a lot of really good books on the subject."

"Sure," said Jay. His face twisted into mask of sarcasm. "Fake books full of fake shit. Or, at best, half-truths. The true history...the real shit that went down...it's here!" He pointed at the screen. "Underground."

"Great..." Deana was not relishing the thought of going on a wild goose chase into some dark cavern. She took a deep breath to calm herself. "So where is Leon? Where did you take him?"

"Ok," said Jay. He held out his hands, as if to say "slow down".

Deana looked as if she was going to smack him.

"He saw images I'd posted. Where I found the best stuff—"

"Where!"

"It's deep—"

"How deep?!"

Jay turned around to his computer. He scrolled down to the deepest level on his map—an area labeled "Undercroft".

"What the hell does that mean? Undercroft."

Jay was squirming in his chair. He looked away. "It's like...the basement of a castle, or something."

"Perfect." Deana dreaded the thought. They don't pay me enough for this shit, she thought. "Ok, let's go—"

"Wait, wait!" cried Jay. "We can't just go down there. You have to prepare for it. I...have to prepare. Set things up!"

"How long?! Leon could be in serious trouble. He could be dying!"

"Ok. I...give me a day. A day at least!"

Deana looked at him closely, to see if she could push him further. Jay's eyes were bulging. He seemed like he was ready to jump out of his skin.

"Fine," she said. She gave him one of her cards. "Call me when you're ready. But please be quick about it. I don't want to find Leon's corpse down there."

*  *  *

Deana went home and ate the remains of her Bison Burg meal. It was cold and greasy—not a good combo. She was in a foul mood, and she jumped when her cell rang.

"It's Mack," said the voice. "Sorry for the late call. I had to do some research. You're gonna want to hear this."

"Ok," said Deana. "What do you have for me?"

"You were followed today."

"Followed? By who?"

"None other than the chief of Eschaton security."

"I'm guessing that's not normal."

"No," said Mack. "Far from normal. They have a small army of security guards. You must be quite important to them, if the big guy himself is following you around."

"Ok," said Deana. "Security was watching me. What else?"

"That's it," said Mack. "But I did some digging on the security chief."

"Lay it on me," said Deana.

"This guy is Stanley Sincline, a career Army Intelligence officer. Lieutenant Colonel. He served in three wars—no combat, but highly decorated. Latest was two tours in Afghanistan. Got out a few years ago."

"So?" said Diana.

"So?!" said Mack. "When I think of college security, I think ex-police officer. If you're lucky, maybe a former FBI agent. Sincline should be in charge of a CIA black site somewhere. He's extremely over-qualified for the position. And over-paid. His tax filings indicate that he makes more than Lynda Shields, the Chancellor of the university. About a hundred-grand more."

"Your kidding," said Deana.

"Not kidding," he said. "And you have to wonder...what he's doing there to pull that kind of check?"

*  *  *

Deana spent the next day pacing around her apartment. She tried to put the thought of Leon dying in a pool of blood out of her mind. No call came from Jay. And that night, she slept poorly.

*  *  *

Deana's cell rang at nine the next morning. It was Jay calling to say he was ready to take Deana down to the Undercroft. He told her where to meet him, and she said she'd be there in 30 minutes.

Deana showered, put on some dark-colored work-out clothes and grabbed her small day bag. It was always packed with some essentials: a flashlight, first-aid kit, multi-tool, a bottle of water and some snack bars. She threw the bag in her car and drove across the Mid-Hudson Bridge. Gold morning light gleamed off the buildings of Eschaton University.

# The Shadow Under Eschaton Part 2

Deana followed Jay's instructions. She was to meet him behind a large greenhouse on the edge of campus, near the woods. She found Jay sitting on the ground, with his back to a matte gray utility box. His face was illuminated by the laptop computer in front of him.

"You're late," he said, as she approached.

"Security was tighter than I expected at the front gate. Had to take the long way around."

They moved quickly through the winding pathways of the greenhouse, ducking behind tall racks of climbing ivy and dense ferns. The humid air was thick with the scent of damp soil, decomposing leaves, and the faint sweetness of blooming orchids. Jay stopped, and Deana crouched beside a cart stacked with empty planters.

Jay motioned for her to follow. "Stay quiet. There's minimal staff on today, but we could still get caught. Come on."

They slipped past the misting stations and into a narrow stairwell that led to a basement storage area. The scent of plants gave way to the musty staleness of old fertilizer and rusting tools. Rows of gardening equipment, bags of soil, and dusty machinery filled the room.

A pair of workers walked through the space, chatting about an upcoming campus event. Deana and Jay pressed themselves against the wall, in shadow, until the voices faded behind them.

In the far corner, Jay found a hatch, which lead to the sub-basement. The heavy iron door groaned as he pulled it open, revealing a steep set of metal stairs descending down into the darkness.

They moved carefully, their footsteps echoing off walls lined with thick electrical conduits, old water pipes, and dusty air ducts. The infrastructure here was minimal—flickering lights, exposed wiring, and rusted grates. It hadn't been used in decades.

Jay led Deana through a maze of passageways, and he constantly referred to the map on his laptop for guidance. Then they came to a corner, and Jay motioned for to Deana to stop. He carefully and quickly peered around the edge with one eye, then snapped back. Then he turned to Deana.

"Ok, this is it," he said. "There's a security door in there. It's hard to see, designed to blend-in. But it's high-tech with a biometric lock. Give me a minute."

Deana waited for Jay to do his thing. After several minutes, she was about ask him what was taking so damned long. As she opened her mouth, Jay looked up and smiled.

"Ok, we can go in," he said. "I spoofed the camera. I'm feeding it looped video of this room before we arrived."

Jay went around the corner and Deana followed. At the end of the passage stood a reinforced steel door, devoid of markings except for a discreet, recessed camera mounted in the ceiling. The door wasn't meant to be seen—set into the concrete with precision, as if the builders had designed it to disappear into the wall.

They were invisible to the camera, but the door's lock, however, was another problem. A panel beside the door featured a complex biometric scanner. Jay exhaled sharply. "This might take a while. Sorry."

Deana glanced over her shoulder. The silence here felt unnatural, like the building itself was watching them. The stale air carried a metallic tinge. "Make it quick!"

"Good thing the wireless network extends to this section. I need it for this."

After several tense minutes, the scanner flickered green. Deana, startled, jumped back.

"Got it," said Jay.

The door hissed, then slid open with a pneumatic whoosh.

"C'mon!" Jay motioned as he ran through the door. "Before it closes again!"

They entered a narrow staircase that led them deeper—past modern reinforcements, and past several concrete barriers—until they stood within the old bones of Eschaton University.

Jay opened his laptop and began to poke at it.

"What are you doing now?" asked Deana.

"Had to release the camera from the feed loop," he said. "Don't want security finding it like that. Also—" A few more jabs at the keyboard. "There. Had to remove a log entry which showed the door had opened."

"Smart," said Deana. She was impressed. Jay really seemed to know what he was doing.

Jay closed the laptop, looked around and smiled. "Wow. Look at those walls!"

Deana looked. "So? Red brick. Nothing special."

"These are the Civil War-era foundations. The walls here are ten-feet thick, designed to withstand the siege guns of the era. Well...resist them. Toward the end of the Civil War, most forts were earthen works— because, you know, rifled artillery could easily blast apart brick."

"Fascinating." Deana rolled her eyes. Then she looked at Jay and smiled. "Sorry. I know you love the history of this place."

The brickwork stretched into the darkness, cracked and eroded in places where time and neglect had taken their toll.

A rusted iron gate hung open to one side, leading to a row of prison cells. Most were empty, their bars long since removed, but one held something unsettling—a skeleton still bound in shackles, slumped against the wall.

Deana swallowed hard. "Jesus."

Jay took a step closer, the beam of his flashlight illuminating a brittle scrap of parchment posted on the wall outside the cell. The ink was faded, but the writing was clear enough to make out:

Condemned for heresy, 1864.

The word 'heresy' sent a chill through Deana's spine.

Further in, the passage collapsed into a jagged hole where the structure had been breached. Beyond it, a crawlspace yawned into the darkness.

Jay stopped to put his laptop into his pack. Then slung it onto his back. He took a deep breath, crouched down, and squeezed through. Deana followed.

Deana was half-way through when she got stuck in the passage. She fought the instinct to cry out, but the rest of her went into full panic. Her blood ran cold, and her vision began to narrow.

"You coming, or what?" said Jay from the other side.

"I..." said Deana. "I'm stuck!" She gave several more pulls, and finally something gave. Her shirt and pants tore in several places, but she was free. She climbed the rest of the way through. She stood up, turned and gave an emphatic double-middle-finger to the hole.

* * *

The old brick gave way to concrete, steel, and remnants of an era of mechanized slaughter. Desks with telegraph sets sat frozen in time, maps tacked to the walls and yellowed pages of The New York Times pinned beneath glass. The light here was intermittent—on steady for several minutes, then wavering or blinking on and off. Deana hated it. She found the effect disorienting.

Jay's eyes gleamed with excitement. "This place is amazing. A total time capsule! In World War I, this part of Fort Highpoint was added and used extensively." He gestured to the walls, covered in wartime headlines:

WAR IN EUROPE!

BERLIN SEIZED! KAISER FLEES TO HOLLAND!

GERMANY SURRENDERS!

## WILSON'S LEAGUE OF NATIONS!

Propaganda posters peeled from the walls, urging young men to enlist or to buy war bonds. A Sears catalog lay open on a desk, pages brittle with age. An oil painting of Woodrow Wilson sat in the corner, its once-proud colors now muted beneath a thick layer of dust. Deana was particularly disturbed by a propaganda poster of the German Kaiser, who was represented as a spider. It said, "Don't Talk - Spies are Listening."

"Not bad for a hundred-year-old basement," Deana muttered, but Jay was already moving ahead.

Deana and Jay reached a lower level, which was in complete darkness. They switched on their flashlights and looked around.

Jay crept forward with Deana close behind. Clearly there was something here Jay was wary of. He was wearing a pair of non-tinted sunglasses, like people wore at a shooting range.

There was an almost inaudible click, followed by the sound of something humming to life. To Deana, it sounded like a charging camera flash.

"Hold on," Jay whispered. "Don't move."

"Shit," Deana whispered back. "We're not going to get blown-up, are we?"

"No," said Jay. "But they'll alert security if I don't act quickly!" He opened his laptop open and began typing.

"Why? There's nothing here."

"There must be something," said Jay, sounding distracted. "Here. Take these."

He held out the glasses without looking at her.

"What?" said Deana. She grabbed the glasses and put them on. "I don't—" Then she saw them. Dim white lines, criss-crossing the floor. Hundreds of them.

"The floor here is lousy with laser trips."

"I don't know what that means...but I'll take your word for it."

\* \* \*

Deana was laying on the floor, giving serious thoughts to catching a nap. Jay was sitting nearby with his computer on his lap. He'd been fiddling with the thing for over an hour.

"There it is," said Jay. He hit a key, emphatically. "Boom!"

Deana heard several low clicks. She sat up and looked around. The white lines were gone.

"Took you long enough!" said Deana. She was more than a little annoyed.

"Sorry!" said Jay. "There's a protocol. Had to follow the steps exactly."

At the far end of the room there were steps down into a larger storage area. Wooden crates and metal storage boxes lined the walls. Some bore the logos of long-dead corporations. Others displayed something more disturbing—modern insignias, belonging to defense contractors still in operation today. Deana read off the names as the beam of her light illuminated them.

"Aventor Aerospace, Global Atomics, Molecular Dynamics, Rayon-Theta, Titan Maritime, Vorpal Industries." Her face hardened. "These shouldn't be here. What the hell is going on?"

"No idea," said Jay. "They do seem out of place. Out of...time."

"They look new," said Deana. "Like they were put here recently."

Deana pulled out a pad and pen and jotted some notes. "I have a feeling this is about to get a lot more interesting."

"Maybe so," said Jay. He moved the beam of his flashlight around the area. "Just so you know...this is officially the deepest I've ever been. This is the Undercroft."

*  *  *

A rusted metal hatch was embedded in the floor, partially open. They pointed their flashlights down inside. It was a small, narrow room with unmarked wooden crates and an array of hand tools and other dull metal objects Deana couldn't identify.

Jay lowered himself down carefully, and then raised his arms up to help Deana. The air was stifling here. It was hot and full of dust. Deana suddenly felt the need to get out of this cramped room.

On the wall nearby was a large, rusty metal handle, which looked like it opened the floor-to-ceiling sliding door it was attached to. Deana threw her weight into the handle, and the door reluctantly slid open with several loud screeches.

Deana and Jay carefully walked down the ramp on the other side of the door. They waved their hands at the billowing cloud of dust that had been stirred up. When their vision cleared, they realized they had just emerged from a train car. It had been left here with two connected cars, one fore and aft. All looked long forgotten, the paint on their sides faded into obscurity. But there was something else. Deana saw white chalk scrawled on the side of the train car:

If you find this, go get help. Do not follow me! - LEON

Deana exhaled sharply. "Leon was here."

Jay looked at Deana. She could tell he was scared. "Maybe we should do what he says."

"It's too late for that," said Deana. "Plus, we don't know what we're dealing with. He could be nearby and need medical attention. We have to keep going."

They were in a cavern that seemed to be hollowed out of solid rock. The walls had vertical lines running down them, a tell-tale sign of dynamite blasting.

The train car they'd emerged from was part of a rail siding where other rolling stock was being kept. The ceiling of the cavern was very close here, but just past the tracks, the ground sloped downward. From here the cavern opened up into a wide open space.

Artificial lights had been strung across the top of the cave, and moored in place with pitons. Each projected wide, white circles on the ground below. Powerful construction lights were set up, illuminating the outer walls. In the periphery, stalactites and stalagmites added an interesting, yet sinister complexion to the place.

As Deana descended into the open area, she noted everything here looked temporary, unfinished. It was like a movie set, or a construction site. The floor of the cavern was covered in dirt, but the central area had been topped with light-gray stone and gravel. On the far side of the cave, against the wall, were two sets of concrete buildings. One set looked like living quarters. The other was more purpose built, like store fronts in a strip mall. Each section had a large glass window, so one could see everything in the room beyond. Most of the rooms were dark. One was lit, and one had a light which was intermittent.

In front of them, set some distance apart, were about ten trailers. Some had the wheels still on them, other had the wheels removed.

One of the trailers was more prominent. It was double-wide, made from two of the trailers hastily welded together, the seams left unpainted. On top, there was a short pole, upon which hung a faded, red flag a single white star.

Deana approached this trailer first, and was rewarded by more of Leon's white chalk.

"HERE", it said, printed in large letters on the side.

There was a placard next to the door, which said:

OSS - General William Donovan

Beside it, several clipboards were hanging. A sign below them announced:

Today's Interrogation Schedule.

Deana and Jay entered the trailer and were amazed by what they found. It was another time capsule, but this time, from World War II. Just inside the door was a large painting of president Harry S. Truman. The walls were littered with framed newspaper pages, with headlines proclaiming:

WAR IS OVER IN EUROPE

VICTORY! JAPAN QUITS

GERMANY SURRENDERS

HITLER IS DEAD

The inside of the trailer seemed to be set up for multiple purposes. It was General Donovan's office, having a very large wooden desk and comfortable-looking chair. It was a small briefing room, with twenty-or-so chairs with built-in desktops, like Deana remembered from elementary school. And it was a monitoring station, with an array of ten dark gray television screens, each marked with a number.

What the hell were they doing here?, thought Deana.

"I found this," said Jay. He handed her several sheets of paper, which looked like they had been ripped out of a ringed notebook. "I think Leon left them for us."

Deana read the pages in disbelief.


I'm leaving these notes for several reasons:

1. Posterity.

2. Breadcrumbs for myself. I don't know how deep this rabbit hole goes, and I might need a trail to find my way out again!

3. If I run into trouble, they're for anyone who comes looking for me.


This place is a revelation. It's existence changes everything we thought we knew about the post-WWII era and who we thought had perished during the war.

I've spent about eight hours pouring over evidence in the camp, and the conclusion is undeniable. Everyone knows about Operation Paperclip, and some remember a similar operation in Japan debriefing members of Unit 731, but I don't think anyone knows about this.

Project Revenant was a classified operation to fake the deaths of high-level Nazi officers, scientists and engineers. They brought them down here with the promise of a new, comfortable life...if they provided valuable information. They got very little of value from these men, but it looks like that wasn't really their plan. They tortured most of them to death. I hate to say it, but that works for me.

The OSS (before they became the CIA) recorded hours of interrogations here. Hans Kammler, Adolf Eichmann, Heinrich Müller, Lorenz Hackenholt...and Hermann fucking Göring! It's like the who's-who of Nazi assholes who either went missing, or died in a way that prevented them from being identified. Very clever. They took most of the evidence with them. My guess is that it's either been destroyed or buried in some secret vault under the Pentagon. Who knows?

Thank god I brought my camera with me. The photos alone will make me famous. There's still blood stains and other...matter...they didn't bother to clean up. I got it all recorded. I'll get the Pulitzer for sure!

I'm moving on. I see light coming from a tunnel to the North, so I'm heading that way. I'll leave more notes there. - Leon


"If you're still alive," said Deana to herself.

"What?" said Jay.

"Did you read this?" asked Deana. "It seems a little over the top."

"I don't think it is," said Jay. "Look here."

Jay was pointing to a button on a console near the bank of televisions. Leon had marked it with chalk.

PRESS!, It said, with an arrow added for emphasis.

"Well?" said Jay.

"Fine," said Deana. "Do it."

Jay pressed the button, and the screen nearest them came on along with a series of protestations from the old equipment. Static, wavy lines, frames flipping vertically, then slowly settling. A gray-scale image finally came into focus.

The image rapidly zoomed out. A man was seated in a chair. The chair was surrounded by pools of black—blood spatters. The blood wasn't from the man, his face and body seemed undamaged. He was dressed only in an undershirt and boxer briefs. His uniform, of the expensive, Hugo Boss variety, was hung neatly on a hanger at the edge of the frame.

"Holy shit," said Deana. "I know that guy! That's Joseph Goebbels!"

"Yeah," said Jay. "Not for long."

A man came into frame. The person operating the camera was careful to keep his identity hidden, his head was always out of the shot. The man was putting on shiny leather gloves.

Goebbels looked up at the man, and said something inaudible.

His answer came in the form of a punch to the face, which deviated his septum. Blood flowed out of both nostrils and dripped down onto his shirt.

"Okay..." said Deana. "That's about all I need to see."

She exited the trailer and caught her breath. Jay came soon after.

"You missed the best part!" he said. "They brought out a drill and—"

"You're not funny," said Deana.

Jay smiled. "Well, you have to admit...the bastards deserved it."

"I don't think anyone deserves to be tortured," said Deana. She looked at him with a severe expression. "Ok. Let's get out of here. Leon said he was heading North. Let's go find him."

\* \* \*

The train tunnel was completely dark, except for the single point of light ahead. It was faint at first, but as they neared the threshold, the brightness became mesmerizing. This was not the dim glow of ancient bulbs or flickering fluorescents. It was Sunlight.

They stepped forward, emerging from the darkness, and into a vast, impossible space.

The opening in front of them stretched for miles, an immense hollowed-out cylinder with towering buildings rising from the rock floor. At its apex, an artificial sun cast golden light over an entire underground cityscape.

Jay's breath caught in his throat. "This is..." His eyes darted around the scene, and he shook his head. "How is this possible?"

"I don't believe it," said Deana. Her fingers tightened into fists. This couldn't exist. And yet, here it was.

A secret metropolis, built deep beneath Eschaton University.

# The Shadow Under Eschaton Part 3

Deana had been watching the sleek trains for hours. Their arrivals and departures, announced over the city-wide public address system, occurred with clockwork regularity. She noted the ceaseless flow—every train bound for the tallest building in the center of the city, a vast, partially subterranean distribution center shrouded in mystery.

Overwhelmed by the scale of it all, her mind reeled. What must it cost? And who benefited? What were they really doing down here—and why? The questions swirled in her thoughts without answer.

From their refuge on a high plateau, she and Jay enjoyed an excellent view of the city. Behind them, the dark, arched mouth of the train tunnel lay abandoned—a silent portal to the unknown. At the bottom of the incline to her left, where the tracks met the city below, a blockade halted the lines. Beyond, several groups of linked cars were spread along the track. A small engine would arrive to retrieve them, pulling the cars down into one of the many dark tunnels feeding the central building's underground labyrinth, only to return shortly after with more.

The city itself held its own surprises. The first revelation was the abundance of plant life. Great swaths below had been transformed into green-space, nurtured by the large artificial star at the apex of the dome overhead. The area around their hideout was lush and overgrown; Deana had even adopted a large, leafy bush at the edge of the terrace as her lookout. How could vegetation thrive in what was essentially an underground cave?

Then two more marvels unfolded. The artificial sun dimmed, fading to a cool blue that mimicked moonlight. With that change, the dome transformed into a sky streaked with drifting clouds, and the outer walls of the city shifted—from a regular pattern of red brick to reveal a breathtaking vista of snow-capped mountains.

For exactly five minutes, rain fell. Deana and Jay dashed into the nearby train tunnel, shivering as the cold downpour seeped into their bones. The rain, both a physical and emotional chill, underscored the day's roller-coaster of sensations, amplifying the constant low-level fear that had shadowed her all day.

Glancing at her watch, Deana noted that night was coming in sync with the world above. As they emerged from the tunnel, a cool breeze and a slight scent of ozone greeted them—a quiet prelude to what might come next. A subtle vibration in the ground and a distant mechanical hum reminded her that the city's heartbeat was never truly silent.

Jay yawned, and for a moment, Deana nearly followed suit. A fleeting thought of backtracking to the interrogation camp they had left not long ago crossed her mind, but she quickly blocked it out. Sleep might have been a welcome escape—if not for the nagging worry that Leon might be in danger.

Then, abruptly, the public address system crackled with static before falling silent. Deana's attention snapped to the shiny black horn of a nearby speaker, a prickle of unease rising in her.

"Ok, listen up," a gruff voice boomed, shattering the calm. "We haven't formally met, so let me introduce myself. I'm Stan Sincline, security chief of the operation you've stumbled into."

In an instant, terror gripped both Deana and Jay. Their eyes widened as they crouched down in tall grass, scanning their surroundings for any sign of danger.

"We don't have an exact fix on your position," the voice continued, "but it doesn't matter. You tripped several sensors coming down here, and we have a general sense of where you are. Do my security teams a solid by turning yourselves in right now. Come out with your hands on your head, and someone will come pick you up. No harm done, no charges filed."

Jay raised his eyebrows in silent questioning, while Deana furrowed her brow and shook her head firmly. She couldn't risk a confrontation—not now. Too much remained unknown. And where was Leon? That question pounded in her mind as Jay's eyes darted nervously, and her heart hammered with fear.

\* \* \*

"Damn it!" said Jay. He kicked at the dirt under his feet. "Too many attempts. I'm locked out. Encryption's too strong."

"Shit," said Deana. She had been watching Jay try to hack his way in to the wireless network for the better part of two hours. "Isn't there something else you can try?"

Jay said nothing, and Deana didn't press him. His face was turning red, and his expression said he wanted to throw his laptop down into the valley below.

"Maybe we could steal something?" said Deana. "Like one of their laptops, or a security badge?"

"Maybe," said Jay. He didn't sound convinced. "But I think there's an easier way. These trains make stops at low security checkpoints, all day, all around the city."

"Yeah," said Deana. "They're scanning the cargo, or something."

"Right. I think there's plenty of time after the scans and before the train departs."

"Time for what?"

"Time for us to sneak on board."

*  *  *

They'd been lucky so far. The progress had been slow sneaking down to the train station. They timed their movements to evade the security patrols, and were now hiding in a narrow alley across from where the trains stopped. In a bit of providence, fog had descended on the area, dimming colors softening sounds and giving them some extra cover, when and if they decided to make the short dash to an open train car.

Deana had plenty of desire, but no will. They were almost sighted several times due to dumb luck and bad timing.

"C'mon!" whispered Jay. "This is the third train! It's not gonna get any better than this. We have to go!"

"I know. I know!" said Deana. Her frustration and self-loathing were reaching peak levels. "I just...you know what? Fuck it!"

Deana broke cover and dashed across the gap. It was no more than fifteen steps, but her dread made it feel like ten times the distance. Jay waited a few seconds, then dashed across to join her. Now they were inside the train car, crouched behind some wooden crates, wide-eyed, panting and grinning at each other like idiots.

* * *

The building's cold corridors were a maze of flickering lights and silent danger. In a cramped, forgotten alcove, Jay found a terminal. His fingers danced over keys until the screen revealed what he feared—and hoped for in equal measure: Leon was indeed in the building. He was confined on sub-level two.

Deana and Jay slipped past patrols, the hum of security systems a constant and oppressive backdrop. But then, fate splintered their fragile plan. An automated door slammed down between them. Deana's breath caught as a nearby monitor flickered to life. It was displaying a live feed from the other side of the door.

Jay was backing up, hands raised. In front of him, several guards armed with submachine guns were advancing on him. Deana watched in silent horror as Jay was ruthlessly gunned down.

"Why—?" Deana screamed, the shock twisting her voice.

A distorted figure materialized on the screen—a man with cold, calculating eyes. It was Sincline. "He was expendable. Not important. You're the one I need."

"Me? Why?!" Deana demanded, anger lacing every word.

"Come up to my office, and I'll explain everything."

"Go fuck yourself!" she spat, pivoting on her heel and bolting down the corridor. She might have imagined it, but Deana thought she heard the sound of Sincline laughing behind her.

As she made her way down to where she believed Leon was bing held, Deana passed through several armored doors. She used the simple interface to shut and lock them behind her.

Sincline's voice echoed over the PA: "Clever, but that will only slow my teams down. You're simply delaying the inevitable."

* * *

"They're all out looking for you, Deana," Leon whispered urgently.

Inside the cell, Leon leaned against the cold metal bars. His eyes glinted with a mix of mischief and regret.  "That's why this block was left unguarded. We've only got a little time. Help me open the cell."

"How?!" Deana stared in at him, her hands gripping the bars. Her adrenaline was ebbing and her sweat was making her feel cold and weak.

"I'll walk you trough it," said Leon. "This story will blow the lid off of everything. I'll win the Pulitzer for sure!"

"I don't care about a headline," she snapped. "I care about getting you out of here. Getting us both out!"

Leon walked Deana through the process of opening his cell via the cell block's security center. Deana's focus was singular, and with trembling determination, she manipulated cold metal lever that controlled the lock to Leon's cell.

As the cell door slid open, alarms shrieked to life. Red lights pulsed like a heartbeat on every wall.

Deana ran back to Leon in a panic.

"Follow me—I know the way," Leon urged.

He led her through several labyrinthine maintenance corridors. The the clamor of alarms grew quiet behind, but their footsteps echoed loudly against metal and concrete around them.

They reached a narrow ladder embedded in the wall. It was connected to a sealed hatch, which loomed overhead.

Leon paused, his gaze heavy with urgency. "Up you go!" he commanded.

Hesitating only a heartbeat, Deana gripped the cold rungs and climbed. With a forceful shove, she sent the metal hatch swinging open. Darkness yawned above her as she pulled herself through.

Deana heard the muffled thud of struggle below. Two security guards appeared and tackled Leon. The hatch slammed shut, sealing away the chaos. "You bastards!" she cried. Her voice ricocheted strangely in cavernous space around her.

Overhead, a single spotlight snapped on, illuminating the imposing figure of security chief Sincline. Two more spotlights revealed armed men, machine guns trained on her.

Deana was torn between the need to cry and the desire to rush Sincline and beat him to death with her fists.

Then Sincline's voice rang out, amplified and disturbingly jovial:

"You made it! Well done!"

Clapping erupted, a monstrous sound that swelled into the cheers of an unseen crowd.

The lights finally came up, and Deana found herself in a vast indoor stadium, packed with smiling, applauding faces. Confusion and dread churned in her gut.

* * *

Later, in an office that defied every expectation of confinement, Deana sat across from Sincline. The room was enormous—walls of black stone tiles, floor-to-ceiling textured pillars, and an entire wall of glass, offering a panoramic view of an underground city. The entire room was bathed in a warm orange glow of the artificial sun.

"How long did you know?" said Deana.

"We were monitoring you the whole time," said Sincline. "It was a test.

"A test? Why? For what?"

Sincline leaned forward, his tone smooth and calculated. "We're extending an invitation for you to join this operation. I think by now you've gotten a good idea about what we're doing down here, and what's at stake."

"National security?"

"That's right. It's been running non-stop since WWII."

Deana's mind reeled. "I—I don't know. This is a lot to take in."

A soft chuckle cut through the tension. "I have something that might help you decide."

A side door swung open. In stepped Leon and, impossibly, Jay—very much alive—and trailing them was her editor-in-chief, Evie Marshall. The revelation was as shocking as it was surreal.

Deana's stomach twisted. She clenched her fists. "But I thought—"

Sincline interrupted with a wry chuckle. "You thought wrong."

Leon sat on the edge of a sleek desk, arms folded. "Consider it a second job interview."

Deana swallowed hard. "A job interview. Ok. But what if I had failed?"

Evie stepped forward, her tone calm and self-assured. "We knew you wouldn't."

"You said this is a matter of national security," Deana pressed. "I've read about some secret operations in the Hudson Valley. Is this...a...a Phoenix thing?"

Sincline considered the question for a moment. "This operation started as an OSS/Donovan holdover. After the war we were rolled into the same continuity organs that eventually became PHOENIX. Most of them dissolved or rebranded. We didn't. We had the prisoners, the artifacts, the trains — too valuable to break up. So PHOENIX filed us under 'legacy asset' and left us buried. We answer to them on paper. Day to day, we run ourselves."

A chill ran down Deana's spine as Sincline continued, "We're tasked with studying and reverse-engineering exotic and occult devices—artifacts from across the globe. Technically, we're part of Arcadia, PHOENIX's cultural continuity program."

"Arcadia," repeated Deana. "Cultural Continuity? Why does PHOENIX need something like that?"

"If civilization falls, its symbols must survive—to remind whoever rebuilds what was lost. Our vaults hold the true relics of human achievement. Authentic history. Authentic memory. Authentic myth. Most of what you see top-side, in museums and secure federal buildings is fake—carefully created duplicates—often down to the molecular level."

"You're kidding," said Deana. "So something like the Mona Lisa... isn't real?"

"I never joke about such things," said Sincline. "And the Mona Lisa is real. It's just not the one that Da Vinci painted."

"You mentioned exotic and occult devices," said Deana. "What exactly are we talking about here?"

"Oh, I'm sure you know some of them by name," said Jay.

"How about the Ark of the Covenant," said Leon. "the Holy Grail..."

"Things the Nazis built," said Evie, "Like Die Glocke. The bell."

"Never heard of it," Deana replied, skepticism and awe mingling in her voice.

"Supposedly an anti-gravity device that never worked—a dead-end pipe dream," Sincline explained.

"Okay, I get it," she said slowly. "You have lots of cool toys down here. But what does this have to do with me?"

"Simple," Sincline said. "Our work is vital. We need allies...people in the media. People who can control the flow of information topside. People like you."

"Each of us was hand-selected," said Evie.

"Consider it a second job," Leon added. "With some excellent benefits and one hell of a retirement plan."

Jay echoed softly, "It's a great honor."

Deana met Sincline's gaze steadily. "And if I refuse?"

Sincline's eyes locked with hers. "Then you stay down here, and the world remains ignorant."

Deana looked off, suddenly feeling very uncomfortable and fearing for her own mortality.

"It's your choice, of course." Sincline said.

"I'm disappointed!" Deana joked, attempting to ease the mounting tension. "I though there would be lots of buried treasure down here!"

Leon's smile widened, and Sincline's eyes twinkled. "Oh, it's treasure you want?" he mused.

*   *   *

Sincline led Deana down a corridor until they reached a massive vault door, a monolith of reinforced steel and hidden power. He pressed his hand to a scanner, and leaned down to let the machine scan his eyes.

With a deep, echoing clank followed by the groan of gears, the door slid open. Inside, the vault was huge—the interior stretching on and on. Deana could only guess, but it seemed at least the length of a football field. But the space was narrow, maybe a hundred feet across, giving the vault the feeling of a wide hallway.

Deana's breath caught at the sight: piles of gold bars, ornate jewelry in display cases and antique tea sets, flags from long-forgotten regimes.

Swastikas were everywhere. Mannequins were clad in various SS uniforms. Nazi weapon prototypes were stacked and dorted into groups by type. Long glass cases displayed swastika-embellished objects of every kind, and strange, organic-looking artifacts were arranged with a precision that spoke of both obsession and expertise. Deana couldn't believe her eyes. The scale of it all was unbelievable. It was truly a macabre gallery of relics.

Sincline's voice resonated with pride. "Behold—the death's head rings from Wewelsburg Castle."

"The what rings?"

"In 1938, Himmler ordered every fallen SS-man's ring be returned to the castle," Said Sincline. "It was supposed to be a symbol of eternal membership. Historians believe they were lost to time. But we have them all here. Eleven and a half thousand of them."

"That's a lot of rings," said Deana. Her brief smile faded quickly, as she thought that so many highly-trained men had sworn absolute fealty to a madman.

Sincline led Deana on.

"This is the most valuable treasure in the vault," he said.

This?" said Deana. "It's just some old metal boxes." There were three olive-drab cases, each with a single, faded black eagle. In its talons, a circular wreath. And within that, a swastika.

"True," said Sincline. But inside is something very valuable. Let me tell you a story..."

Deana sighed. "If you must." She liked history, just not this history.

"In April, 1945, at the end of WWII, an aircraft crashed south of Dresden near Börnersdorf. Only one person survived. An SS Wehrmacht unit secured the crash site and retrieved three crates of sensitive material. The orders came from Hitler himself. The crates were stored in a nearby farmhouse, until they could be transported to Berchtesgaden, a town in the Bavarian Alps. From there, they are taken to Alpenhof, a hotel in Hintersee.

"Ok, but what..."

"I'm getting to that," said Sincline.

"The Hintersee area became the final command post of the Berchtesgaden/Obersalzberg Nazi leadership. The crates were guarded until word of Hitler's death arrived in early May of 1945. The Nazi commanders escaped into Austria. They left the crates behind, abandoned."

"That's interesting," said Deana. "But how did they get here?"

"Well...it's a long story, but I'll give you a hint. It involves a special commando unit called Task Force Kestrel."

"Kestrel?" Deana laughed.

"Yes. They packed the crates out by hand, through the Bavarian alps to Austria."

"The contents, huh?" said Deana. "Ok, I'll bite. what's inside? It must be very valuable."

"Some people think so," said Sincline. "I read some of it. It's a lot of nonsense."

"Read? Wait a minute. Are these... the Hitler Diaries?"

Sincline nodded, his smile almost imperceptible. "The day-to-day musings of a dictator. Both tedious and boring."

"I thought the diaries were a hoax," said Deana. "I saw a documentary about it in the 1980s."

"The hoax was real," said Sincline. "Part of an operation we ran to muddy the waters, hide the trail, discourage people from looking for the real documents. It was quite effective!"

Deana: "Well you had me convinced."

"We have them all scanned and cataloged, of course," said Sincline. "You can read them sometime, if you're interested. You'd uh...have to agree to work with us, of course."

Deana raised an eyebrow. "Of course."

"But here is, by far, the least valuable part of the collection." Sincline indicated a mannequin bust which was off by itself, against the far wall of the vault.

"Least valuable?"

"Yes," said Sincline. "But it's my favorite."

The bust was mounted at head-height, so observers had a straight-on view of its face. The figure was limbless—just a head and torso which had been mounted on an ornate wooden display stand. It was dressed in a black SS uniform, the silver medals still gleaming.

The figure seemed despondent. Its head was bowed, eyes glassy and unfocused, looking off into the distance. And it was...drooling.

"Ugh," said Deana. "It's really creepy and realistic. Is it wax?" She stepped closer, her pulse slowing, her skin crawling with cold horror.

"Oh, he's quite real," said Sincline.

Without warning, the mannequin's head lifted.

Deana jumped back. "My God!" Recognition and horror collided in her mind. "Hold on. I know that face..."

"Oh please. Miss! Help me!" Said the man in a thick German accent. The voice was weak, and sick sounding, like his lungs were full of phlegm. "I'm being held here against my will by these...mad men! Please, get me out of here!"

"Deana," said Sincline, "let me introduce you to Joseph Mengele—The Angel of Death".

"No. It can't be. How—" Deana began, voice trembling.

"The technology is sophisticated. I can explain later."

Deana's mind reeled. "But his bones were verified by forensic experts in the mid-1980s!"

Sincline smiled thinly. "We grew those bones using his own DNA—buried them south of São Paulo. A confirmation that our technology works, and more importantly, a safeguard ensuring no one ever comes looking for this son-of-a-bitch."

"Amazing...and horrible," Deana murmured.

Sincline's tone hardened. "Horrible indeed—a physician, once trusted, who performed unspeakable acts at Auschwitz. He even selected victims for the gas chambers. Didn't you, you piece of shit?"

Mengele's face reddened. He spluttered in a mix of fury and loathing, curses filling the air in guttural German. He stopped only long enough to cough up a voluminous gout of greenish bile, then continued his tirade.

Sincline's hand shot out, delivering a resounding slap that silenced the old Nazi.

Terrified and disgusted, Deana could only watch as Sincline grabbed her arm and led her away.

The vault door closed behind them, abruptly cutting off the distant cacophony of shouts and curses.

*  *  *

Back on a balcony overlooking the sprawling underground city, Deana stood silently with Sincline. The artificial sun cast a comforting glow over the skyline, a stark contrast to the darkness of the secrets below.

Sincline's voice was soft, almost gentle. "So. What do you think?"

Deana stared out at the engineered horizon, her thoughts a tangled mix of disbelief, horror, and reluctant awe. For a long, silent moment, she could only watch—unsure if she was ready to embrace this new, dangerous world or forever retreat into the shadows of what she once knew.

# INFECTUS Part 1

## Operation Ice Dagger

**PHOENIX INTERNAL BRIEFING MEMORANDUM**

**CLASSIFIED – OMEGA**

**DO NOT DUPLICATE – PHOENIX EYES ONLY**

TO: Command Directors – West, Central, and East

FROM: Archivist M. LeClair, Department of Containment & Recovery

DATE: October 19, 1997

RE: OPERATION ICE DAGGER / CONTAINMENT ARTIFACT ["INFECTUS"]

STATUS UPDATE & RECOMMENDATION FOR DESTRUCTION

# I. BACKGROUND: UNIT 731

During World War II, the Imperial Japanese Army operated a covert biochemical weapons division known as Unit 731, headquartered in Pingfang District, Manchuria. Under the false pretense of water purification research, Unit 731 conducted extensive human experimentation, including:

- Weaponized disease vectors

- Live dissection without anesthesia

- Frostbite testing using prisoners of war

- Aerosol and waterborne delivery of chemical agents

As Soviet forces advanced into Manchuria in August 1945, Unit 731 personnel initiated a full evacuation and site purge. However, certain materials were preserved for strategic leverage in surrender negotiations with U.S. forces. Among them was a clandestine underground laboratory designated Site 10-Kyokko, which conducted anomalous research.

# II. OPERATION ICE DAGGER

Emergency intercepts from residual Japanese command in August 1945 included repeated requests for highly-trained commando units to prevent an unknown catastrophic outbreak. Fragmented transmissions referenced a "breach of nature." The unit went dark on August 19th, 1945. No further transmissions. Aerial recon flights revealed nothing but stillness—and ice.

This prompted OSS leadership to authorize Operation ICE DAGGER, deploying an elite black-ops team called Task Force Kestrel, under direct orders from General William Donovan.


Task Force Kestrel – Personnel Manifest:

Maj. Calvin Grissom – Commanding Officer, combat strategist, survival specialist

Sgt. Mack "Stitch" DeSoto – Field medic and flamethrower specialist

Lt. Emory "Dust" Lockhart – Explosives and demolition expert, fluent in Japanese and German

Agent Roland Thorne – Intelligence analyst and infiltration specialist

Jael Winterbourne (SOE, British) – Cultural anthropologist and occult researcher; trained paratrooper

Cpl. Eugene "Boxcar" Voss (U.S. Signal Corps) – Field communications and radio specialist, cryptographer, attached last-minute due to transmission anomalies

Their orders:

- Investigate Site 10-Kyokko
- Obtain any surviving Axis weapons research
- Neutralize emerging anomalous threats

Upon insertion into Site 10-Kyokko, the team encountered:

- Localized extreme cold—subzero blizzards despite summer conditions
- Environmental anomalies, including: indoor snow, freezing rain, fog as well as various sensory disruptions

A partially functional cryogenic suppression device was identified in the lower facility, later confirmed as KÄLTEFAUST, developed under Projekt K-Einheit by the Nazi Ahnenerbe Division in 1944.

## III. KÄLTEFAUST – PROTOTYPE ORIGIN & DEPLOYMENT

Projekt K-Einheit ("Cold Unit") was a German engineering initiative aimed at developing battlefield temperature-manipulation weapons to disable enemy forces.

There were two prototypes:

Einheit-01 was recovered in the Western theater post-war, now in Phoenix custody following Operation Paperclip.

Einheit-02, equipped with an advanced Overfrost mode, was smuggled to Japan via German submarine, U-234, and installed at Site 10-Kyokko as part of an emergency request to deal with an unknown entity.

Kältefaust's primary function was to create a focused atmospheric collapse, flash-freezing biological organisms at the molecular level. However, the machine was found damaged. Its instability led to a wide range of complex weather anomalies, both inside and outside the facility.

Kestrel found evidence that the machine was obtained and deployed in a desperate attempt to contain a threat within the facility. That threat had a name. It was scrawled in fractured English and Japanese across a wall near the main lab: INFECTUS.

## IV. INFECTUS

The primary anomaly, later designated INFECTUS, is a polymorphic, nano-crystalline parasitic entity, exhibiting:

- Perfect mimicry of biological and inanimate structures

- Rapid bootstrapping of genetic code across multiple species

- Behavioral intelligence, including voice replication, ambush strategy, and false distress signaling

Recovered Kestrel footage and Jael [SOE] debriefing confirm:

- Visual distortions, fractal patterns
- Extreme psychological strain due to infiltration-based paranoia
- Victims absorbed and repurposed at the cellular level

Entity was successfully flash-frozen after the last three surviving Kestrel members reactivated Kältefaust Overfrost mode, sacrificing themselves in the process. A complete collapse of the substructure occurred, entombing the anomaly under meters of frozen debris.

## V. FURTHER CONTAINMENT

INFECTUS was later retrieved and quarantined by Phoenix operatives. It remains sealed within OMEGA-VAULT 6, a maximum quarantine chamber in the Ozark Containment facility GRAYNEST, located under Mark Twain National Forest.

Containment protocols include:

- Triple-vessel dewar system cooled by liquid helium

- Electromagnetic isolation field

- No-network zone: All AI systems removed from the perimeter

- Automatic and Manual purge systems, with a plasma incineration array

Notable anomaly: Spores have been detected in several exterior access corridors since the last maintenance cycle. Although the spores were detected and neutralized, it's just a matter of time before a breach occurs.

## VI. RECOMMENDATION

It is my professional conclusion that INFECTUS represents an extinction-level threat. All research requests, extraction efforts, or containment upgrades represent an unacceptable risk. Infectus is not a specimen. It is a mistake we buried. It learns and it waits for us to slip-up, make a mistake. I hope this report is a sobering reminder of the potential for harm and loss of property. Even a small, regional outbreak would require a nuclear detonation.

## Recommended Action: Immediate Termination.

Utilize Vault 6's full plasma array and seismic collapse protocol.

Further, let no record of its existence survive. We should do ourselves and humanity a favor—forget about Infectus entirely.


Respectfully submitted,

M. LeClair

Archivist, Department of Containment & Recovery

Phoenix Central Command

# INFECTUS Part 2

## Containment Crisis

**BLACK ANNEX ADDENDUM //
OMEGA-VAULT 6**

**OPERATION ICE DAGGER: INFECTUS
BIOFORM DOSSIER**

**CLASSIFIED – OMEGA-TIER ACCESS ONLY**

**DO NOT TRANSMIT – DO NOT REPLICATE
– DESTROY AFTER REVIEW**

TO: Command Directors – West, Central, and East

FROM: Archivist M. LeClair, Department of
Containment & Recovery

DATE: October 22, 1997

SUBJECT: INFECTUS – Addendum to OPERATION
ICE DAGGER

SUB-CODE: THETA-ZERO-ONE "INFECTUS" –
Bioform Threat Dossier

## I. INTRODUCTION

The following dossier represents a classified
addendum to the Operation Ice Dagger final brief,
provided under Omega-level security clearance. The
contents herein are not to be digitally stored,
replicated, or referenced in any interdepartmental
correspondence.

This material is provided by request of the Tri-
Command to clarify the true scope and nature of
THETA-ZERO-ONE: INFECTUS, beyond the limited
details included in the original mission summary.

The data below has been assembled from:

- Extensive documentation from Unit 731, Site
10-Kyokko

- The Jael Winterbourne debrief, conducted 15
days post-recovery

- Recovered Task Force Kestrel audio logs

- Internal post-retrieval research conducted
between 1945–1996

The documentation details an archaeological dig
site in Manchuria at the end of WWII. An artifact of
extraterrestrial origin and extreme age was found and
transferred to Site 10-Kyokko, one of several Unit 731

biological and chemical warfare sites. There, Unit 731 studied the artifact and subsequently lost containment.

Task Force Kestrel, a team of highly trained OSS operatives, infiltrated the site and neutralized the threat—but at great cost. All but one Kestrel team member died, sacrificing themselves to contain the entity.

It is critical to note: entire research teams, Phoenix branches, and containment divisions were lost in the years following retrieval. This is not exaggeration—it is a matter of historical record.

## II. PHOENIX LOSSES – POST-RETRIEVAL

The initial phase of Infectus study (internally referred to as the "Cold Cell Initiative") resulted in the following:

- 43 Phoenix personnel absorbed during the containment breach of Vault 3-C (1947)

- Termination of monitoring systems due to irreversible data corruption (1948)

- Full decommissioning of a bio-circuitry wing after the entity mimicked control node architecture and attempted to override purge protocols (1951)

- Memory compromise in two senior researchers—both became cognitively unstable, claiming they were "not alone in their own thoughts"

- Complete psychological collapse of Containment Chief Henrick Lozano, who self-immolated inside a sealed vault after stating:

  "It's using my voice now. And my skin... is it my skin? I can't tell."

In response, Phoenix established new containment protocols that introduced the following operational precedents:

- The OMEGA-Vault system
- The no-computer zone law
- Triple-phase cryogenic isolation

In short: Infectus changed the way we do containment.

## III. BIOFORM CLASSIFICATION – INFECTUS

Codename: INFECTUS

Designation: THETA-ZERO-ONE

Origin: Unknown

First Contact: Pingfang District, Manchuria, 1945

Composition: Polymorphic nano-crystalline structure; semi-organic, semi-mechanical

Dormancy: Estimated millions of years

Growth Phases:

- Mycelial Tethering – Fiber-thin tendrils seeking life and energy

- Spore Bloom – Airborne dispersal; mimics snowfall, fog, or ash

- Mobile Camouflage Phase – Imitation of small organisms (rats, birds, fish, etc.)

- Complex Mimicry Phase – Perfect simulation of higher lifeforms and inanimate objects

- Genetic Synthesis – Once sufficient biomass is collected, the entity assembles a colossal polymorphic form using dominant local genetic materials. This is its true form.

Key Abilities:

- Complete mimicry of any object, animal, or human down to the cellular level

- Voice and behavioral replication, including emotional nuance

- Database functionality: At its core, the entity possesses an internal database of genetic and inorganic matter blueprints. The structure contains over 23 million unique species records and 180 million individual genetic entries

I cannot stress enough the importance of this discovery. There is an entire catalog of extinct alien species inside.

Ambush intelligence: Known to reproduce screams or simulate injured humans to lure responders

Sensory & Environmental Cues:

- Victims report overwhelming cold at the moment of initial contact

- Can generate high-fidelity sound patterns, including but not limited to: industrial machinery, ambient natural sounds, breathing, digestive noises, animal calls, and human speech. Its mimicry of sound appears limitless

## IV. THE PSYCHOLOGICAL COMPONENT

Infectus doesn't just attack—it studies, then ambushes its prey. It has demonstrated the ability to:

- Replicate the voices of deceased loved ones to disarm emotional defenses

- Alter its physical form to simulate wounds or distress

- Induce paranoia, extreme stress, and sleep disruption

Prolonged exposure to Infectus has been observed to cause:

- Personality fragmentation
- Identity erosion
- Full psychosis

## V. STRATEGIC DANGERS

If Infectus escapes current containment, it will not act immediately.

It will study. Learn. Build.

It will appear weak, pitiful, even helpful.

Then it will become us.

Or rather, we will become it—after it takes us over.

Simulations predict a minor containment failure would require sterilization of a 50-mile radius, including all human populations, wildlife, and infrastructure.

An urban outbreak—even in a remote region like the Ozarks—would lead to loss of control within 96 hours, requiring a tactical nuclear detonation. Even then, containment would not be guaranteed.

A full-scale manifestation of its fifth growth stage could initiate a Gray Harvest Event, absorbing enough biomass to achieve planetary-scale mimicry. Earth's entire biosphere would be lost.

Research suggests this was likely the fate of other worlds before it arrived here.

## VI. FINAL STATEMENT

INFECTUS is a mistake we unearthed.

It is not a creature, a virus, or a weapon. It is a cosmic disease—one that outlived its creators and now waits for us to repeat their error.

It is sickness made sentient.

Recommended Action:

- Initiate Vault 6 full incineration purge

- Activate seismic collapse protocol

- Eliminate all surviving documentation—physical or digital

- Detain and debrief all personnel with exposure exceeding 0.4 cumulative hours

- Burn the root. Salt the soil. Forget its name. Then move on.

Respectfully,

M. LeClair

Archivist, Department of Containment & Recovery

# PHOENIX CENTRAL COMMAND

* * *

## PHOENIX COMMAND MEMORANDUM

RE: INFECTUS – COMMAND RESPONSE TO
DESTRUCTION RECOMMENDATION

CLASSIFIED – OMEGA PRIORITY

PHX-CMD-RSP-247A


TO: Archivist M. LeClair

FROM: Deputy Director Alan R. Graile

Phoenix Eastern Command – Oversight Division

DATE: October 27, 1997

RE: CONTAINMENT ARTIFACT "INFECTUS" –
STATUS OVERRIDE


Archivist LeClair,

Your concerns regarding containment artifact
THETA-ZERO-ONE ("INFECTUS") have been
reviewed and acknowledged. Your thorough
documentation—including the Black Annex
Addendum to Operation Ice Dagger—has been filed
accordingly.

Please be advised: while your recommendation for full incineration and structural collapse of Vault 6 is noted, it is disapproved.

The continued containment, analysis, and application of THETA-ZERO-ONE now fall under Project EIDOLON, a cross-divisional directive governed by the Viridian Island Research Complex.

Effective immediately:

All materials, field data, and personnel associated with THETA-ZERO-ONE are to be transferred to Viridian Island under maximum-security escort.

Your department will oversee all containment and transport preparations.

Any required resources are to be submitted via Priority Channel 9. They will be provided without delay. Your operational budget is considered unrestricted.

You are to cease all further inquiry into this matter unless specifically summoned for audit or testimony.

Let us be clear: while your work is valued, the scope of this artifact's potential exceeds your department and clearance authority.

You were assigned to document the past.

We are tasked with shaping the future.

Should you continue to voice opposition to this directive, your access privileges will be reviewed and may be revoked.

The world is changing, Archivist.

We intend to meet it prepared.

All Hail Columbia.


— D. Director A. R. Graile

Phoenix Eastern Command – Oversight Division

\* \* \*

VIRIDIAN ISLAND RESEARCH COMPLEX

Internal Memorandum – Eyes Only

CLASSIFIED – OMEGA

VIR-COMM-ALERT-77D


TO: Deputy Director Alan R. Graile, Phoenix Eastern Command

FROM: Dr. Emilia R. Voss, Director of Operations, Viridian Island, Oceanus Division

DATE: November 3, 1997

RE: Incoming Artifact Transfer – THETA-ZERO-ONE

Deputy Director Graile,

We have received the classified cargo manifest scheduled for arrival at Viridian Island under Dimensional Isolation Protocol V-I-44. After a thorough review of the submitted biological and incident dossiers—particularly the Black Annex Addendum compiled by Archivist LeClair—I am compelled to formally state:

We are not prepared to accept this.

Our current secure storage modules were designed for passive materials and theoretical phase anomalies, not for an active, polymorphic, sentient biocrystal with a documented history of containment breaches, cross-domain mimicry, and cognitive contamination.

Let me be absolutely clear:

INFECTUS is not a curiosity to be stored. It is weaponized extinction.

And I strongly recommend that it not be housed at Viridian Island.

We are a physics-forward facility. We study and build portals. None of our personnel are trained to handle an organism that can infect a floor tile or become an undetectable copy of a person.

You are asking us to place this entity into a dimensional buffer—a space not fully observable, not fully testable—and expect it to remain dormant.

You are betting that it will stay asleep inside a box that was never designed to hold a nightmare.

I urge you to reconsider.

Infectus belongs in permanent cryogenic stasis, not in proximity to a functioning aperture array capable of transdomain transmission.

I understand this directive comes from above. I understand resistance may result in reassignment—or worse. But you asked for our cooperation.

This is our response.

If anything goes wrong, there won't be time to contain it.

The best we'll be able to do is warn the mainland before we're gone.


Respectfully,

Dr. Emilia R. Voss

Director of Operations

Viridian Island Research Complex, Oceanus Division

\* \* \*

AUDIO TRANSCRIPT

Recorded by facility sensors and compiled for Phoenix Eastern Command

November 3, 1997 – 21:47 Local Time

Location: Dr. Emilia Voss's Private Office, Sub-Level 19


VOSS (on phone): He's out of his fucking mind.

[silence on the other end]


VOSS: Did you read the same memo I did?

"Dimensional storage"? I don't need to remind you that "storage" implies inanimate objects—not something that's actively rewriting matter on a subcellular level.


DR. EZRA CALLEN (voice-only):

It gets better. He wants it housed in Annex C. Just a reminder—that's the same array where we had the breach last quarter.


VOSS: Oh, excellent. Let's just throw an end-of-the-world party there. Maybe set up a gift shop across from it too!

[pause]

Sorry. The gallows humor's just... how I deal with the horror of all this.

CALLEN: I know. I feel the same.

We're prepping the containment area in Lab Seven now. Triple-layer cryogenics, active magneto-suspension—just like the protocols say. It's the best we can do on short notice.

But Emilia... this is bad.

Like "call your lawyer and write your will" bad.


VOSS (pacing): Worse than bad.

This thing learns. That's what LeClair's report says. Mimics everything. Organic, synthetic, psychological patterns... voice, memory, emotion.

It makes you think it's your brother.

Your favorite book.

The voice in your head telling you you're safe.

If we make just one mistake—we're fucked.


CALLEN: Yeah.

It's not just mimicry.

This could trigger the end.

And I mean THE END.

The kind of end where everyone's dead and no one's left to wonder what happened—or how it happened so fast.

[brief silence]

CALLEN (softly): I've got people threatening to quit.

Kerrigan locked herself in the biosuit chamber when she found out what was coming.

I don't blame her.

But don't worry.

I'll take care of it.

VOSS (dryly): Well, tell her to pace her breakdown.

We're all in this together—and we've got a monster to babysit.

[sound of a cabinet opening, a bottle being retrieved]

[Voss pours herself a drink—Lagavulin. No hesitation.]

CALLEN: You know this was supposed to be a particle harmonic lab, right?

String theory. Gravitational edge modeling. Maybe even earn us a Nobel if we got lucky.

Now we're a goddamn prison.

VOSS: We're not a prison, Ezra.

We're a gamble—and a bad one at that. One with long-ass odds.

And we're stuck.

We have to comply.


CALLEN: Comply or die.

So this is self-preservation now.

I'll let the rest of my team know they're in for some long hours.


[Voss pauses. Swirls the glass.]


VOSS: Thanks, Ezra.

I'll make sure everyone gets a little extra stipend for the overtime.

I know it's not much, considering.

God help us.


CUT TO:

A blinking light on the island's southern docking bay monitor.

TRANSFER: THETA-ZERO-ONE — EN ROUTE

ETA: 08:19 HOURS

# INFECTUS PART 3

The Viridian Incident

Yesterday, 9:23 PM.

E verything on the surface of Viridian Island was blasted flat and incinerated by a 50-kiloton airburst—delivered by a Tomahawk cruise missile, courtesy of the United States Navy.
It was the beginning of the end of the world.

The Chairman of the Joint Chiefs of Staff—an Army general and thirty-five-year veteran of three wars— had been so shaken by the footage from Viridian that he bypassed protocol and ordered the strike himself.

Ordinarily, this kind of action required the President's direct authorization. But there was no time.

What he saw wasn't a threat to national security.

It was a threat to the species.

Whatever was loose on that island could end humanity faster than all the weapons in the U.S. arsenal combined.

He would deal with the fallout—political, moral, and literal—later.

For now, he bowed his head and whispered a prayer for the hundreds of good men and women he had just condemned.

\* \* \*

Twenty minutes earlier...

Marie Wong barely made it out of the lab before the reinforced glass doors slammed shut behind her.

Klaxons still howled in her ears. The brightness of the hallway fluorescents stabbed at her vision.

The thing had grabbed her arm. She'd torn free before it got a solid grip—but the others hadn't been so lucky.

She had to get out.

She had to warn someone.

My God, she thought. What if it got out?

Could it get out?

She sprinted for the elevator. When it finally arrived, she slapped the button for the ground floor.

The ride took five minutes.

It felt like fifty.

Adrenaline surged through her, clouding her thoughts. She shivered uncontrollably, arms wrapped tight across her chest.

The elevator doors slid open.

A wall of military police stood waiting, rifles raised.

"Step out of the elevator!" one barked. "Slowly!"

Marie obeyed, hands up.

"Check her."

One of the MPs broke from the line, weapon lowered. He approached her cautiously, scanning her up and down.

To her surprise, there were no marks on her arm. She could have sworn it had drawn blood—hadn't it?

The MP pulled a scanner from a pouch on his thigh. She tried to glimpse the screen, but the data meant nothing to her—just pulsing colors and glyphs.

"She's clean," the MP said.

"Alright," the lead officer replied. "Get her outside. Wait for the Marines."

\* \* \*

Marie climbed the steps of a matte-gray school bus—normally used to ferry personnel around the island on a timed schedule.

Outside, muffled shouting and thudding boots echoed between houses as nearby neighborhoods received unexpected Marine Corps visits.

She passed a heavily armed Marine posted at the front, avoided the gazes of the others onboard, and made her way to the rear.

When she could go no farther, she slid into a seat by herself.

She felt feverish and cold—like the flu had hit her all at once. Sweat broke across her skin, and she began to shiver.

The spot on her arm where the thing had grabbed her started to itch. She scratched at it absent-mindedly.

The sensation was off—like pressing on your face while still numb from Novocaine.

A few minutes later, the bus door closed and they began to move. It stopped again in a residential sector, where Marines escorted more civilians from their homes—ready for war, judging by their posture and gear.

A man and his wife boarded and took the seats across from Marie.

He looked composed.

She looked like she was falling apart.

"What's happening, Gary?" the woman asked, voice trembling.

"Something's not right," he said. He pulled her close and rested his forehead against hers.

"They said there's been some kind of containment breach."

"Containment breach?" someone echoed.

Marie recognized the voice—it was Tom Flannery, a neighbor and colleague from a sister department.

"That doesn't make sense," Flannery said. "We do high-energy physics here. If there was a real breach, we'd be getting the debriefing from Saint Peter."

The bus filled rapidly. The doors sealed. The interior lights went dark.

They moved again—stop-and-start, then fast. Marie had no idea where they were headed, but she guessed helicopters. That's how she'd arrived on Viridian last year.

As dusk gave way to darkness, tension thickened in the bus. Armed Marines stood like statues at the front. The whispering started—fragmented, desperate.

"I'm Diane," the woman across from her said, attempting a strained smile. "This is my husband, Gary."

"Marie," she croaked.

"Oh, sweetie..." Diane leaned forward, concern etched into her features. "You don't look good."

"I'm okay," Marie whispered. "Just a little scared."

"There's nothing to be scared of," someone whispered.

Marie stiffened. "What—did you...?"

Diane and Gary looked at her, confused.

"Never mind," she muttered.

"I think it might be that new project down on Twenty-One," someone whispered from the dark.

"Yeah," said another voice. "Hey, Marie—you work down there. What's going on?"

All eyes shifted toward her. Moonlight glinted on her sweat-slick skin. Her face was frozen in a silent panic.

"I... I'm just an admin assistant," she said. "Barely got out. Something... came through. I... everyone..."

Her voice cracked. She covered her face and began to cry.

"Came through?" Gary asked. "Came through what?"

Marie looked up, wild-eyed. "I don't know. A circle of light. They kept turning it on and off. They called it a quantum... quantum something."

"Quantum?" said Gary. "Quantum what—computer?"

"Dimension," she said. "It had 'dimension' in the name."

"Wait. Whoa, whoa, whoa," said Flannery. "You guys have a dimensional gate or something down there?!"

"I don't know!" she snapped—then softened, trying to breathe. "I don't know. I saw something. It came out. They turned it on, and something..."

Her voice trailed off. Her eyes widened, caught in the memory.

"This is not good," Gary muttered, clearly wanting to say more—but the bus jerked to a sudden stop.

They had reached the shoreline.

Beyond a sparse line of palm trees, three Navy hovercraft loomed on the sand—hulking, melted-looking shapes with twin circular fans mounted at their sterns.

"Cool!" Flannery said, eyes wide. "I've always wanted to ride in a hovercraft."

"Elsee Aye see, sir," said the Marine at the front of the bus.

At least that's what Marie thought she heard.

"Right, right," Flannery nodded. "Landing Craft Air Cushion. L.C.A.C."

The Marine said nothing, but nodded once.

\*  \*  \*

The U.S. Navy's assault hovercraft loomed like dark silhouettes against the shimmering Pacific.

Circles of artificial light danced across the sand— cast by handheld flashlights wielded by flight-suited men in headsets, each tethered by long comm cords to mobile consoles nearby.

Passengers were ordered off the bus and directed toward the waiting LCACs.

Gary took Diane's hand and led her across the narrow beach at a stumbling jog, heading for the nearest ramp. Marie followed close behind.

On the deck of the lead hovercraft sat a large, gray, metal container—bolted down with thick cargo chains. Three open doors lined its front, each manned by a Marine.

The group was divided into three columns and ushered in—most went willingly. Those who hesitated received quiet encouragement from the armed escorts.

Inside, each corridor resembled the hold of a military transport plane: long rows of nylon webbing for seats, bolted to both walls beneath dull fluorescent lights. The overhead fixtures were cylindrical, explosion-proof, and bathed everything in a sickly greenish hue.

By chance or design, Marie, Diane, and Gary were placed in the same compartment. Gary and Diane took seats near the far end, beside what looked like the only window. Marie sat directly across from them.

There were small observation windows at either end of the container, but none along the walls—just a few rectangular cut-outs connecting the adjacent sections. If you stood, you could see through them into the other compartments.

A tinny but pleasant-sounding female voice came over the PA:

"Standby. We're Oscar Mike. Going feet wet."

A pause.

"I mean—we're moving out. Trip should only take about ten minutes. For your safety, please remain seated until instructed otherwise."

Outside, Marie heard the high whine of turbines spooling up.

The LCAC's massive air skirt inflated, lifting the craft and kicking up roiling clouds of sand and mist.

Diane clutched Gary's hand, her breaths rapid, eyes darting.

"Hey..." Gary said gently. "We're going to be fine."

"I'm just a little... claustrophobic," she said, glancing around the tight interior.

"Look." He pointed toward the door at the opposite end. "See? There's plenty of room."

Diane followed his gesture. She exhaled and nodded, visibly trying to calm herself.

Gary and Diane were holding it together—barely. Others weren't. Across the aisle, couples whispered fiercely. A few passengers had to be physically settled by nearby Marines, who didn't seem particularly happy about the assignment either.

The container sealed. The LCAC pushed off.

Through the rear-facing window, Marie watched Viridian Island shrink against the moonlit sky—just a jagged silhouette fading into the sea.

Two other hovercraft fell in line behind them, their blocky shapes joining the convoy.

Then—

Everything is fine. Don't worry.

The whisper wasn't in the cabin.

Marie stiffened.

Who— she began, but stopped herself.

Who are you?

I have been called many things, the voice said.

But my true name is INFECTUS. You may call me... friend.

You are not my friend, Marie thought. What... what are you?

I am time—come across the eons. Come to help you. Let me help you.

"I don't need your help!" Marie snapped.

Diane looked over, startled. "Everything okay, sweetie?"

Marie hesitated, then nodded and looked away.

Ten minutes passed. The passengers tilted as the LCAC began to slow.

She wasn't sure if they were docking or simply turning, but the shift in motion was unmistakable.

The PA crackled again.

"Okay everyone," said the same woman. "We're docking at the ship. Apologies for packing you in like sardines, but it was the fastest way to get you out of harm's way. Once aboard, we'll get you assigned bunks and something to eat."

Her tone lightened—cheerful, almost absurd.

"On behalf of the United States Navy and Marine Corps, thank you for riding with us today. The crew of the U.S.S. Highland welcomes you aboard! The Highland is a San Antonio-class amphibious—"

A different voice cut in, sharp and annoyed: "Give me that."

Several Marines chuckled. The tension didn't break—it just shifted.

*　*　*

A bright light pierced the compartment, flooding everything in white.

For a moment, it felt like a spotlight had been turned on from outside—blinding, unnatural.

Marie shielded her eyes. The beam shifted downward, crawling across the floor like a searchlight on a slow arc.

She imagined a crane lifting the source, hoisting it toward the sky.

Then—

A sharp, metallic pop.

A single syllable of violence:

PING!—amplified to deafening levels.

The hovercraft jolted hard. Everything inside lurched down and sideways. People cried out as heads collided. The LCAC bounced twice, the engine's pitch spiked, then settled again into its steady roar.

Marie stood unsteadily and turned to the window.

Outside, a massive fireball was blooming over Viridian Island—spherical, yellow-orange, impossibly wide.

Her brain couldn't register it.

It didn't look real.

She'd only ever seen mushroom clouds in old documentaries or science fiction films. This wasn't cinematic—it was wrong. Too bright. Too complete.

It broke something inside her.

"Oh my god," she whispered. "What the hell is happening?"

"What is it?" Diane asked.

"Let me see!" someone shouted from behind. A rough shove sent Marie tumbling back into her seat. She fell against the man beside her, both of them pressed against the wall as people swarmed the window.

"They... they nuked it!" someone yelled. "Oh my god! It's the end of the world!"

"Everyone sit the fuck down!"

A Marine had drawn his sidearm, arms locked and aimed at the growing chaos.

Other Marines rose, weapons drawn, barking orders.

It didn't take long. Fear—military fear—restored order. The crowd retreated to their seats, shaken and silent.

But Marie was already gone.

Her vision tunneled. Bright sparks danced at the edge of her sight.

A static roar swelled in her ears.

Then she slumped forward.

Her clothes were drenched with sweat. Her hands clenched into rigid claws, spasming in tight jerks—like a machine shorting out.

"Dear lord," Diane gasped. She scrambled across the aisle, instincts overriding fear.

Gary turned just in time to see Marie's head rise.

Her eyes had vanished.

There were only sockets—voids of inky black.

"You are not my friend," she said.

But it wasn't her voice.

Then her head split.

Not like bone breaking, but like a flower blooming wrong—petals of skin peeling outward in fractal layers.

Beneath the flesh: a spiraling mass of black coils, slick and geometric, folding in on themselves like living machinery.

Gary and Diane didn't move.

They couldn't.

There was no scream. No last words.

Only silence—and the shape of something ancient stepping into the world.

*  *  *

Roughly twenty Navy personnel in blue coveralls and hardhats marshaled the hovercraft into the Highland's aft well deck.

From the gangways above the massive open ramp—still lowered into the Pacific—they had a clear view of the incoming LCACs.

Those carrying radios shouted excitedly about the view.

Some took pictures with their phones.

The mushroom cloud behind the hovercrafts cast an otherworldly glow over the scene.

Photos of LCACs docking in a well deck were nothing new.

But with a nuclear explosion in the background?

Nobody would believe it wasn't Photoshopped.

The awe didn't last long.

Gunshots—muffled but unmistakable—echoed from inside the personnel container.

Then came the screams.

Not human.

Moments later, the pilot and co-pilot burst from the flight deck, wading onto the half-submerged platform like men fleeing a sinking ship.

They didn't shut down the engines.

They didn't speak.

They just jumped off the ramp—and swam.

Above, radio chatter turned frantic.

Supervisors were called.

Warnings relayed.

Within minutes, the Highland sent an encrypted message to Command:

Compromised.

Then the door on the container opened—and black smoke billowed out, thick and choking.

A Marine stumbled through it—blood-soaked, coughing, her sidearm gripped in one shaking hand.

It wasn't her blood.

She backed away from the opening, firing into the darkness.

When the shots failed to land—or matter—she holstered her weapon and pulled two grenades from her rig.

Pins popped.

She tossed both.

The twin explosions rocked the deck. The container's door blew clear off its hinges.

A sound rose from within—layered and impossibly deep.

Not a roar.

Not a scream.

Something between a modem shriek and tectonic plate shear.

The container shook violently.

Something inside was striking the walls with colossal force, warping the metal.

The roof buckled outward—trembling like it might rip open at any second.

Then came the tendrils.

Hundreds of them—dark, barbed, twitching—shot from the doorway like living wire.

The Marine barely had time to turn her head.

The first wave struck her hand and forearm.

The second buried into her face and neck.

A third volley hit her legs and pulled her clean off the deck—dragging her back into the smoke.

Screaming, she drew her Ka-Bar and slashed at the threads.

They didn't cut.

Instead, they began to merge—melting into her flesh, fusing with her.

She disappeared into the shadows of the container.

A moment later, the world turned white.

A nuclear warhead–tipped torpedo, launched from deep underwater, struck the Highland centerline with flawless precision.

The ship didn't break apart.

It ceased to exist.

Most of her was vaporized instantly.

Molten debris was flung a mile into the night sky, scattering across the South Pacific.

Some of it rained down on islands hundreds of miles away.

For the third time that day, sunlight bathed the ocean.

* * *

The captain of the U.S.S. Louisiana was furious—at the world, yes, but mostly at himself.

He'd commanded the Los Angeles–class submarine for over a decade. In all that time, he'd never been ordered to do anything like this.

Not that he'd questioned it.

He and his crew had carried out their orders with precision, without hesitation.

But now they were holding position in contaminated waters... and he had just killed every man aboard.

A thousand thoughts ran through his head at once.

Was this a suicide order?

Was he being sacrificed?

It didn't matter.

He just hoped it accomplished whatever the brass thought needed doing.

His executive officer stepped up beside him and placed a hand on his shoulder.

"Not my proudest moment," the captain said, eyes fixed on the deck. "We buried a lot of our own today."

"Goes without saying," the XO replied softly. "Command to dive? We should take evasive action."

The captain shook his head. "No point, Jim. We were set at minimum safe distance from the island. I didn't plan on leveling the Highland too."

He looked his XO in the eye.

"This was supposed to be a rescue mission. The incident shock's gonna catch us."

The XO exhaled and looked away. "Great."

He pulled out his wallet and slid a photo from inside—his wife and two kids. He stared at it for a long moment.

The captain picked up the PA mic.

After the Boatswain's call sounded through the sub, he spoke into the silence:

"Godspeed, gentlemen.

It's been an honor."

A moment later, the shockwave hit.

Hydrostatic pressure folded the Louisiana like paper—twisting steel and flesh into silence.

# ARCHANGEL

The story broke at 7:03 a.m.

By 7:30, the newsroom phones were screaming.

Sam Griffin watched the chaos unfold from his desk at The Dutchess Sentinel. His name sat beneath the headline in bold black font:

**LOCAL HOSPITAL LINKED TO PATIENT DISAPPEARANCES.**

Reporters stared at him like he'd just pulled the pin on a grenade. One of the interns whispered, "The governor's office is on line two—again."

Evie Marshall, the editor-in-chief, burst from her glass-walled office clutching her phone. Her eyes were dark with exhaustion and anger.

"Sam, get in here. Now."

Inside, the blinds were half-drawn, sunlight cutting her face into sharp planes. The governor's voice rasped from the speakerphone—accusations, legal threats, words like defamation and sanctions. When she finally hung up, the silence felt heavier than the shouting.

"You had one job," Evie said. "Facts, not firebombs."

"It's all sourced," Sam answered. "Names, dates, patient logs—"

"Which you stole," she snapped. "And half your sources recanted overnight. Archangel's lawyers sent a twelve-page cease-and-desist. The hospital's donors are threatening to pull advertising. The governor wants my head on a spike."

She took a slow breath, then softened—just enough to sound human again.

"I'm putting you on leave. One week. No calls, no emails, no stories. Go home."

Sam stood there a moment longer than he should have, jaw tight, fingers twitching toward his camera bag. "So that's it? I tell the truth, and we hide under the desk?"

Evie's eyes flicked to the window, where rain had begun to streak the glass.

"Sometimes survival looks like cowardice," she said. "Get out before I make it official."

* * *

Outside, the parking lot was slick with drizzle. Sam sat behind the wheel of his Bronco, engine idling, the glow of the Archangel billboard bleeding through the mist ahead.

RESILIENCE AND RENEWAL, it read in towering white letters.

He laughed once—short, humorless.

"Yeah," he muttered. "Something like that."


He drove home through the rain, radio silent, phone buzzing with messages he ignored. Every ring felt like another hand reaching to pull him deeper below the surface.

At a red light, he opened his laptop, pulled up the published story, and read it again. The words felt heavier now—too certain, too final. He wondered how many people had already decided he was crazy.

A new comment appeared at the bottom of the article:

You don't know what you're cutting into, Mr. Griffin.

— JANUS.


Sam stared at it until the light turned green. Then he closed the laptop, tossed it into the passenger seat, and kept driving.

He didn't know it yet, but the incision had already been made.

*  *  *

Sam didn't sleep that night.

He sat on his apartment couch surrounded by empty coffee cups and printouts—medical records, patient rosters, transcripts of interviews he'd recorded on his Sony voice recorder. The glow of his monitor painted the room in cold light. Every time he closed his eyes, he saw those missing names floating in the dark.

At sunrise, the phone rang.

"Man, what the hell did you do?" his friend said, voice thick with disbelief. "You've got cops nosing around my shop asking about you. You pissed off the governor?"

Sam rubbed his temples. "It's fine. Just noise. I'm right about this, J.D.—you know I am."

There was a pause. "Maybe. But right doesn't keep you breathing. Drop it, Sam. Just this once."

"I can't."

"I know," J.D. said quietly, then hung up.

By afternoon, Lydia called. Her voice was soft, careful—like she was handling a wounded animal.

"They told us at the hospital not to talk to you."

"I figured," Sam said. "I'm radioactive now."

"I mean it, Sam. Security's tightening. There's talk about restraining orders. Please just stop. For me."

He almost laughed. "You think I can walk away from this?"

"Yes," she said. "If you want to live long enough to publish anything again."

Her voice broke slightly on the last word. He didn't notice until later.

* * *

Rain again. Always rain.

He drove to J.D.'s garage, just wanting to talk—to depressurize.

The bay doors were closed, but the lights were on inside. Through the slats he saw his friend talking to someone—tall, female, wearing a red coat. For a moment, Sam thought it might be Lydia, but when the woman turned, he recognized the profile of Vanessa Caldwell, Archangel's PR officer.

She smiled as she handed J.D. something—an envelope, maybe. As she left, her eyes flicked to Sam's car before she climbed into her own and drove off.

When J.D. stepped out into the drizzle, Sam stayed hidden. He didn't feel like talking anymore. He just watched J.D. lock up the garage and leave.

Something twisted in his gut.

By the time he got home, the rain had stopped, and the street was silent.

But there was something new waiting for him—an envelope, slid under the door.

* * *

The envelope was plain and unmarked—no return address, no postage. Just his name, printed in clean block letters: SAM GRIFFIN.

He hesitated before opening it. Every instinct said it was a bad idea. But instincts hadn't stopped him before.

Inside were three things.

A security badge, laminated, pristine—his photograph printed above the words ARCHANGEL MEDICAL CENTER – CONTRACTOR.

An antique skeleton key, heavy and cold to the touch, its dark metal worn smooth by decades of use.

And a folded map, slightly yellowed at the edges, showing the hospital campus from above.

One area was circled in red ink: SUB-LEVEL ACCESS: LIFELINE CONDUIT.

At the bottom of the map, a single handwritten note:

Truth demands witness. You are close.

— JANUS

Sam stared at the badge for a long time. The photo was perfect, down to the subtle gray streak in his hair and the line of his jaw. The timestamp read 07/31/24—last week.

He hadn't sat for a photo in years.

He turned the badge over. QR code. Embedded microchip. Nothing counterfeit about it. Whoever made it had access to the real thing.

The skeleton key didn't fit with the rest—an old-world relic beside precision security tech. He traced its grooves with his thumb, wondering what kind of door it could possibly open.

\* \* \*

That evening, he packed his camera, notebook, and the little black USB drive where he kept everything he didn't trust to the cloud. He laid everything out on the table, staring at it like evidence from a crime scene.

Outside, thunder rolled across the Hudson Valley, rattling the windowpanes. He could almost hear Evie's voice in his head: Facts, not firebombs. But what if the facts were buried beneath a mile of concrete?

He picked up the badge. The laminate caught the glow from his desk lamp. In its reflection, for a split second, he thought he saw something move behind him—just a flicker of motion in the shadows.

He spun, heart hammering.

Nothing there.

Just the soft hum of the refrigerator and the steady tick of the wall clock.

When he turned back, the note seemed to have shifted slightly closer to him.

He exhaled, shaky. "Get a grip, Griffin."

He poured a shot of whiskey, tossed it back, and opened his laptop. Archangel's security database wasn't public, but he knew a backdoor through the county's vendor registry system. He typed in the badge ID.

Result: Active Credential. Valid through September 30, 2024.

His breath caught.

Someone inside the hospital wanted him to go back.

The storm outside broke wide, rain hammering the roof. For a long minute, he just listened to it, letting the sound fill the room.

Then he folded the map, pocketed the badge and key, and slung his camera bag over his shoulder.

"One last time," he said. "Get solid evidence tying Archangel to Phoenix, then blow the whole thing wide open."

* * *

ARCHANGEL Medical Center occupied ten city blocks, its facilities spilling into several others. It was half a mile wide and almost two miles long. Sam had only been inside three of the many buildings that made up the Poughkeepsie campus, so it had taken him more than thirty minutes to find his target on the map.

It was nearly midnight when Sam pulled into the staff lot behind the Spiritual and Religious Center, his designated entry point.

Rain slicked the asphalt, reflecting the floodlights and the tall, partially mirrored windows of the hospital's dark, Brutalist façade. The building loomed above the trees, its tall structure louvered like Devil's Tower in Utah. There were few windows, but every pane glowed a different shade of sterile white. It looked less like a hospital and more like a castle keep.

Sam sat in the Bronco with the engine off, heart thudding against the silence. The badge and key lay on the passenger seat beside his camera. He could hear the faint hum of the hospital's generators and, beneath it, the low rhythmic whoosh of ventilation fans—like the building itself was breathing.

He slipped on his jacket, clipped the badge to his chest pocket, and stepped out into the cold drizzle.

*  *  *

The main lobby was quiet except for the soft drone of ambient music and the distant rattle of a janitor's cart. He flashed the badge at the front desk without slowing down. The night clerk barely looked up.

"Late shift," Sam muttered.

The badge reader by the elevator blinked green.

No alarm. No questions.

He rode down three floors to the service level, where the air was colder and the lights more mechanical. The hallways were a maze of polished concrete and humming fluorescent tubes. Door after door passed—Storage, Maintenance, Medical Waste—until he found the one from the map.

**SUB-LEVEL ACCESS – AUTHORIZED PERSONNEL ONLY**

He pressed the badge against the reader. It clicked open with a hiss.

Beyond the door, a narrow stairwell spiraled downward into darkness. The hum of machines grew louder, mingled with the faint, echoing sound of something moving far below. He drew his flashlight and started down.

The stairs ended at a steel corridor. Faded paint on the wall read:

## LIFELINE CONDUIT – PATIENT TRANSFER

He could feel the temperature drop, his breath fogging in the beam of his light. The floor vibrated slightly underfoot—a deep mechanical pulse that reminded him of a ship's engine room.

He followed the sound.

The corridor opened into a long underground tunnel—metal walls, cables snaking along the ceiling, rails embedded in the floor. A transparent tube ran parallel to the walkway, sealed and illuminated from within.

Inside it, something was moving.

Sam froze.

Through the frosted surface, shapes slid by slowly—capsules the size of coffins, each lined with a faint blue glow. For an instant, he saw a pale face within one, eyes closed, mouth slack. Then another. And another.

Each capsule bore a stamped serial number and a faintly glowing symbol:

**ASPHODEL**

His stomach turned.

He took a photo. The flash lit the tunnel like lightning—and in that brief moment, he saw something else at the far end of the passage. A figure, watching him.

Then the lights flickered, and the figure was gone.

Sam's pulse pounded in his ears. He backed toward the stairwell—but the door had sealed itself. A red light blinked above the lock.

**ACCESS DENIED**

He turned back toward the tunnel. The conveyor belt beside the tube whirred to life, crawling forward into the darkness.

The only way out was forward.

\* \* \*

Sam stepped onto the motorized walkway.

It hummed beneath his boots, moving at a steady pace toward the far end of the tunnel. The glass tube beside him pulsed with blue light, carrying its silent cargo deeper underground. The pods floated by like translucent coffins, each one containing a sleeping shape—faces serene, almost peaceful. The hum of machinery was constant, like the murmur of a distant heartbeat.

Every thirty feet, dark camera domes dotted the ceiling. In his mind, every one was tracking him as he passed.

He kept walking.

Halfway down, he found a maintenance alcove—a wall terminal, old and dust-covered. He brushed the grime away and tapped the touchscreen.

## SYSTEM ACCESS – LIFELINE CONDUIT / TRANSFER

### ROUTE: ETERNAL TAIGA

Below it:

## STATUS – ACTIVE / SECURITY OVERRIDE ENABLED

He stared at the word Active for a long time, then opened the map overlay. The conduit stretched for nearly a mile beneath the Hudson River, terminating at another facility labeled only ET-1.1.1.9.5. The blueprint looked more like a bunker than a hospital—rings within rings, deep underground.

He felt the hair on his arms rise.

The system pinged.

Unauthorized login detected.

The screen went black.

A voice echoed through the corridor—female, calm, synthetic.

"Please remain on the walkway. Assistance is on the way."

Sam froze. "Shit!"

He turned, sprinting back the way he came. The conveyor fought him, dragging him forward as alarms began to pulse through the tunnel. Red lights flared. Behind the glass, the pods continued sliding past, oblivious.

When he reached the sealed stairwell door, it was locked solid. The badge reader flashed ACCESS DENIED.

"Come on," he hissed, slamming his fist against the panel. "Come on!"

\* \* \*

The walkway shifted beneath him—reversing course, speeding up. It carried him forward whether he wanted it to or not. He grabbed the railing, fighting for balance as the tunnel walls blurred around him. The voice returned, soothing as ever:

"Transport in progress.

Destination: Eternal Taiga.

Estimated arrival: four minutes."

He looked down at the glass tube beside him. Through the frosted surface, a pale hand floated close—fingers twitching slightly, as if waving.

Sam stumbled back, eyes wide. "Jesus..."


The tunnel began to slope downward. The hum of the motors deepened into a thunderous vibration that shook his bones. The pods moved faster now, rushing past like ghostly bullets. The air grew colder, metallic, tinged with the scent of ozone.

Then came the pressure—subtle at first, then crushing. His ears popped. Condensation gathered on the glass, streaming downward like rain.

Ahead, the tunnel curved into a massive vertical shaft. At its center, the conveyor belt merged into a rotating platform—an elevator system, carrying both pods and personnel into the abyss below.

There was nowhere else to go.

He took a deep breath, steadied his flashlight, and stepped onto the platform.

* * *

The descent began.

As the platform lowered, the tunnel walls fell away, revealing the vast machinery of the underground complex—tangled pipes, spinning turbines, skeletal catwalks suspended over endless depth. Through the faint blue haze, he saw other conduits converging from different directions, each one feeding into the same dark heart.

At the edge of hearing, voices whispered—a hundred overlapping tones, human and not.

Fragments of speech. Numbers. Prayers. Code.

And far below, a faint white glow pulsed like a heartbeat.

When the platform finally slowed, he saw it—engraved on the curved wall ahead, massive and backlit:


**ETERNAL TAIGA — 1.1.1.9.5**

**PHOENIX / NEO COLUMBIA**


Sam lifted his camera and took the shot.

Then the lights went out.

\* \* \*

When the lights returned, they were colder.

The elevator doors slid open with a hiss, revealing a corridor lined in glass and steel. Everything was spotless—too spotless. The air was dry, antiseptic, humming faintly with electricity. Every few seconds, a soft tone chimed from somewhere distant, like the pulse of a patient monitor.

Sam stepped forward, boots echoing on the tile. The corridor stretched ahead into infinity, branching into sealed laboratories and observation rooms. Behind the glass walls, he caught glimpses of equipment—MRI machines, cryo pods, racks of roughly spherical canisters glinting like diamond under surgical light.

At the end of the hall stood a security checkpoint, empty but active.

A single door marked:

## ASPHODEL / STASIS ACCESS – AUTHORIZED PERSONNEL ONLY

The moment he read it, his stomach turned.

ASPHODEL.

The word from the pods.

He raised his camera—and froze.

A reflection moved behind him.

"Don't bother," said a voice, calm, measured. "It won't record in here."

Sam turned.

A man stood in the center of the corridor, wearing a gray suit and an expression carved from marble. Late forties, lean, eyes the color of dust. His ID badge read SPENCER R. MACKEY.

But Sam knew the name beneath the name.

"Janus," he said.

The man smiled faintly. "You've been quite useful."

Sam's heart thudded once, hard. "You sent the badge. The key. The map."

"Yes." Janus stepped closer, hands clasped behind his back. "We needed to test the system. Identify vulnerabilities. And you... well, you've always been good at finding loopholes."

Sam backed up a step. "So you used me as some kind of—penetration test?"

"Precisely." Janus nodded toward the sealed lab doors. "Every security alert you triggered, every bypass you exploited—it all made us stronger. You helped us close the gaps."

He let the silence stretch, then added almost kindly,

"You should be proud."

* * *

There was movement down the hall.

They emerged together, composed, silent, like actors taking the stage—Lydia, J.D., and Vanessa Caldwell in her signature red coat.

Sam felt his breath catch. "Lydie...?"

She didn't meet his eyes. "I told you to stop."

"You're one of them," he said, voice breaking. "Both of you?"

J.D. exhaled, looking genuinely pained. "They have my daughter, Sam. I didn't have a choice."

Vanessa smiled—professional, hollow. "Oh, you all had choices. You just didn't understand the stakes."

Janus clasped his hands behind his back. "Mr. Griffin, do you know what the word Asphodel means?"

Sam didn't answer.

"In Greek myth, it was the field where ordinary souls wandered after death—neither damned nor saved. Just... preserved." He gestured toward the glass walls and their diamond vaults. "Eternal Taiga serves the same function. Preservation of consciousness. A bridge between mortality and the future."

Sam's throat was dry. "You're harvesting people. Stealing their brains."

Janus tilted his head. "We're saving them. The human brain is the only vessel proven stable for long-term memory continuity. We extract, encode, and store. The minds you saw in those pods will one day awaken—reborn. Free of pain. Free of decay."

He smiled.

"You will join them."

\*  \*  \*

Two guards appeared beside Sam and took hold of his arms.

He looked at one, expecting to see something inhuman. Instead, he saw a young man of about twenty-five—bright-eyed, clean-shaven, smiling faintly. His badge read Brian Gray.

As the guard turned his head toward the corridor lights, Sam caught a strange yellow glint in his eyes—catlike, reflective. Sam told himself it was the lighting. But a chill crept down his spine all the same.

Sam struggled, but their grip was iron.

"Enough," Janus said softly. "You've given us everything we need."

They led him down the corridor past observation bays and glass chambers filled with silent machines. Behind one pane, he saw rows of mechanical arms tending to brain-like structures suspended in fluid—

each encased in diamond, marked with serial numbers and the PHOENIX sigil.

A sign overhead read:

## CORE-TEX / NEO COLUMBIA ARCHIVE
## UNIT CAPACITY: 312,480

Beyond, the corridor opened into a cavernous space.

It was endless.

Circular columns extended downward into the depths. Each slot in their sides held a human brain, glowing faintly blue. Technicians in white ceremonial garments took inventory with handheld tablets or carefully installed new units into the lattice.

The sheer magnitude of the operation was beyond comprehension. The air vibrated with a low, resonant hum—like the sound of thought itself.

Sam whispered, "Oh, God..."

Janus smiled beside him. "God has nothing to do with it."

* * *

They reached a platform surrounded by medical equipment.

Lydia's expression was pale, trembling. "They'll make it painless," she said quietly.

He looked at her with disbelief, then at J.D. "You're really going to let them do this?"

J.D. swallowed. "You should've walked away when you had the chance, brother. Now we're all committed."

Janus placed a reassuring hand on Sam's shoulder. "Don't fight it. You're part of something larger now."

They strapped him to the table. The lights dimmed. Cold mist coiled from vents above.

"I wanted to save you," Lydia whispered. "I just... didn't know how."

Janus leaned close.

"Resilience and Renewal," he murmured. "That's what we promise. And now—you will endure forever."


A needle pierced Sam's neck. The world tilted sideways, color draining from everything. Through the haze he saw Lydia's tears, J.D.'s guilt, Vanessa's perfect stillness.

As darkness closed in, Sam tried to speak, but only one word came out.

"Why?"

Janus smiled. "Because we need you, Sam. Your country needs you."

The world was fading to black. He managed to whisper, "For... what?"

"When the Day of Fire comes," said Janus, "and it will come—citizens like you will rise from the ashes to form a new nation. A glorious republic."

He turned his gaze to the vault stretching into infinity, his voice filled with quiet awe.

"Neo Columbia."

# EPILOGUE

August 22, 2024

The Dutchess Sentinel — Front Page

## LOCAL REPORTER MISSING UNDER MYSTERIOUS CIRCUMSTANCES

Law enforcement refuses to comment on active investigation.

\* \* \*

The following are excerpts from a photocopied Dutchess County Sheriff's report, filed by Sheriff Tom Barrett. The document is partially redacted, stamped FBI ARCHIVAL REQUEST – PRIORITY LEVEL ALPHA.

Incident Report – Case 24-0815-MIA

Filed: August 21, 2024

Reporting Officer: Sheriff T. Barrett

The following items were recovered at a bus stop approximately one-quarter mile south of Archangel Medical Center.

Items were delivered to my office by a good Samaritan [Name Redacted by Request].

The Samaritan reported the items were found "stacked neatly" on the bench at approximately 05:45 hours.

Items recovered include:

- One dark gray Carhartt Storm Defender jacket
- One pair of blue jeans, folded
- One Field Notes notebook (black cover, dot-graph paper)
- One telescoping Fisher Space Pen (black)
- One Corsair Flash Survivor USB drive (black)
- One pair Gatorz ballistic sunglasses
- One Kangol wool cap (dark flannel)
- One small digital voice recorder, Sony ICD-UX570
- One laminated press ID, The Dutchess Sentinel — Samuel Griffin
- One handwritten Post-It note: "I knew the risks. – Sam Griffin"

All items were sealed and transferred to evidence locker 3-B.

No trace DNA, fingerprints, or signs of struggle detected.

All items were clean, laundered, and dry despite rain the previous night.

\* \* \*

### Addendum – August 22, 2024

Ms. Vanessa Caldwell, Public Relations Officer at Archangel Medical Center, contacted this office.

She stated the hospital would not pursue trespassing charges against Mr. Griffin.

All prior citations have been dropped.

\* \* \*

### Law Enforcement Summary

Based on testimony and materials provided, Samuel "Sam" Griffin was an experienced journalist and U.S. Army veteran.

Colleagues describe him as "driven," "paranoid," and "obsessed" with Archangel Medical Center."

His immediate supervisor, Evelyn Marshall, confirmed that Griffin had been suspended following publication of a controversial article linking the hospital to patient disappearances.

No corroborating evidence has been found.

Several hospital staff members confirmed that Griffin had repeatedly entered restricted areas without authorization.

No record of his presence exists on internal surveillance footage from the dates in question.

As of this report, Griffin remains missing.

Investigation continues pending FBI review.

\* \* \*

## Addendum – August 24, 2024

This case and all related evidence were formally transferred to federal jurisdiction following a call from the New York State Governor's Office.

The request came directly from FBI Manhattan Field Headquarters, citing "national security interest."

I have complied with the order.

Case closed at the county level.

— Sheriff Tom Barrett

* * *

INTERNAL MEMO – CLASSIFIED / EYES ONLY

PHOENIX Systems Internal Communications Archive

1.1.1.9.5 — Eternal Taiga

ASPHODEL Section ET-01


STATUS: ARCHIVAL COMPLETE

ASSET DESIGNATION: CORE-TEX 514,912-B — Griffin, Samuel P.

CONTAINMENT: Level 3 / Cognitive Preservation – Stable

ASSIGNED ARCHIVE: NEO COLUMBIA – MEMORY VAULT SECTOR 11G


"Subject assimilated successfully. Neural lattice preserved at 99.97% fidelity.

Awaiting integration into the collective."


— Dr. L. Cross, ASPHODEL Division Lead

— Supervisor Authorization: Spencer R. Mackey (Janus)

End of File.


Deep within the vaults of Eternal Taiga, Core-Tex unit 514,912-B flickered once, almost imperceptibly.

Then, silence.

\*      \*      \*